THE
DREAM THIEF

HELEN A. ROSBURG

Gold Imprint
Medallion Press, Inc.
Printed in USA

DEDICATION:

This book, as usual, is dedicated to my husband James, the love of my life, who did not steal my dreams but made them all come true.

And to my best friend, my buddy, who told me to take my little short story and turn it into a novel. Good call, Leslie.

Published 2005 by Medallion Press, Inc.
225 Seabreeze Ave.
Palm Beach, FL 33480

The MEDALLION PRESS LOGO
is a registered tradmark of Medallion Press, Inc.

Copyright © 2005 by Helen A. Rosburg
Cover Illustration by Adam Mock

Printed in the United States of America

Library of Congress Cataloging-in-Publication Data

Rosburg, Helen A.
  The dream thief / Helen A. Rosburg.
    p. cm.
  ISBN 1-932815-20-1
  1. Women--Crimes against--Fiction. 2. Venice (Italy)--Fiction.
  3. Dreams--Fiction. I. Title.
  PS3618.O7824D74 2005
  813'.6--dc22

                        2005025282

ACKNOWLEDGEMENTS:

I would like to thank Karen Syed
for her generosity of spirit.

PROLOGUE

Venice lay beneath the velvet pall of a moonless night. Though the city's mood throughout both day and evening was carnival-like, no sound of revel disturbed the midnight hour. What boats remained on the canals glided silently through the dark water. Even the lap of tiny wavelets against the wooden hulls and stone steps seemed muted.

Within the Villa Santonini, only the plaintive cries of the *doge's* daughter could be heard. Valeria cried out in her sleep, but did not wake. She lay soaked with sweat, her thin, silken shift sodden. Her tongue flicked in and out of parched lips, and her hands kneaded her breasts. Her back arched, lifting her body from the bed, and she tossed her head from side to side.

He was back again, in her dreams. There, at the foot of her bed. He wore a ruffled white shirt, its ties undone so she could see a tantalizing bit of his well-defined chest. Thick, wavy, sun-streaked brown hair kissed the tops of broad, muscular shoulders. Knee-high black boots of the softest leather embraced his calves. Skin tight leggings caressed his heavily muscled thighs. Her eyes moved to the V of his groin.

He followed her gaze. His hand moved lazily downward; he touched himself.

Valeria watched him harden. The sight inflamed her, sending rivers of molten blood through her veins. He reached out to touch her where he had touched himself and she arched to meet him, pulling up her night shift. Then, suddenly, he was gone.

Groaning with the pain of loss, Valeria pulled herself upright. Where had he gone? She looked desperately about her bedroom, but he had vanished. Just like every night before. But this night was different. This night she had to have him. Had to. She could not wait any longer.

The tapers in the silver candelabrum had long since guttered, and no light came through the tall, gold-draped windows. But she would have known her way through her father's palace had she been blind-folded. Valeria tip-toed to her door and opened it.

"You," she gasped. "You're here. You're really here."

By way of reply, he raised a finger to his lips. He reached for her hand.

Valeria shuddered with desire when she felt his fingers twine about her own. His cool flesh surprised her. She had thought his touch would burn her.

Together they moved silently down the long, window-lined gallery. Valeria felt as if she moved in a dream. And as if it were, indeed, a dream, she did not pause, did not question. What happened went beyond her control.

The night air was cold against her skin when they left the palace. She smelled the canal, and let him lead her down the steps to her father's dock. A strange boat swayed gently atop the water. She noticed it was not secured, yet waited like a patient horse for its rider. It was painted black, one with the water on which it rested. Gilt paint decorated its sides in whorls and flourishes. Its small cabin was completely enclosed and windowless. The man at her side gestured and she stepped down into the vessel. It barely rocked. It moved not at all when he followed her.

Silken pillows lined the floor. She could not see them in the darkness, but she felt them. When he placed his hand on the small of her back, passion surged through her entire body and her knees turned to liquid. She sank down into the pillows.

He did not have to court her body. She came to him. Ready. Her thighs glistened with moisture when she opened them to him.

Suddenly he was naked before her. He knelt between

her knees, his flesh gleaming palely in the dark, as if he were illumined by a magical light within. And he was ready, as ready for her as she was for him. He was hard and very large, within her delicate hand. Small animal sounds came from the back of Valeria's throat.

Beautiful. He was so beautiful. And he had seemed to become more so each night. Gaunt and pale when she had first seen him, he had come each night to tempt and torment her, growing more and more beautiful each time, irresistible. She had thought him a dream, only a dream. But here he was. Entering her.

Valeria screamed. He filled her, ignited her. When he moved against her she screamed again. The pleasure grew too intense, too overwhelming. Her entire body became composed of strings, all being pulled down at once, down and down to the secret place between her legs. Tighter and tighter they wound as they rocked together until the cords suddenly snapped, and she was released in a spasm of pleasure, an explosion of sensation. Heat poured from his body into hers.

And then, suddenly, the warmth began leaving her. Even as she floated, she felt herself growing cold, colder. She tried to move, but her body had no strength, no power. And she had no sight. Everything was black, black. . . .

He pulled down her shift, covering her naked legs. Her arms he arranged over her still breast. Carefully, almost lovingly, he pulled her long, brown tresses artfully about her shoulders.

He left her, a single passenger. The black boat drifted along through the night and into the dawn.

CHAPTER

1

The streets of the Ghetto Nuovo teemed with life. Pina picked her way around market carts stalled in the throng of humanity, piles of offal left by numerous equine drudges, and lean, opportunistic dogs and cats staying alive on fat waterfront rats. Uncountable bodies pushed past her; Jews with the circle of yellow sewn onto their outer garments; well dressed merchants visiting the money lenders; dandified young men taking in the sights. Pina glanced back to make sure her servant, Andrea, still followed, and quickened her pace.

It was still cool so early in the spring. Early in the morning as well. It had been barely two hours since the beadle, the Shomerim la-Boker, Watcher for the Morning, had been round from house to house knocking on doors to wake the ghetto denizens. The street was shady, too, as the Jewish population had nowhere to build but up, and haphazardly constructed buildings towered over the busy streets. Pina clutched her shawl more tightly to her breast.

The poorly built housing was the reason she hurried. Another building had collapsed recently, killing scores and injuring more. Her skills, and coin, were sorely needed.

Pina turned a last corner and found herself in front of the unimposing façade of The Scola Grande Tedesca. Externally, the Venetian synagogue did not present features of particular merit or interest. It was not prudent to attract the attention of the Rulers of the Republic, who had explicitly forbidden the construction of synagogues. She looked up at its five windows and hesitantly pulled open the massive door.

The synagogue's benign exterior belied the sumptuous, gilded interior. She glanced up at the women's gallery, then heard the sharp click of footsteps on the beautifully inlaid floor.

"Rabbi Levan?" Pina called tentatively.

"Oh, good. You're here, child. I am grateful. As many others will be." The traditionally garbed Ashkenazi teacher took Pina's hands in his own and squeezed them gently. He tilted his head in acknowledgement of her servant. "We should leave at once."

"Of course." Pina's eyes drifted to the large basket Andrea cradled. "I brought as much as I could. I know it's not enough. It's never enough. But . . ."

"Hush, child." The Rabbi held a finger briefly to his lips. "Come. They're waiting."

Pina followed the black clad figure back onto the street. His slightly hunched back became the center of her focus as they wound their way along the crowded, narrow thoroughfare. Several minutes later the Rabbi opened the door to a tall, shabby tenement and gestured her inside.

The stench assaulted her immediately; unwashed bodies; the coppery odor of blood; human waste and vomit; the pungency of fear and despair. Pina heard the moans of the injured and dying, the murmuring of prayers. She followed the Rabbi out of the corridor and into a room packed with too many bodies to count.

Almost all the furniture had been removed. People lay in rows on the floor, only inches separating them. Several women, all with the yellow circles sewn on their breasts, moved among the maimed, offering what comfort they could. Two men working in blood-stained outer coats were doctors she recognized from previous missions to the ghetto. One of them looked up when she entered.

"Thank the Lord," he groaned, and pushed to his feet. His yellow patch was nearly obliterated by his patients' effluvia.

"God's angel has visited us once again in our time of need," the Rabbi said. His coal black eyes pinned her, and she looked away. She felt absurdly guilty, as if the plight of the people was her fault.

"You are not the cause of this," Rabbi Levan said softly, startling Pina with the accuracy of his statement. "Neither will you be the cure. But you are a blessing, and a light in the darkness."

The doctor who had risen stood before Andrea, who offered him the basket.

"There is material for bandages," Pina said shyly. "Herbs and salves as well. It's so little, but it was all I could manage. We're running low as well, and. . . ."

"We know your dilemma," the doctor interrupted in a kindly manner. "We thank you for your generosity. And your courage." With that he turned away to resume his work.

"Can I . . . can we help?" Pina looked up at Rabbi Levan. "You know my skills. I've helped before."

But the Rabbi shook his head. "You must not risk yourself by tarrying."

Pina couldn't disagree. It was becoming harder and harder to think up excuses to leave the villa, particularly for any length of time. And with the recent murders her mother was getting more and more protective.

"All right," she conceded reluctantly. "But I'll be back as soon as I can gather more supplies. Oh, and take these." Pina dug into the velvet sac tied to her belt and withdrew a few gold coins. She pressed them into the Rabbi's palm. His black eyes glittered, and she turned away before his tears of gratitude could spill.

Back on the street, Andrea turned to her mistress. She shuddered and wrapped her arms tightly across her breast. "I can't do this any more," she whispered. "It's horrible. I don't know how you stand it. And we're going to be caught, Miss Pina. Someone's going to notice the missing stores, or. . . ."

"I'm so sorry, Andrea." Heart going out to her maid, Pina put her arms around the dark-haired young woman. "I know this isn't easy for you. I'm so grateful for your loyalty. And your companionship. Thank you. With all my heart, thank you, Andrea."

The girl sniffed, genuinely afraid. Eventually they would be caught; her mistress took too many chances. And when her complicity in her mistress' escapades was discovered, she would undoubtedly lose her job. Yet Andrea knew she could never deny Pina, whom she had served since they were both children. Pina Galbi was, as the Rabbi had said, an angel. As long as her mistress continued to serve the poor, downtrodden, and oppressed of the city of Venice, she would remain at her side. Andrea pushed a hand under her nose and stepped away.

"We'd best get back to the villa, Miss Pina. We've

been gone too long already."

Pina placed a quick kiss on her servant's cheek and broke into a long-strided walk. Andrea was right. She was definitely pushing her luck. Her absences had been too frequent of late. Several of the other servants were growing suspicious, not to mention her mother.

Thoughts of her mother brought Pina another prick of guilt. Francesca Galbi, frail and nervous since the death of Pina's father, had become even more high-strung and anxious since the mysterious deaths of several young women, daughters all of wealthy and respected families.

Once outside the ghetto, the streets broadened and the crowds thinned. The noxious odors faded, replaced by the everpresent, liquid fragrance of the canals. The elegant facades of the buildings in her neighborhood were familiar and comforting, and the sun was warm on her back. Yet suddenly Pina was struck with unaccountable unease. Gathering her skirts, she hastened her steps.

The gates to the courtyard stood ajar. It was not a reassuring sign. Since the murders began, her mother had been adamant about keeping the gates locked at all times. Pina slipped inside, Andrea at her heels.

Two flights of stone steps arced gracefully upward to the wide double front doors. They were closed, but Pina's premonition deepened. She ran up the stairs and pushed the heavy door inward.

The sound of keening came to her ears, a high, thin sound that stretched her nerves taut. It came from the direction of the grand salon. Pina bolted.

Her mother, dressed in her habitual black, stood in the center of the elaborately inlaid marble floor. Both hands were pressed to her temples and her normally perfectly groomed silver hair streamed around her milk-white face. She tilted her head back and uttered another animal-like cry.

"Noooooo . . ."

"Signora Galbi . . . Signora, please," the steward, a portly, balding man, pleaded. "You cannot carry on like this. You will make yourself ill."

"*Si*. Sit, Signora," her maid added to the chorus of importunities. "Sit and let me bring you a glass of wine."

Francesca remained apparently oblivious. Pina strode quickly across the floor.

"Mother!"

"Ahhhhhhh . . . Pina!" Francesca Galbi seemed to have been jerked sharply back to reality. She took her hands from her head and held them out to her daughter. "Pina!"

"What is it, Mother? What has happened? What's wrong?"

"Pina . . . my daughter . . ." Signora Galbi choked. It was all she could say. Throwing her arms around Pina's shoulders, she broke into wild, uncontrollable sobs.

It was several minutes before the older woman was able

to rein in her explosive emotion. All the while, a half-dozen servants hovered with pitchers of iced wine, lavers of water, and linen towels, anything they thought might be of aid or comfort to their hysterical mistress.

When her mother had calmed somewhat, Pina's hands constantly stroking her back, she glanced over her shoulder at the steward. "Tell me what has happened," she demanded in a level voice. "What has happened to upset the Signora so?"

The steward merely looked uncomfortable. He exchanged glances with the other servants.

"Stefano!"

The steward visibly flinched. Signora Galbi broke into a fresh spate of weeping.

"It's Valeria!" her mother cried, pulling away, snatching at the few strands of hair left in the remains of her chignon. "Your cousin . . . my niece . . . my sister's baby!" Another shriek echoed through the cavernous, sumptuously decorated salon.

"Mother!" Pina grabbed her mother's forearms and forced her to look at her. "What about Valeria? What has happened. Tell me!"

"Dead!" An unearthly sound issued from Signora Galbi's throat. "Dead, like all the rest. Deeeeaaaaaaad . . ."

Pina staggered under her mother's weight as she collapsed into her daughter's arms.

CHAPTER

2

An arm slung over the side of the bed, head tilted to one side of the pillow, Francesca Galbi snored softly. Servants had closed the windows and drawn the heavy, indigo drapes, but there was still a chill in the air. Pina rose from her chair by the bed and pulled the coverlet up around her mother's shoulders. The older woman stirred briefly and settled back into her deep, exhausted sleep. Pina returned to her chair.

Though hours had passed, it was still incomprehensible. Valeria. Gone.

Pina tried to swallow past the painful lump in her throat, surprised there were apparently more tears to shed.

Valeria. They had been like sisters. They'd grown up together, playing, laughing, crying together. Their mothers were sisters, their fathers the closest of friends, fellow members of Venice's ruling council. Pina felt as if she had a hole in her heart. How could it be? She recalled Stefano's account of the events in her absence, once her mother had been put to bed.

"There was a messenger, Signorina," he had said. "A messenger from Villa Santonini. He asked to be brought to your mother. I tried to intercept the message, to spare the Signora a stranger's presence, but he was insistent." The steward wrung his hands. "And his news, when the Signora heard it . . ."

Pina well imagined her mother's initial reaction.

"I called for her maid," Stefano continued, "But even Sophia was unable to . . . to calm her."

"Did the messenger have anything else to say? Did he know how Valeria died? Where she was found?"

The steward paled visibly. "The Signora was incapable, but I . . . I questioned the man . . ."

"And?"

"And," Stefano cleared his throat. His eyes flickered briefly in Pina's direction, then returned to his tightly clasped hands. "And he told me she . . . Miss Valeria . . . was found in a boat. . . ."

"Oh, no." The beat of Pina's heart abruptly seemed to rise to her throat.

"Si, Signorina. Like two of the others."

"No." Pina shook her head in denial, but the steward

continued, warmed to his task.

"And there was no obvious cause of the death. She was just found . . . in her nightclothes. Dead."

Five others had been found in their nightclothes as well. Two, as Stefano had said, floating on the canals in a strange, black boat. Three, she amended mentally. Now three. Three others had been found on the grounds of their fathers' villas, in remote garden locations. No cause of death was evident. Pina shivered.

The first five had been horrible, of course. Tragedies. But they had not touched her. Now the terror had entered her own home. Valeria. Her cousin.

Pina glanced at her mother, still deeply asleep. She could not imagine her parent would awaken any time soon. She had not only finally taken wine, but wine laced with the ground leaves of a certain flower. Her slumber would be dreamless. And long. Pina turned from the bed.

It was time to see to herself. A soothing, warm bath perhaps. Her own glass of wine. A soft knock on the door drew Pina from her planning.

"Signorina?"

It was Andrea. Pina went to the door and opened it. "What is it, Andrea?"

Her servant's expression said it all.

"Who is it?" she asked, though she knew.

"Signor Antonio," Andrea replied timidly. "He's

determined to speak with you, Miss Pina."

Pina sighed wearily. "I'll see him in the grand salon, Andrea. Have someone bring us refreshment. And . . . thank you."

Andrea nodded briefly and withdrew. Pina sighed deeply.

Of course Antonio had come. Of course. She should have known.

It did not make it easier. Pina took another deep breath and left her mother's chamber.

The grand salon was vast, even by the standards of the prosperous Venetian elite. The chamber was round, half of it a bank of windows opening onto a balcony overlooking the Grand Canal. Draperies of heavy gold brocade hung between each set of the partially open doors, their lengths pooling on the marbled floor. On the opposite side of the room, the wall segments were divided by giltwork; in between each section hung a painting by a European master. Every piece of furniture was decorated with gold, chairs and settees covered in gold-embroidered, off-white silk. A clavichord graced one end of the room, a harpsichord the other. Vast bouquets of spring blossoms filled gold filigreed vases scattered about the room. Their perfume filled in the air, and a night breeze stirred the heavy curtains.

Pina could hear the hiss of the material as it moved on the floor. The sound was immediately covered by the noise of someone impatiently clearing their throat.

"There you are," Antonio said brusquely. "Do you know how long I've been waiting?"

He stood by one of the open windows. The breeze moved his light, thin hair, lifting it from a prominent brow. His pale blue eyes were wide, brows arched. Pina moved to his side.

"I came as soon as my servant summoned me," she said placatingly. "I'm sorry if I kept you waiting. I was with my mother."

Antonio sniffed. "How is *la signora*?" His tone bordered on grudging. Pina had to make a conscious effort not to tighten her fists.

"She is as well as can be expected . . . under the circumstances," she replied levelly.

"Ah, yes. Which is why I came. The circumstances, I mean. Tragic. Absolutely tragic."

"Then you've heard about . . . about Valeria?"

"Of course. And I came as soon as I could." Antonio composed his features into what he apparently thought was an appropriate expression of concern. He reached for her hands. "And you, my love. How are *you*?"

It was all Pina could do to keep from pulling her hands from his slightly clammy grip. *This is the man I'm to marry,*

18

came the sudden, panicky thought, *and I cannot even bear his touch.* Pina took a deep, steadying breath.

"I mourn my cousin, as you would expect," she replied. "We were . . . we were very close."

Antonio's grip on her hands tightened. He moved a little closer. Pina dropped her gaze.

"I am well aware of your relationship with Valeria. And it is why I fear for your safety now, my Pina."

Her pulse quickened, but not because of his nearness. Reluctantly, Pina glanced up. "What do you mean? Why should you worry for *my* safety?"

Antonio's grip tightened again. It was painful now. He leaned into her, his tall, thin body towering over her petite form.

"Because Venice is no longer safe." Antonio's voice was harsh, his tone menacing. "Young women are not even safe within the walls of their family villas, much less wandering the streets as you and your . . .."

The sound of footsteps clicking on marble was a welcome distraction. Although she knew she had only escaped him momentarily, Pina drew abruptly away from her fiance'.

"Set it over there, please, Andrea." Pina gestured at a low table. "And thank you."

The maid set the tray down; a bowl of fresh fruit, a decanter of wine and two goblets. "Is there anything else, signorina?"

Pina shook her head half-heartedly. "No. No, you may . . . you may leave now."

Andrea curtsied and withdrew. Pina turned back to the man at her side. "Antonio, may I pour you a. . . ."

His hand latched on to her wrist. Pina gasped. "Antonio, what . . . ?"

"Don't play the innocent," he growled. "I know where you were this morning."

Pina felt her jaw drop. "You . . . what?"

"You heard me. I know you were in that vile, filthy ghetto."

Though her temperament was generally serene, Pina felt a flame of anger spark in her breast. "And just *how* would you know, Antonio?"

His grip on her wrist relaxed. He crossed his arms over his narrow breast and snorted derisively. "We're betrothed, Pina," he replied, as if it explained everything. "You will be my bride. It is my duty to see to your safety and well being."

"You had me followed." Icy fingers seemed to be climbing up her spine.

"With your best interests at heart," he said smoothly. But the half-smile on his thin lips faded, belying his tone. "Yes, I had you followed. And not for the first time."

Pina drew a sharp breath.

"Nor the last." Antonio's voice was flat, hard. "I forbid

you to visit the ghetto again, Pina. I forbid you to leave this villa, in fact, unless you are in either your mother's company, or mine."

"You can't . . ."

"Oh, yes. I can," Antonio interrupted. "I will speak to your mother first thing in the morning. I know she will support me entirely in this."

Pina straightened her back, pulling herself up to her fullest height. "My mother is in mourning," she said coldly. "I doubt she'll even see you."

"Your mother's been in mourning since your father died. Nothing whatsoever has changed."

Pina felt as if she'd been slapped. Before she could speak, however, Antonio continued.

"One of the last things your father did was to arrange our marriage. The slightest wish your father ever had was considered a sacred obligation by your mother. I think, therefore, that when I plead my case to her, she will be more than happy to listen, and restrict your comings and goings. All in the interests of your safety, of course."

The half-smile returned to his lips.

"Or, I could tell her about your visits to the Jews. Does she know that's where you go when you leave with your little maid? Do you tell her all about the money and supplies you bring them? Money and goods you steal right from under her very nose? Does she know, Pina, or should

I tell her? And make certain you never leave these walls again. Until our wedding, that is."

Pina found herself literally trembling with fury. "How *dare* you invade my privacy in this fashion?"

Antonio made a clucking sound with his tongue against his teeth. "Is that any way for a well-bred young woman to speak to her affianced? I think not, my love." Yet again, his features abruptly hardened. "And you would do well to remember it."

A small cry erupted from Pina's throat when Antonio's fingers wrapped once more around her wrist. The strength of his grasp made it obvious he intended to cause her pain. It was all she could do to keep her knees from buckling.

Antonio released her as suddenly as he had grabbed her, and Pina staggered. A low chuckle emerged from his throat.

"*Buono notte*, my love. Sleep well. I will see you, no doubt, in the morning."

With that, Antonio whirled and strode from the room. Pina heard him bark an order at some hapless servant in the entrance foyer, and the sound of the massive front door opening and shutting. The door to a lavish prison.

CHAPTER

3

Pina sat in front of her dressing table mirror, concentrating on her image to banish thoughts of Antonio, and brushed out her long, honey-colored hair. She wore it longer than was fashionable, but it had been her father's pride and joy. *Father*.

Though it had been over a year, the pain of his loss was still sharp. Signor Eduardo Galbi had been not only an enormous force in Venetian politics, but in his home as well. A loyal, loving husband and doting father, he had been a rarity in their circle. His sudden death had been a terrible blow. Worse, Pina had been consumed with guilt as well as grief, for only days before his death they had quarreled. Over Antonio. Pina squeezed her eyes tightly shut, but the memory was achingly persistent.

They had been in his study; scrolls, books and

parchments lined the floor-to-ceiling shelves. The heavy, crimson drapes had been pulled aside and the window to the interior courtyard was open. Birdsong drifted in, mingled with the perfume of orange and lemon trees blooming in their ornamental tubs. But the mellow beauty of the day had been lost on Pina.

"You . . . you've done what?" she had demanded uncharacteristically of her father.

"I will not deign to repeat myself, Pina. You heard me well enough."

Yes, she had. Had she also heard a tinge of regret in his voice? "But you can't mean it, Father," she whispered. "Please tell me you don't mean it."

He had risen from his desk and walked to the window, his back to her. His long, elegantly embroidered camicia stirred in the breeze. "It is long past time I did this, daughter," he continued firmly. "I'm not getting any younger, and neither are you. It's my obligation and your duty."

"But Antonio Fontini . . . why? Why Antonio?"

He had turned then, patrician brow creased. "I thought you looked on him with favor, Pina."

"I was polite, Father. I treated him as I did every guest in this house. How could you possibly mistake . . ."

"Enough!"

Pina took an involuntary step backward, stung. She watched her father run a hand through his thick, silver hair.

"The marriage will be an excellent one. The Fontinis are one of the few families still prospering in overland trade. Signor Fontini is clever, resourceful, and has taught his son well. Antonio is your equal, both in wealth and breeding. His prospects are brilliant, his manners impeccable. And he is not ill-favored. It is a suitable match. It will be done."

There had been nothing to say to him. Not at the moment anyway. She knew better than to argue with him when he was making an initial point and taking his stand. Later she would be able to work on him, soften him with her subtle entreaties and endearments. He would change his mind about Antonio, whom she not only didn't love, but didn't even like. He would come around to her way of thinking, unconventional as it was. He would agree, eventually, that there was someone special out there, waiting for her, waiting to find her. Someone she could love, spend her life with happily. Later she would convince him. Later . . .

Pina stood so suddenly her padded stool tipped and fell over, thudding dully on the Turkish carpet. She dashed the tears from her cheeks, crossed to her high bed and blew out the tapers in the candelabra. The darkness was a balm, and Pina prayed it would help her sleep. She climbed beneath the covers. Continuing grief for her father, and fresh anguish for her cousin warred with anger toward Antonio. The knowledge he had had her followed felt no less than a personal violation. How dare he take it upon himself to have her watched? she silently fumed. Pina pulled the silken covers around her shoulders and turned restlessly onto her other side.

And it was not, he had admitted, the first time he had had her followed. How long had it been going on? Anger dissolved suddenly into fear for her friends in the ghetto.

Her father had told her Antonio's manners were impeccable. And so they were — on the surface. But his moods were mercurial, and when the smile slipped from his lips, as it did all too often, a seething, simmering anger was frequently revealed. Antonio, she had discovered, was vindictive, cruel even. His closest friends regarded him warily. Should he decide to blame her Jewish friends for something, perhaps just for her seeing them, or helping them, the consequences could be terrible for the already persecuted minority.

The darkness no longer seemed comforting. She suddenly longed for sunlight and sound, the companions of her day, things that turned her thoughts from black to white.

But the hours 'til dawn were long, and she was alone with the knowledge of her imprisonment. It was very late before Pina finally slept.

Sleeplessness took its toll. It was Andrea who awakened Pina, pulling back the sky blue, gold-edged drapes and throwing open the shutters.

"Good morning, signorina. Are you well? I don't think I've ever seen you sleep this late."

Pina sat up and rubbed her eyes. "What time is it?"

"Two hours since your mother broke her fast," the dark-haired girl replied. "Would you like me to bring you tea?"

"Two hours!" Pina thrust her legs over the side of the bed and slipped to the floor. "Why didn't you waken me?"

Andrea looked crestfallen. "With respect, signorina, you are in mourning for your cousin, and . . ."

"Never mind. I'm sorry." Pina pulled open a carved chest and began rummaging through her clothes. "My mother hasn't had any visitors yet, has she?" she asked distractedly.

"Why, yes. Signor Fontini is with her even now."

Pina's fingers curled tightly on a pale green velvet gown, and for an instant she felt frozen to the spot. Then she pulled it abruptly from the chest without noting what it was. "Help me dress, please. Quickly."

Pina found them in her mother's favorite room, a smaller

reception chamber off the grand salon. Everything was in her mother's favorite shade, from the pink-veined marble floor to the damask drapes. Roses bloomed on silk-covered chairs, and on the chaise where her mother reclined.

Francesca raised a heavy-lidded gaze to her daughter. "My child," she gasped hoarsely. Pressing one pale, blue-veined hand to her breast, she held out the other to her daughter. "Pina . . ."

"I'm here, Mother," she replied quickly, and moved to her mother's side. The fingers she clasped in her own felt too warm, and she noted her mother's face was flushed as well. She raised her eyes at last to the man standing on the opposite side of the chaise.

"Antonio," Pina bit out tightly. He nodded, a slow smile creeping across his lips.

"Good morning, Pina, my dear," he drawled. "I trust you slept well?"

Pina pressed her lips firmly together and redirected her attention to her mother. "You feel warm to me, Mother. Shall I get you a compress?"

Signora Galbi rolled her head from side to side. "No. No . . ." she moaned. "I want . . . I just want. . . ." Tears overwhelmed the older woman and she pulled away from Pina to bury her face in her hands.

"Perhaps I can help," Antonio put in smoothly. His smile was still in place, but a tic jumped under his left eye.

Pina had to use all the force of her will to keep from gnashing her teeth. So. It was as she had feared.

"Your dear mother wants what I want, Pina," Antonio continued. His watery gaze was unblinking. "Your safety."

"Oh, Pina," Francesca took her hands from her face and clasped them in an attitude of supplication. "How could you take such chances? How could you do such things when terror is abroad in our city, a murderer is preying on our young women . . . your own cousin!"

Pina's blood chilled. Her eyes shifted to Antonio. How much had he told her mother?

"I've told *la signora* about your . . . 'charitable works'," Antonio said.

Pina watched him lick his thin lips, prolonging, and savoring, her anxiety.

"I've informed her of your generosity to those less fortunate than ourselves . . ."

"Oh, Pina," Signora Galbi interrupted. "You are so good hearted. No mother could ask for a better child. But Antonio is right. You must not put yourself at risk any longer. I will have servants deliver our scraps to the Catholic poor, if it is your wish to continue this good deed. But you . . . you cannot go out again . . . not with the murders . . ."

The storm of weeping resumed. Pina put her arms around her mother to comfort her, but her heart felt leaden. She glanced up at Antonio.

His grin said it all. He had lied for her, yes. Rather, he had withheld the truth. But not from any goodness in his soul. The truth, the whole truth, about her activities would be a hammer held over her head. Antonio had given her mother just enough information to ensure her imprisonment. It was what he wanted . . . for now. But what might he wish from her in the future? What might she have to do to keep from her mother knowledge that would surely devastate the older woman?

A shiver traveled up Pina's spine and she hugged her mother tighter. "Sssshhh, Mama," she soothed. "Everything will be all right. I'll stay home, I promise. I'll be safe. Nothing will happen to me. Nothing . . ."

CHAPTER

4

A freshening breeze stirred the drapes in Pina's room. Restless, she walked to the window and gazed down at the traffic on the canal. The sight of the boats, people hurrying about their business, served merely to depress her further. She paced the width of her chamber to the window overlooking the courtyard.

Guards at the gate. Guards at the front steps. Guards, undoubtedly, by the front doors. Her mother's paranoia was full blown. And probably nurtured by Antonio. Pina's hands clenched at her sides as she seethed.

The situation was untenable. A prisoner! In her own home! And soon she would have to marry her jailer. She hated him! She hated him so thoroughly the emotion eclipsed even her grief over Valeria's death. Pina whirled toward the door just as it opened.

Andrea's heart instantly squeezed with pity at the sight of her mistress' expression. "Miss Pina," she began, "I . . ."

"How is my mother?" Pina interrupted, wanting to forestall Andrea's offer of sympathy. It only made her feel worse. "Did she take any lunch?"

Andrea nodded. "A little. But what about you, Miss Pina? Can I get *you* anything?"

Pina started to shake her head, then paused. "I need nothing. But what about Rabbi Levan? What about all those poor people injured in the building collapse? Oh, Andrea . . . I can't stand this any longer! I have to get out of the villa. There's so much to do. I can't remain locked up forever!"

If she'd hoped to see confirmation in Andrea's gaze, Pina was disappointed. The maid's round, dark eyes glistened as tears welled.

"Please, don't cry, Andrea," Pina said, more sharply than she had intended. Fists still clenched, she turned away. "Damn him. *Damn* Antonio."

Andrea gasped. "Miss Pina!"

Pina smiled grimly and her fingers relaxed. She felt a little better. Maybe she'd be able to think more clearly as well.

"Getting angry isn't going to get me out of here, and it isn't going to help our friends in the Ghetto Nuovo." Pina turned back to Andrea. "You'll have to go in my stead."

Andrea's eyes widened until Pina could see white all the way around the irises.

"Go without you?" The maid slowly shook her head. "Oh . . . oh, no. I couldn't. I . . ."

"You have to," Pina said firmly. "I can't just abandon the people who need our help so desperately, little as it is."

"But . . . but the *ghetto*, Miss Pina. I don't mind going with you, but . . ."

"You'll be just fine, you know you will. We can't abandon those people, Andrea!"

Andrea visibly shrank, shoulders seeming to cave inward. "What . . . what do you want me to take?" she asked reluctantly.

"Thank you, Andrea," Pina said, grasping her maid's hands. "Thank you so much. I feel better already."

Andrea listened while her mistress reeled off a list of items she'd have to pilfer from the dwindling stores, knowing they were going to be caught sooner than later. But there was no way she could deny her mistress. With a heavy sigh and a heavier heart, she left to do Pina's bidding.

Andrea's sense of foreboding grew as she made her way through the bustling streets toward the ghetto. She adored Pina and loved Signora Galbi as if she were her own mother.

Indeed, Signora Galbi was the only mother she had ever known. Her own mother, a cook in the Galbi kitchens, had died at her birth, unwed. Andrea had been reared in the household and her loyalty was unquestionable and undying. She would do anything for Pina, but felt guilty at the same time going behind Signora Galbi's back. Perhaps that was why she felt as if a black cloud hovered over her head, despite the warmth and brightness of the day.

The huge gates to the Ghetto Nuovo loomed ahead. It was true, what Miss Pina had told her, Andrea realized. She *did* know she'd be fine as soon as she made it inside. The ghetto's denizens really were their friends. It was out here, on the streets of Venice, she was in the greatest peril.

The thought quickened Andrea's steps. Clutching her basket of purloined herbs and linens, she moved within the shadow of the towering gates . . .

. . . and felt cool fingers curl around her wrist. The grip immediately tightened. Cruelly.

Andrea's cry died in her throat when she looked up into Antonio's slitted gaze. Tiny lines appeared at the corners of his eyes as his smile broadened. A chill ran down her spine, and as swiftly returned to its origin. She could almost feel the blood drain from her face.

"Ah, the little maid," Antonio drawled. "Running an errand for your mistress?"

Andrea's tongue had cleaved to the roof of her mouth.

She couldn't even blink.

"How droll. And what have we in the basket?"

Andrea tried to cringe away, but Antonio held her fast. She managed to squeeze her eyes tightly shut when he lifted the muslin covering.

"Well, well, well. Let's see." The fingers of his free hand trailed over the items in the basket. Andrea could not help thinking they had just been tainted beyond use.

"Does *la signora* know about this, hmmm? Does she know how generous she's being to the . . . *citizens* . . . of the Ghetto Nuovo?"

Andrea's instinct was to close her eyes again. But that wouldn't make him go away. Although she made an effort to speak, her throat felt paralyzed.

"In the absence of your response, let me guess. No." The smile slipped instantly from his lips. Andrea felt her hand begin to go numb as his grip, unbelievably, tightened further.

"How much do you like your job, little maid?" Icicles of fear penetrated Andrea's flesh. "Do you love it? Will you miss it when you're out on the street?"

It was getting hard to breathe. "Please." Andrea squeaked.

" 'Please' what?" Antonio mocked. "Please don't tell Signora Galbi of your thievery? Your disloyalty?"

Had she managed to nod? Her muscles were so tight

she wasn't certain she had actually moved her head.

"I might, actually, be able to help you." Antonio's tongue swept lasciviously over his thin mouth. "If you were to help me, that is."

Andrea realized the grip on her wrist had loosened. She watched his hand, in horror, as it reached for her breast. Cupped it. Caressed it. When she tried to pull away, his free arm went about her waist, pulling her to him. She felt the evidence of his arousal against her thigh. Desperate, she cast about her for help.

The crowds were anonymous, indifferent. A single passerby, a dandified gentleman, cast his gaze briefly in her direction. His brows arched and a half-smile tilted one corner of his mouth. He looked away.

"No one will help you, you know. You're a servant, and I . . . well." Antonio chuckled obscenely. He squeezed her nipple. Painfully. "And *I* am the man who will make you beg for more . . ."

She was going to faint. His words caused a terrible nausea to churn in her belly. Words that were vaguely familiar. Where had she heard them? And why did they make her head swim?

Antonio released her abruptly as her knees started to buckle. She staggered away from him. He laughed aloud.

"That's it, little maid. Run along home now. Run along and wait for me. Because I'll come. You know I will. And I want you to be ready. Very, very ready. Go on, now. Go."

She didn't need to be told again. The sound of his laughter followed her.

For the first two hours of Andrea's absence, Pina contented herself with visions of her maid's mission. Andrea would be fine, just as she had assured her. She would find Rabbi Levan in the synagogue. Being the recipient of his gratitude would be a balm to the state of anxiety she had worked herself into. Perhaps she would accompany him to the makeshift hospital.

But no. Andrea didn't have the healing instincts Pina had. She certainly hadn't the stomach for the inevitable stench. No, Andrea would hand over the all-too-meager supplies, and return to the villa. She should be back at any moment.

But Andrea didn't appear, and the afternoon stretched onward. Soon shadows gathered in the corners of her chamber, and the breeze that had once refreshed now made Pina shiver. She fetched a shawl that had been carelessly flung over the back of a chair and wrapped it around her shoulders. Taking a deep breath, she left her room.

Servants stalked the corridors, carrying tapers with

which to light numerous candelabra to dispel the early evening gloom. Pina stopped a young boy, Pietro, the son of her mother's personal maid, and laid a hand on his shoulder.

"Pietro, have you seen Andrea?"

"Si, signorina. She's in the grand salon with Signora Galbi."

Puzzlement and concern warred in her breast. Why hadn't Andrea returned to her? Had she been unable to leave? Had something gone wrong? Had she been caught taking the stores? Remembering to thank Pietro, she sent him on his way and changed directions to head for the salon.

Pina's eye was immediately drawn to the long bank of windows. Only one of them was open now, and Andrea was pulling the drapes closed over the rest. Pina's mother sat by the huge marble fireplace, sipping wine, and staring into the nonexistent flames. Casting Andrea a worried sidelong glance, she crossed to her parent.

"Mother, how are you?" Pina brushed a kiss against Signora Galbi's cheek and took the chair next to her.

The older woman turned her head slowly in Pina's direction. Her eyes seemed to refocus, and she offered her daughter a wan smile. "Pina," she acknowledged.

"How are you?" Pina repeated, taking her mother's hand. It felt cold.

The older woman shrugged, then gave her head a little shake. "I grieve for Valeria," she replied simply. "My heart bleeds for my sister. And I fear for you . . ."

"Mother . . ."

Francesca gave Pina's hand a little squeeze. "I know it's difficult, remaining confined in the villa, my dear. But it gives me a small measure of peace. Antonio is so wise, so kind."

Pina had to will herself to remain calm. She heard Andrea knock against a small table; its legs scraped gratingly on the marble floor.

"He came by a short time ago," the older woman continued as if she'd heard nothing amiss. "Andrea said you were sleeping, dear, or I would have told you."

"What did he want?" Pina managed to ask stiffly. She cast a glance at Andrea, who visibly paled.

"Naught but to inquire after our needs." Signora Galbi sighed, a faint smile touching her lips.

"And . . . is there anything you need, Mother?"

"I'm feeling stronger now. I wish to go to the basilica tomorrow and pray for Valeria's soul."

"I'll accompany you, Mother," Pina said quickly. "You don't need Antonio."

"Yes. Yes, that's right." Francesca released her daughter's hand and returned her gaze to the empty hearth. "That's what I told him. He's a busy man, an important man. He needn't dance constant attendance on us. We shall go to pray together, as it should be. And we'll take some of the household guards."

Pina felt a curious mixture of relief and irritation. Antonio's noxious presence still hovered, but her mother had kept him at bay, however temporarily. And she was going to leave the villa, however briefly.

Keeping one wary eye on Andrea, who puttered about, straightening bric-a-brac and arranging the folds of the drapes, Pina chatted with her mother for several more minutes. She was grateful to see her parent's mood had indeed improved. Even her color was better. But she was anxious to speak with Andrea. Finally able to excuse herself to dress for dinner, Pina hurried from the room. She was not at all surprised to hear Andrea's footsteps clicking along behind her.

"Where were you all afternoon?" Pina cried the instant Andrea had shut her chamber door. "I was worried sick!"

Andrea clasped her hands together in front of her breast. "I'm so sorry, Miss Pina."

"Sorry for what? What happened?"

"As soon as I returned, Sophia asked me to help her with some mending for La Signora, then ."

"No," Pina said impatiently. "I mean what happened when you went out?"

Andrea swallowed, as if the action might arm her with courage. "I . . . I never saw Rabbi Levan. I never made it to the synagogue."

Icy fingers curled around Pina's heart. "It was Antonio, wasn't it?" she asked slowly.

Andrea nodded. "He must have followed me."

Pina resisted the urge to close her eyes. By the expression on Andrea's face, there was more. A lot more.

"Go ahead, Andrea. Tell me."

"Oh, Miss Pina . . ."

"Tell me."

Andrea found herself completely unable to speak. The memory of his hand on her was too fresh, too horrible. He was an evil man, and her beloved mistress was going to be forced to wed him. Andrea hiccoughed on a sob and pressed her hands to her mouth.

"Andrea!" Pina said sharply, and gripped her maid's shoulders. "Did Antonio hurt you? Did he . . . *touch* you?"

Another strangled sob was her only reply. Pina gave her a little shake, and Andrea finally nodded.

"He . . . he. . . ." Andrea glanced down at her breast, then burst into sobs. "Miss . . . Miss Pina, you . . . can't . . . you can't marry him! He . . ."

"Never mind," Pina hissed, and drew Andrea fiercely into her arms. "You'll be all right. And I'll be all right. I'll find a way, Andrea. I'll never marry him. Never!"

But as Andrea wept and trembled in her arms, Pina knew her prayers on the morrow would have to be for more than her cousin's soul.

CHAPTER

5

Though the spring day had dawned with little warmth, it was stifling in the church. Not only had her mother insisted they walk to the basilica in the company of a half-dozen household guards, but she had wrapped herself, head to toe, in a flowing black cape. Nothing would do but for Pina to do so as well. Furthermore, she had not allowed her to let the hood fall from her head, or loosen the clasp at her throat. Miserable, Pina sat and felt miniature rivers of sweat run from beneath her arms, down her back, and between her thighs.

Compounding her misery was the heavy, nearly stifling perfume of incense. She tried to concentrate on the words of the Mass, but felt too lightheaded to concentrate. Yet, she had to pray. She had to.

It wasn't hard to repeat the ritual prayer words. It wasn't

difficult to send heartfelt grief for her cousin heavenward as a wordless prayer. But when it came to Antonio . . .

Was it even right to pray to be released from an alliance her parents had made? Was it right to pray *against* something rather than *for* it? It somehow felt wrong, and selfish.

Steeling herself, Pina remembered Andrea weeping in her embrace. She had never told her exactly what Antonio had done, and Pina didn't need to know. She could imagine. She recalled how Antonio had had her followed, how he held the truth of her charitable works over her head to keep her a prisoner. He was cruel, sadistic even. This was the man she was supposed to spend the rest of her life with? Pina squeezed her eyes tightly shut.

Heavenly Father, she began formally in her mind. Then, as fear and revulsion clamored in her breast: *Please, God, please . . . help me. Save me. I'll do anything to prove my devotion, my faith, if you'll just free me from this horror. I can't marry Antonio . . . my soul will die. I'll do anything, face anything. Just please don't make me marry him. Please, O Lord, please . . . help me. . . .*

"Pina?"

It took a moment for Pina to pull herself from the depths of the trance into which she'd spiraled. Her mother was tapping her forearm.

"Pina," she whispered. "The Mass is over."

Pina looked up at the splendor of the basilica's interior;

the soaring, domed ceiling, and priceless stained glass windows streaming warmly hued sunlight. Her face felt flushed. Her clothes were wringing wet and plastered to her body. Flashing her mother a faint smile, she struggled to her feet.

Sweat rolled down her legs to her ankles. Concentrating on taking deep, regular breaths, Pina took her mother's arm as they made their way down the wide aisle, through the double wooden doors, and out into the sunlight. Despite its brightness, its heat, there was at least fresh air on her face. The lightheadedness receded.

The guards fell in step around them and the women started back toward the villa, a relatively short walk. Pina longed for the cool comfort of the airy rooms and quickened her step. But dizziness assailed her overheated body once again, and she faltered. Her mother grabbed her hand and tugged her along.

"Come along, Pina. Hurry." Her light brown eyes darted from side to side furtively, as if someone might jump at them from out of the shadows.

But it was impossible for Pina to keep up. Her gown beneath the cloak was wringing wet and its weight dragged at her. She stumbled, and her hand pulled loose from her mother's. Pina fell to her knees.

For the space of several heartbeats, Signora Galbi's entourage continued to move forward. Those in front moved on ahead; the guards behind were still several steps away. The world lagged. Time seemed to slow. Pina felt someone watching her and slowly, slowly turned her head.

Directly perpendicular to her was a dark, narrow alley. She saw nothing at first. The she saw his eyes.

Golden brown, they bored into her. Gilded flecks appeared to dance within their depths. The very beat of her heart became sluggish and her blood thickened within her veins. It was with supreme effort only Pina was able to move her gaze to the rest of him.

He was tall, very tall. Thick, unruly hair cascaded to his shoulders, hair almost the color of his eyes, with streaks of sun-kissed gold. His face was well-proportioned and his features refined, lips full and elegantly sculpted.

But he was pale, so pale, and gaunt, with purple bruises beneath his eyes. Pina's gaze started downward, but the guards had caught up with her. She was assisted to her feet and moved briskly forward. The alley was behind her.

The gold-flecked eyes burned in her memory.

As soon as Pina had stripped out of her sodden clothes, she bathed, and felt almost returned to normal. Andrea wrapped her in a linen bath sheet and went about tidying the chamber while Pina sat at her dressing table.

The mirror reflected a young woman whose features were as distinguished as her lineage. Pina turned her face to one side, then the other. Her nose was small, cheekbones high. Her skin was pale and flawless, her eyes blue, her hair a rare shade of gold. People called her beautiful. Her mother had told her that her beauty, combined with her dowry, would bring the richest prince of the city to their door. She had not been wrong. The villa had been besieged with the most eligible applicants for her hand. The money Pina had always been able to understand. But her physical attractions? She supposed Antonio thought her comely enough. There was no question he found her dowry suitable.

Pina continued to stare at her reflection. Was she pretty, in truth? She had never really thought about it, never considered it important, or even relevant to her life. Her father, whom she had adored, had told her education mattered, intellect was important, knowledge was relevant. Her pursuits therefore had been cerebral ones. She had been so unlike Valeria, always concerned with her hair, her complexion, clothes. So why did she now stare at her reflection so critically?

Gold-flecked eyes suddenly looked back at her. Pina blinked.

"Are you all right, signorina?"

Pina turned from the mirror, feeling slightly stunned.

"I . . . I'm fine." Why did Andrea look at her so curiously? She wanted to be alone. "But I find I have a . . . a headache. Would you draw the drapes, please, and leave me?"

"Would you like to put on a night dress, or . . ."

"Just leave me. Please."

Andrea did as she was bid and hurried from the room. When she was gone, Pina locked her door. Barefoot, she crossed to her bed and let the bath sheet fall to the floor. She climbed between the sheets, reveling in the feel of her naked skin against the clean linens, and closed her eyes.

She didn't have a headache. Not at all. She just wanted to be alone. Alone with the memory of golden brown eyes. Alone until night fell, and she could . . .

What? What was she thinking? Why were her thoughts spinning?

Pina tried to rise from her bed, but her body felt weighted. Fatigue tugged at her eyelids. She slept.

Francesca sat alone at the head of the long mahogany dining table. Candlelight flickered in silver candelabra, reflecting off the crystal and sterling laid for dinner. It was elegant, and delicious smells wafted from the kitchen, but the Signora frowned.

"Where is my daughter, Tita?" she asked the maid

who served the table. She knows this is the dinner hour."

"I don't know, Signora Galbi. Shall I fetch Andrea?"

"Please." The white-haired woman drummed her fingertips impatiently on the tabletop until Andrea appeared.

"I'm sorry, signora. Pina is asleep."

"Still? She slept all afternoon."

Andrea clutched her hands together. "She felt unwell, as you know, when you returned from church."

Francesca nodded. "Very well. I'll dine without her. But, please, see if she'll eat something when she wakes."

"Very well, signora." Andrea ducked her head and left. She too was worried about Pina. Especially since her door was locked. In all the time she had served the family, Pina had never once locked her door. When Andrea had knocked, she had called that she was sleeping . . . or trying to. Andrea had never even heard that tone of voice before. What had happened in the space of time Pina had accompanied her mother to the basilica and returned?

Andrea tried knocking on Pina's door one more time, but got only a muffled response. Pulling a chair from a nearby guest chamber, she sat down by her mistress' door to wait. But for what, she didn't know.

Pina lay staring into the darkness. She remembered falling

asleep, but didn't think she had slept long. When she awoke, she had been able to think of only one thing.

She had to go back to that alley. She had to go back and see the man with the gold-flecked eyes.

All throughout the remainder of the afternoon Pina had lain in her darkened room. When Andrea had called to her, she told her to go away, that she was trying to sleep. Andrea had returned later to see if she needed help to dress for dinner. Pina had declined, of course, feigning lingering fatigue. When Andrea had come back a third time, undoubtedly on her mother's orders to see why she had not appeared for dinner, she had merely mumbled a reply that Andrea could interpret as anything she wished.

Every hour, on the hour, the clock on her fireplace mantle chimed. Ten. Eleven. Twelve. Pina rose from her bed.

The air was chill on her still naked skin. Pina dressed swiftly, and pulled a hasty brush through her waist-length hair. She tip-toed to her door.

It opened soundlessly to reveal Andrea sound asleep in a chair. She snored softly and did not stir when Pina moved past her.

The corridor was deserted, as she had known it would be. The servants were all asleep. The guards were all posted on the exterior of the villa. She made her way down the long, dim hallway.

Once, when she was very young, she had wanted to see a fireworks exhibition in the plaza, despite the fact she had developed a case of the sniffles. Her mother had been adamant in her refusal to let her daughter attend. The night air was cool, the excitement would be too much, she was ill already . . .

Her father had come for her after she had been put to bed. Hand in hand they had sneaked down the corridor and through the villa to his library. On the short wall to the right of the doorway hung a floor-to-ceiling portrait of some distant ancestor. Her father had touched it and it sprang away from the wall, revealing a hidden door.

"Sssshhh." He had raised a finger to his lips, hearing her delighted giggle. "Mama must never know. This will be our secret."

On the other side of the door, stairs led down to the dock. To avoid being seen by the household guards, they had simply walked along the retaining wall to their neighbor's dock, then up the narrow alley between the two villas. It would have been impossible to do during daylight hours; the guards would have seen her. But now . . .

Pina shivered when she stepped out into the night air. She climbed up onto the wall and began walking.

CHAPTER

6

Though it was past midnight, Venice was a lively city. Late-night revelers roamed the streets, almost exclusively male. They eyed her curiously, and Pina drew the hood of her cloak up over her head. This time when she shivered, it was not because of the briskness of the air, which did in fact seem unnaturally warm. The tremor was accompanied by a brief moment of clarity.

What was she doing? Was she mad? She was on her way to meet a stranger. Even some of the people she knew were dangerous. And this was a perfect *stranger*.

Furthermore, there was a killer loose on the streets of Venice, someone who murdered young women. And there were undoubtedly many who would have no compunctions about simply pulling her into an alley to have their way with her. What had she been thinking?

And just what made her assume the stranger with the hypnotic eyes would still be in the same place? How could she ever have thought he would remain there, waiting for her?

No sooner had the thoughts whirled through her brain than they were gone again.

He would be there. She was absolutely certain. It's why she had come out; why she had been compelled to leave the safety of the villa and return to the alley. He would be there.

The route to the basilica was a familiar one and Pina walked rapidly. The alley was not far ahead.

Near the plaza the street became more crowded. It was an easy feat to slip, unnoticed, into the alley.

Pina's heart pounded as heavily as if she had run all the way. She put a hand to her breast. Took a deep breath. Peered toward the darkened end of the alley.

No one. Just a puddle of water, some debris. Shadows.

A war of emotions raged in Pina's breast. Relief. Disappointment. An overwhelming urge to feel completely foolish and irresponsible. She turned to leave.

"Please, don't go."

The voice was low, mellifluous. It shuddered through her, a physical presence, rooting her to the spot.

"Pina."

Tendrils of fear wound languidly around her heart.

She was not moved to bolt. But how could he know . . .?

"How do you know my name?" She did not turn to face him.

"I . . . don't know. I saw you. I knew."

Pina closed her eyes. The sounds from the street faded away. "How do you know me? Who are you?" Silence. "Answer me."

"I told you. I don't know."

"You don't know who *you* are?" Pina whirled then, so swiftly her skirt swirled out around her. The sight of him shocked her.

She remembered his handsome but gaunt face, the dark smudges beneath his eyes, the pallor. He had looked starved, ill perhaps. But this man appeared to be dying.

Pina's heart clenched and she reached out to him, the gesture instinctive. He flinched away from her.

"What's wrong with you? Are you ill?"

He shook his head. His thick, wavy hair brushed the tops of broad shoulders.

"You must tell me your name," Pina demanded, "so I can help you."

"I . . . I don't know," he repeated.

"You don't know your name? Truly?" This was impossible. Everything was impossible. He had remained in the alley. Waiting for her? How had she known to come? How had she been so certain? And he didn't even know his name. What was happening?

The man made no reply, merely sent her a gaze of such intensity it rocked her. She immediately forgot her questions, her wonder. She even forgot where she was, what she was doing. Pina shook her head. Collected her scattered thoughts.

"Perhaps you've had an accident," she replied at length. "Hit your head, so you can't remember your name."

The eyes stared, unblinking.

"You . . . you need help," Pina faltered. "Please, let me help you."

"Yes. Help me." He held out his hand.

Pina responded without thinking and extended her arm. Their fingers touched.

Once, in a violent thunderstorm, lightning had struck close to the villa. The shock of the concussion had stunned her at first. Next came the adrenaline of fear, hot and wild in her body. The same thing had just happened again.

Pina withdrew her hand as if she had been burned. She stared at it, as if expecting to see the mark of the fire. When she looked up again, he was gone.

CHAPTER

7

Moon and stars were obscured in an overcast night sky. Somewhere out over the ocean a storm brewed, and occasional flickers of far-off lightning illumined the purple-black sky. The air was heavy and humid, fulfilling the promise of the unusually warm evening air.

Pina had kicked the covers from her legs. Sweat beaded her brow and upper lip. Her eyes were tightly closed, but her sleep was not restful. She tossed from side to side, and groped the air, reached out for something like a drowning man reaches for the surface of the water. Deep within her subconscious, awareness struggled to pierce the veil of sleep and bring her up from the abyss into which she had fallen.

Out at sea, thunder rumbled low and ominously. It was enough sound to bring Pina back from the edge. Her eyes opened and she sat bolt upright, panting.

Six candles still clung to life in the ornate candelabrum set on the carved marble mantle. But even as Pina woke, a cool, stiff storm breeze blew through the open windows on either side of her room and extinguished the pale illumination. She got up at once and hurried to relight the tapers, wardens against all night fears.

The fragile light, however, did not dispel the horror of what she had dreamed. Or, rather, *hadn't* dreamed.

Pina stood, one hand on the cool mantle, and tried to remember exactly what had so terrified her. It was, in fact, nothing, she realized with a shiver. She had dreamed nothing, although she was absolutely certain she had been in the place of dreams. But it had been empty. Void. Cold. And she had felt more alone and vulnerable than she had ever felt in her life.

When she finally stopped trembling, Pina made her way to the dressing table where Andrea had placed a silver carafe of water along with a crystal goblet. Pina drank, then pressed the glass to her temples. She finished the water and climbed back into her bed.

What was wrong with her? What was happening?

Trying to ease the strange pounding of her pulse, residual fear from the black place she had been in her sleep, she tried to organize the scattered puzzle pieces of her memory. She had done something out of the ordinary this night — what was it? *Think, Pina, think.*

She had wakened — but had she been asleep? — and had left her chamber. Andrea had been in a chair outside her door. Yes! She remembered. And she had left the villa by the secret way her father had once shown her. She had gone in the direction of the plaza, the basilica . . .

Horrified remembrance clutched Pina's entire body as if she had just been taken in the grasp of a giant's hand and squeezed.

Golden brown eyes. He was ill. He needed her help . . .

Had she really gone there? Had she really done that?

It was no dream, though she wished it. It was in the very core of her nature to help those in need. She had gone out, in the middle of the night, and returned to the alley. Somehow she had known he needed her, and she responded.

But how had she dared? Sneaking from the villa in the dead of the night was a great deal different than making a foray to the Ghetto Nuovo with Andrea in broad daylight. Where had she found such courage?

And why was the memory so hard to catch and hold on to?

Shivering now as the breaking storm lashed at the villa, Pina pulled the covers up to her chin.

It was a long time until she slept.

CHAPTER

8

It was not quite dawn when Andrea awoke, painfully aware of a kink in her neck and a dull ache in the small of her back. Yawning, she stretched and nearly fell out of the straight-backed chair. Instantly fully awake and alert, Andrea jumped to her feet and tried her mistress' door. To her surprise, the handle turned and Andrea stumbled into the chamber. Taking in the scene, she gasped in dismay.

Rain-driven water puddled beneath the window facing the canal. When she touched the drapes, she found them cool and damp. Pina had been so deeply asleep the violence of the storm hadn't wakened her, or she would have summoned Andrea to close the windows. And she had slept away the entire previous afternoon! Andrea hurried to her mistress' bedside. Once again, she had cause to suck in a sharp breath.

Pina was obviously still in a deep sleep, her lips slightly parted. Her hair was in disarray on the pillow, accentuating her startling pallor; the pallor highlighted the deep bruising beneath her eyes. Andrea touched a tentative hand to Pina's shoulder.

"Miss Pina? Miss Pina, please, wake up."

Andrea held her breath for the fraction of a moment until she saw eyelids flutter. "Miss Pina!"

"Andrea," Pina replied groggily. "What's wrong?" Awareness settled slowly into her features, tightening them. "Is it Mother? Is she all right?"

With gentle pressure, Andrea held her mistress down when she tried to struggle to a sitting position. "Sssshhh. Everything's all right. Signora Galbi is fine . . . nothing's wrong. You were just sleeping so deeply, I . . . I was worried, that's all."

Pina glanced about her room, noting the pink light of dawn just creeping over her window sills. "But it's so early, Andrea. Of course I was sleeping."

Andrea stepped away from the bed and Pina blinked away the final edges of sleep clinging to her eyelids. She had been deeply asleep indeed, and waking felt as if she were climbing up from a deep canyon. She rubbed her eyes with the backs of her hands.

"Do you . . . do you feel all right?" Andrea asked hesitantly.

Pina licked her lips and let her mind travel through her body. She felt a bit sluggish, but fine otherwise.

"I'm fine. Maybe a little tea . . ."

"Right away. I'll get it right away, Miss Pina."

Andrea scurried from the room, a worried frown creasing her normally smooth brow.

"Andrea, call the doctor. At once," Francesca ordered. She looked down at her daughter's face, whiter than the white satin pillow against which she lay, and hugged her arms to her thin bosom.

"I'm all right, Mother," Pina protested. "I just didn't sleep well, that's all."

Andrea and Signora Galbi exchanged swift glances, which Pina didn't miss. Suddenly uncomfortable, she squirmed.

"I . . . I was up several times during the night," she offered. "That must be why I felt so groggy this morning."

"If you were up, Miss Pina, why didn't you call me to close the windows against the rain?"

Rain? Pina creased her brow. Yes, it seemed she remembered hearing thunder, just as it seemed she had spent a restless night. But . . . doing what?

"Pina?"

Her mother's voice brought her head up. "Please . . . please, don't worry, Mother. I think all I need is a bit of fresh air."

"You'll not be leaving this house. You'll not be leaving this *bed*." She turned to Andrea. "The doctor, Andrea. Send for him *now*."

Francesca sat in the smaller room off the grand salon and worried the handkerchief she held in her lap. "But she looks so pale, Doctor."

"I agree, but it could be, as Pina insists, the result of a restless night." The doctor patted his thinning gray hair in a nervous gesture. "I find nothing physically wrong with her."

"Wrong with who?"

"Antonio!" Signora Galbi exclaimed. "What . . .?"

"I said, what is wrong with *who*?" In three long strides, he stood in the center of the room, towering over the diminutive doctor and the seated woman.

"How did you . . . who let you in?" the *Signora* asked, affronted.

"I am your daughter's affianced, if you recall. The servants know me quite well. They certainly know to let me in when I come to your door."

Francesca swallowed, taken aback by her future son-in-law's abrupt manner. Well-trained, however, she fought to retain her composure and smooth over the awkward moment.

"Antonio, do you know Doctor Malmo?"

Antonio acknowledged him with a curt bow and pinned him with his watery gaze. "Is it my betrothed you've come to see?" he demanded, trampling niceties.

"I . . . well, if you mean Miss Pina . . . yes. Yes, I have."

Antonio turned sharply to the signora. "And why wasn't I notified Pina is unwell?"

Pina's mother felt her hackles rise. "I do not know Pina is unwell," she replied crisply. "That's why I sent for Doctor Malmo. To make sure that she is *not*."

The ghost of a smile touched Antonio's thin mouth. The old woman had more spirit than he had imagined. He turned his regard back to the doctor.

"Well? Your diagnosis?"

"There's . . . there doesn't appear to be anything physically wrong with the signorina. Perhaps . . ."

"Perhaps I just need to get out, away from the villa, for a little while."

It was Antonio's turn to be surprised by an unannounced entrance. With a swift glance, he took in Pina's dove gray gown decorated with pink ribbons and pink lace at the bodice . . . and her pale, pinched expression.

"How lovely to see you, Pina," Antonio said levelly.

"Seeing you however, I understand you mother's concern. The last thing I would suggest is for you to leave the villa."

Pina locked gazes with Antonio. How she loathed him! But her hatred of him did not occlude her sensibilities.

"Doctor Malmo, thank you so much for coming to see me this morning. I regret it appears to have been a waste of your time. May I have someone show you to the door?"

The little doctor couldn't have appeared more grateful. When he was gone, Pina returned her attention to Antonio.

"How thoughtful of you to take time from your busy day to check on my well-being," she said. "But I am quite fine, as you can see. You needn't squander any more valuable time."

Antonio's eyes narrowed, but he managed to control his voice. "Time spent in your presence I would hardly consider as time . . . 'squandered'."

"I must agree with my daughter," Signora Galbi spoke up suddenly. "Let us not detain you any longer."

Antonio took a deep breath, barely able to control the retort that begged to be loosed from his tongue. He forced a smile to his lips.

"Very well. As I do indeed have important affairs to attend, I will leave you. For now."

"Shall I summon a servant, or . . . ?"

"I know the way out."

Mother and daughter stared at one another until the

footsteps had receded.

"Mother . . ."

"Sit down, Pina." She patted the vacant side of the settee. When Pina sat, she took her hand. "How do you feel? Truly?"

"I feel fine. Truly." Her mother's brows remained arched. "Well, maybe just a little tired." Then the excuse came to her like a flash of brilliant light. "I . . . I have to confess that I've been stressed about . . . about my betrothal . . ."

Francesca sighed heavily and looked away. "I know this isn't a love match, my dear. And I've seen a side of Antonio that . . . well, that shocked me a little, I must admit."

"Why?" Pina asked abruptly. "What happened?"

The older woman debated with herself a moment, and said finally, "He just arrived so suddenly, almost on Doctor Malmo's heels. It was almost as if he . . . as if he were . . ."

"Watching us?" Pina finished for her mother. A stir of excitement surged in her breast. "Oh, Mother, yes. Yes, of course he has been. How else did he know about my . . . how I was helping the poor?"

"And his tone," Signora Galbi went on as if she hadn't heard her daughter. "I didn't like his tone."

"Mother, was he rude to you?" Pina asked, mounting excitement warring with affront.

"Yes, yes, actually, he was."

"How dare he!" Pina rose, paced to the entrance to the

grand salon and back again. "What exactly did he say?"

"It matters not," Francesca said dismissively. "I just . . ."

"Just what, Mother?" Pina asked hopefully.

"Nothing." The older woman sighed and rose slowly to her feet. "Your father was very sure of this match, you know. He knew what he was doing. He always knew what was best."

"But, Mother, what about *my* feelings?" She couldn't help it. The question simply burst from her lips. "Father thought I liked Antonio because I never said anything to the contrary. But I've never liked him, and now . . . now he follows me, watches my every move, barges into our home . . ."

"Pina, Pina, calm yourself." The older woman took her daughter's hands. "Perhaps Antonio is merely concerned about you, as I certainly am, what with the murders and all. He is right about that; you shouldn't be out on the streets, even with Andrea as company. We must take every precaution. When I think how protective my sister was of Valeria, and still . . . still she . . ."

Pina watched her mother's eyes swim with tears and knew conversation about Antonio was over. She put her arms around her parent and hugged her tightly, acutely aware of how frail she felt.

"Don't worry, Mother," she whispered into the snow-white hair. "What happened to Valeria isn't going to happen to me. I'm safe here. We're both safe. I love you."

Outside a sultry breeze lifted from the Grand Canal and blew through the windows in the grand salon, almost as if in response to Pina's declaration. The curtains ruffled, sounding like feet shuffling on the marble floor.

A chill ran down Pina's spine.

CHAPTER

9

Once Signora Galbi's tears had subsided, Pina spent a pleasant day with her mother. They each picked up sewing projects, long abandoned, more for the companionship than the work, and talked and laughed quietly for the remainder of the morning. They had lunch together, although Pina found her appetite diminished, and during the afternoon played cards until the heat overcame them.

It was unusual for such weather in the spring, and had come upon them so unexpectedly. There was no breeze, and to escape the too-warm interior of the villa they lounged on the loggia overlooking the water. Mother and daughter hadn't spent so much time together in too long a while, and they reveled in their new-found closeness. Pina was relieved her mother was now able to speak about her departed husband without weeping, and it was wonderful to share stories of their happy times together as a family. The subject of Antonio was studiously avoided, but Pina was glad of it. Unpleasantness should be avoided during these happy hours. There would be plenty of opportunity to speak of him, and the betrothal, later.

When the sun finally dipped below the horizon, and the heat bled from the air, they moved inside. Pina kissed her mother's cheek and hugged her briefly.

"I'm going to bathe and change for dinner. Thank you, Mother, for one of the happiest days I've ever spent."

"Oh, my dearest daughter." Francesca took Pina's face in her hands. "It is I who should thank you. I haven't been good company since your father's death. I know it, and regret it. Every moment with you is precious. And not just because you are my daughter. You are a very, *very* special woman, Pina. You are a gift, and I am grateful every day of your life."

Pina blinked back her tears, unable to speak. She watched her mother turn and proceed down the corridor to her chamber, and turned toward her own.

It felt good to sink into a tub of lukewarm water. Pina let Andrea scrub her back, then dismissed her. Although she normally loved the girl's company, she was feeling strangely lethargic and wished to be alone. It was probably just the heat, she mused. And now with the added warmth of the bath, she simply wanted to stretch, and enjoy the feel of her body submerged in the rose-scented water. Pina closed her eyes.

Had she ever been so aware of her body before? She didn't think so. She felt as if she longed to be touched, stroked. With the tips of her fingers, she tentatively touched her breasts, surprised when her nipples instantly hardened. Teeth grabbing her bottom lip, Pina ran her palms down over her ribcage to her flat belly, drew her legs up and caressed the outside of her thighs. Moving up again, she stroked the insides of her legs, and felt something clench deep inside.

A sudden clatter in the courtyard outside her window brought Pina sharply back to reality. What had she been doing? Her skin tingled, but with embarrassment, not pleasure. She sat up straight in the tub, water sloshing, then stood up and got out, calling for Andrea.

"Yes, Miss Pina, I'm here." Andrea scurried into the room and wrapped her mistress in a bath sheet. Over the next half hour, as stars became defined in the night sky and the moon appeared over the rim of the world, Andrea helped Pina complete the evening ritual of dressing for dinner.

"There, miss, you look lovely." Hands on her shoulders,

Andrea leaned down, caught her mistress' gaze in the dressing table mirror, and smiled. But Pina didn't acknowledge her, and Andrea was somewhat concerned to see the usually bright eyes were heavy-lidded.

"Miss Pina? Are you . . .?"

"I'm fine," Pina said smartly, straightening. She smiled back at Andrea's reflection. "I was . . . daydreaming, I guess." She rose and headed toward her chamber door.

Never had she felt less like eating. As much as she had enjoyed her mother's company, and had anticipated a similarly pleasant evening, with the darkness had come a lassitude that was difficult to ignore, to fight. With dragging steps, she made her way to the dining room.

It had been an effort to keep up the front at dinner, but she had done her best. Her mother had enough sorrow and worry in her life. She would do anything to keep from adding to her burden. Yet, when she was finally able to excuse herself from the table, she could no longer hide the inexplicable fatigue that caused her to stumble.

"Pina!"

"Silly me," she said quickly. "Tripping over my own feet. Good night, Mother. I love you." She blew her a kiss.

The corridor seemed a hundred miles long. Pina's footsteps dragged. What had come over her? Never in her life had she felt such enervation, such longing to simply fall into her bed and close her eyes.

It took supreme effort of will to remain upright while Andrea helped her out of her clothes and into her night-dress. The dark-haired girl pulled back the bed covers and Pina literally fell onto the mattress. By the time Andrea blew out the candles, Pina was asleep.

The night deepened. It was overcast again. The stars and moon were obscured and the moisture-laden breeze stilled. Pina woke abruptly.

The man with the golden brown eyes. How could she have forgotten him? What had become of him? Did he linger still in the alley, waiting for her? He had wanted her to help him. She had agreed. Did he expect her to come to him again?

A dreadful fear engulfed her. What if she had let him down and he never returned to the alley, never gave her the chance to make it up to him? What if she never saw him again? In the next moment, Pina was appalled at herself.

A stranger. She was obsessed with a stranger. A stranger, moreover, she hadn't spared a thought for all during the day. What was wrong with her? She had to get a grip on herself. Take control of the situation. She forced herself to relax, concentrating on her toes, then her legs, her hips . . . quieting her mind, her muscles . . .

Pina was never sure whether she had crossed over the threshold of sleep and was dreaming, or if it was real. One moment she drifted. The next he was standing beside her bed.

Pina sat bolt upright, heart pounding furiously. "How did you . . .?"

He laid a finger to his lips.

"I won't be quiet. Tell me how you got in here," Pina demanded. She pulled her silken coverlet up to her chin.

"Do you want me to leave?"

That voice again. She remembered it now. It flowed like warm, scented water through her veins. She trembled with the heat of it. "I want you to leave unless you tell me how you got past the guards."

She said the words, heard them, but knew they were mere artifice. Another, different part of her was telling her what to say. It was not what she meant in her heart.

"Does it matter?" he responded at length to her demand.

She knew it did not. "Then tell me how you know where I live."

The quirk of a smile appeared at the corners of his sculpted mouth. Pina felt her own lips respond.

"All right . . . why are you here?"

Slowly, deliberately, he lifted his hand and laid it over his heart. A bolt of pleasure shot through her limbs. But it was wrong. So wrong.

"You . . . you shouldn't be here," Pina protested half-heartedly.

"Do you want me to leave?" he asked again.

Yes, she did. This was wrong. But she found she couldn't say the words. Couldn't. He still didn't look well. A tiny bit better, perhaps, but still not right. She feared for him. And, truthfully, she did not want him to leave.

"You look . . . better . . . than the last time I saw you."

"Because of you."

A flush crept into Pina's pale cheeks. She tried to deny it — it was so bizarre, so surreal, speaking to an almost perfect stranger, a man, who had stolen into her bedchamber in the dead of night — but she was absolutely powerless to do anything except reply as if all were normal.

"Since you're standing in my bedchamber, won't you be good enough to tell me your name?"

"I have no name."

A chill went through her. It was not of pleasure. "Of course you do. Tell me. Or you must leave."

"I told you before . . . I don't know."

"Then I shall give you a name. At least until we find out who you are, and what has happened to you."

His entire demeanor changed, softened somehow. His

brown, amber-flecked eyes widened slightly. "You would give me something?" he asked softly.

"Yes, a name."

"And what would you call me?"

Unmindful of her sheer lace nightdress, Pina let the coverlet drop to her lap. "My father had a hunting lodge in the country. He often took me with him when he hunted stags. Your hair, the color of your eyes, is so like the coloration of a deer. And you're so tall. I shall call you Tallhart."

His smile widened. Everything about his expression bespoke vulnerability, and Pina's heart went out to him. Just like that. Despite the wrongness or rightness of what was happening, despite the dream-like quality of the experience, the very impossibility of it, her heart flew free of her breast and embraced the being whose haunting, haunted need reached out to her.

"You are . . . very kind," he said, haltingly. The stranger newly named Tallhart extended his hand and touched Pina's cheek.

Pina remembered the first time had had touched her and what had happened, how she had felt. This time the feeling was completely different, but just as powerful.

Where his fingers touched her flesh she felt a burning, though not unpleasant. Her whole face felt warm, and the feeling reached down into her neck, her breast. Pina was aware of her nipples stiffening. Somewhere in the back of her mind, modesty cried out for her to cover herself, but she found she was powerless. The heat continued downward into her belly, and to the site of her womanhood. The heat turned into a flame.

Though the smile remained, Tallhart's eyes had narrowed. All traces of vulnerability vanished. His tongue flicked over his lips.

"Now I wish to give you a gift as well," he said in a voice so soft Pina was scarcely sure she had heard it. Tallhart's fingers lifted from her cheek. He touched her forehead.

Pina slipped immediately into sleep.

When she opened her eyes again he was still beside the bed. Nothing about him had changed. He appeared exactly as he had before. Even his expression. No trace of the vulnerability she thought she had seen remained. His gaze was hard, predatory.

But his face was beautiful, so beautiful. She loved the symmetry of it, the strong jaw and aristocratic nose, the meltingly soft brown eyes. Was there just the tiniest cleft in his chin? Pina wondered how she hadn't noticed it before. Perhaps because his face appeared less gaunt, the features fuller somehow.

As he regarded her in turn, Tallhart touched a finger to his throat. He let it move lazily downward to the hollow, then to the open V of his shirt.

Pina was transfixed. She watched him loosen the remaining laces. Tallhart shrugged the shirt from his back and let it fall to the floor.

It seemed he regained his health and vigor before her very eyes. Gone was the frightening pallor of his flesh. It now appeared a sun-touched golden hue. His shoulders were broad and his upper arms well developed. The musculature of his chest was well defined. His finger ran down over the thin line of silken hair that disappeared into the waistband of his leggings.

They were skintight. Nothing was left to the imagination. Pina saw the outline of his manhood, heavy and engorged. The flame in her belly turned to a raging fire. It seared every nerve in her body as she watched him touch the mass straining for release. He ran a finger up and down the impressive length of it.

Pina couldn't help herself. Her hand went to the fire burning between her legs. She touched herself and felt the silken wetness, her body's response to the incredible male animal who stood before her.

What would it be like to feel his lips against hers, his hot breath on her mouth? How would the hard, male part of him feel as he probed her nether lips, taunting, teasing, begging entry? She had to know, had to feel his flesh beneath her hungry hands, had to open herself to his need like a flower to the sun.

Pina threw back the coverlet and swung her legs over the edge of the bed. Her feet touched the cool, marble floor.

Tallhart vanished.

CHAPTER

10

Barely two hours past sunrise, in Pina's chamber, Andrea stood at the foot of the bed and quietly wept as Doctor Malmo once again examined the now semi-conscious girl. Her mother stood at the bedside across from the doctor, holding her daughter's hand.

At length the thin, graying man straightened and exhaled a deep breath. He shook his head.

"Again, nothing," he said. "I can find nothing physically wrong, signora. I'm sorry. I cannot tell you why she will not wake, or why her color is so poor. Her heart, her pulse, everything is normal. There is not a mark on her . . ." He threw up his hands in exasperation.

"But *some*thing is wrong. As you see!" Signora Galbi said, desperation in her voice. She stroked her daughter's forearm. "And this is exactly how her cousin, Valeria, was before she . . . before she was found . . ."

Andrea put comforting arms around the signora. "Ssshhh. Do not speak of it," she said softly.

"I agree." Doctor Malmo moved away from the bed. "There is absolutely no reason to believe that the two conditions are connected. Although this is puzzling, Pina is young and healthy. I do not think her life is in danger."

"Valeria was young and healthy too! Francesca cried. "Until she developed these very same symptoms. And then was found dead!" A tear dropped from her cheek to the back of her daughter's hand.

"Signora Galbi, you must try to calm yourself," the doctor urged. "There's nothing you can do at the moment. Why don't you lie down for awhile? I'll stay with Pina."

"No," the older woman said curtly. "I'll not leave her side."

"A wise decision."

Heads turned as Antonio entered the room. Francesca's lips tightened into a grim line.

"Please leave my daughter's chamber," she said stiffly. "This is not fitting."

"What isn't fitting is neglecting to notify her fiancé of what appears to be a significant illness," he retorted abruptly.

"There was no time." Signora Galbi drew herself up. "As soon as we realized something was wrong, we sent for the doctor. *Not* her fiancé. You're correct."

Inwardly seething, Antonio forced his facial muscles to remain completely still. He had never dreamed the old woman would prove so adversarial. It was a problem he would have to consider. Her attitude could simply not be tolerated. Having reined in his temper, Antonio smiled obsequiously.

"I apologize, signora, for both the intrusion and my words. My concern for my betrothed caused me to act and speak without proper thought. Forgive me."

Francesca bit back the reply she would like to have made, reminding herself that Antonio had been chosen for Pina by her late, revered husband. She managed to incline her head graciously before returning her attention to her daughter. What she saw quickened her pulse.

Pina's eyelids fluttered. Her tongue flicked over too-dry lips.

"Mother?"

"I'm here. I'm here, my precious." Signora Galbi clutched Pina's hand in both of her hers and pressed it to her heart. "Mama's here, my dearest."

"Mother, please . . . Antonio . . ."

"Do you want him, dearest? He's here. He . . ."

"No." Pina's rolled her head sluggishly from side to side. "No. Tell him . . . tell him to leave . . ."

Francesca glanced at Antonio, quickly enough to catch the searing flash of anger that momentarily distorted his features. Her eyes narrowed.

"Please respect my daughter's wishes."

He hesitated only a moment; the time he needed to collect himself and appear to exit, rather than retreat. He bowed briefly, to both Signora Galbi and the doctor, turned on his heel and strode from the room.

Francesca didn't realize she'd been holding her breath until she exhaled. She glanced down at her daughter.

Pina somehow found the energy for a wan smile, and her heart squeezed when she saw the relief wash over her mother's tense expression.

"Thank you," she whispered.

Still holding her daughter's hand to her breast, the Signora merely smiled.

"This is a good sign," the doctor announced needlessly. "How do you feel, Miss Pina?"

"Sleepy." Pina let her eyelids close, long, dark lashes brushing her cheeks. "I just want to sleep."

"Won't you eat something, my darling? Please?" her mother entreated.

Pina wanted to say yes. She wanted to do whatever she could to please the mother she adored. But fatigue pulled at her, dragged her down as if it were almost a living thing. She only wanted to sleep away the day until she could embrace the night, and . . .

And what? Why was it so hard to remember?

Sinking finally into slumber, she was able to recall. As her mother and Dr. Malmo watched, puzzled, Pina smiled.

The night was still and warm. Pina wakened slowly, aware her nightdress was damp with sweat. Aware as well someone was in her room.

He stood at the foot of the bed, handsome features illumined by the guttering candles on a table near the bed. He wore the same clothes; a loose, white muslin shirt, open at the neck, black leggings, and boots. He looked the same, yet did not. Pina studied him.

As if he had spent the day in the sun, his skin had turned a deeper bronze, and there was more color in his face, a pinker tinge to his cheeks. His lips seemed fuller, chest broader, biceps larger. How was it possible?

And how was it possible that she was so overwhelmingly glad to see him?

"You . . . you look better," she offered haltingly.

"Because of you, Pina."

The words, the sultry tone of his voice, stroked her like a caress.

Was she blushing? Was that the heat she felt in her cheeks?

Somewhere in the back of her mind, the voices of her

rational mind and her conscience tried to speak to her. In far-off, but insistent whispers, they warned she had a stranger in her bedchamber. A strange man she knew nothing about. A man who made her feel and want things she had never even considered before.

But she didn't listen to the voices. Her attraction to the stranger was too powerful. The mere thought of him leaving sent a thrill of desperation through her.

"Do you want me, Pina?" Tallhart asked, as if he had plucked the recent thought straight from her mind.

She almost said yes. Almost. Some last vestige of virginal modesty and sense of decorum stilled her tongue.

When she didn't respond, he smiled slowly. "You want me. I know you do."

Pina dropped her eyes to his crotch. She couldn't help it. When she saw he was fully aroused, straining against the thin fabric of the black leggings, something jolted in the feminine core of her. She watched him languidly reach down and cup his genitals.

The voices in the back of her mind gabbled frantically.

This was indecent. Wrong.

But she burned.

Through the leggings, he grasped his erection, fondled it.

Pina could bear it no longer. She reached for him.

Tallhart laughed softly. He stretched his fingers toward hers, still cupping the fullness of his masculinity.

The distance between them closed.

And in the space of a heartbeat, he was gone.

CHAPTER

11

Signora Galbi was deeply asleep when Andrea came to her. She had lain awake long into the night worrying about her daughter, unable to stop making comparisons between Valeria's symptoms and Pina's, and her slumber was profound. Andrea had to shake her gently by the shoulders before she roused. When she opened her eyes at last, it was to see sunlight pouring in through her windows. And Andrea's stricken expression. She sat up abruptly, coverlet clutched to her breast.

"What is it? Pina?"

Andrea nodded mutely, tears swimming in her huge, dark eyes.

Francesca pulled on her robe as she ran down the corridor to Pina's room. The door was ajar and and she ran through to her daughter's bedside.

The pallor of her skin was frightening. Her eyes were sunken, cheeks gaunt. Francesca tried to rouse her.

"It's no use, Signora," Andrea wailed. "I've tried to wake her . . . tried and tried . . ."

"Pina." Francesca's skin instantly became clammy with terror. "Oh, dear God." Her legs buckled and she sank to her knees. "Pina . . ." Her hand groped for her daughter's breast and she held her breath, shaking, until she found the heartbeat. "She lives . . ."

Andrea's heart broke as she watched the signora break down and weep. A sob tore from her own throat and she pressed her hands to her mouth.

This couldn't be happening. It just couldn't. Pina couldn't die, not like her cousin. There had to be someone who could help, someone who would know what to do, what was wrong . . .

Andrea's tears dried, but she kept her hands pressed to her mouth. Her pulse pounded with growing apprehension. Did she dare?

Did she not?

"Si . . . Signora Galbi . . ."

Francesca wiped her eyes on her sleeve and looked sidelong at Andrea. The lady's eyes were twin pools of dread and desperation.

"Signora, I . . . I think I know someone who might be able to help."

The band tightening around her chest, making it difficult to breathe, loosened a little. Francesca pushed to her feet.

"Who? And how do you know?"

Andrea's heart quickened yet again. "A doctor . . . in the Ghetto Nuovo . . ."

"A Jew!" Francesca's hand flew to her heart. "How do you know this man?"

Andrea felt herself begin to tremble. "We . . . Miss Pina and I . . . we've . . . we've helped him," she stammered. Then, in a rush: "Oh, signora, he's a good man, a great doctor! He works with Rabbi Levan. We've seen him do such good, miracles almost. He . . ."

"Fetch him," Francesca ordered curtly. She rubbed her arms as if chilled. "Fetch him at once. And Andrea . . . Have the guards deny Signor Antonio, should he try to enter."

Andrea fled.

Francesca had never considered herself a person of prejudice because she had never actually thought about it. The Jews were an entity unto themselves. They lived in a designated part of the city. They affected her world not at all. Until now.

She recalled the morning Antonio had informed her of

her daughter's "charitable works". How she had assumed the recipients of Pina's generosity had been Catholic. Why had no one corrected her misapprehension?

Francesca shook her head. That was a question for another time. For now, all that mattered was Pina. She never took her eyes off the man examining her thoroughly from head to toe.

He had been introduced as Dr. Mazzetti; he was accompanied by a man Andrea had introduced as Rabbi Levan. He seemed a kindly person. And the doctor, despite the emblem sewn onto the front of his garment, appeared capable. He certainly inspired more confidence than Dr. Malmo. Francesca took a deep, steadying breath when he straightened and stepped away from the bed.

"I find nothing physically amiss," the doctor said, "other than her obvious pallor and evident coma. Her heartbeat is strong, breathing regular. I do find her skin somewhat cool to the touch, but . . ."

"But she wastes."

"Yes. She wastes. Without obvious signs of illness, I've never seen anything like it."

Neither had Francesca. But she had heard. Her sister had told her of how Valeria had begun to waste in this very same way. She had become pallid and thin, her flesh cool to the touch. And she had started to have dreams.

Hot color rose to Francesca's cheeks as she recalled her

88

sister's words. "Dr. Mazzetti, I . . . I didn't think it important before. I didn't think Pina's symptoms could have anything to do with the way her cousin Valeria died . . ."

"A young cousin?" the doctor interrupted.

Francesca nodded. "She was one of the young women found . . . dead."

Dr. Mazzetti closed his eyes briefly. "I have heard of these tragedies. Please, go on."

"But now I . . . I realize that this is very much how my sister told me Valeria was before . . . before . . ." She trailed off, cleared her throat painfully and continued. "There was something else, however. She said . . . she said . . ."

It was impossible. She couldn't confide the intimate details to these men.

Seeing her distress, Rabbi Levan moved to her side.

"I will pray for God's mercy to heal your spirit, Signora Galbi, and to heal your daughter's body. These miracles do not always come straight from His hands, however. Sometimes they are gifted through the hands of man. If there is something else we need to know, please do not fear our learning it. There is little either Dr. Mazzetti or myself has not already seen or heard."

There was something indefinable about the Rabbi, something serene and gentle. It flowed into her and lent her courage. Still, she clasped her hands and lowered her eyes when she spoke.

"My . . . my sister said that, toward the end, Valeria moaned in her sleep. And she spoke aloud, as if to some man, and . . . and touched herself."

A whimper escaped Francesca's horrified lips. She felt the Rabbi's hand brush her shoulder, feather light, and heard Dr. Mazzetti sigh.

"Does your daughter do this as well?" he asked quietly.

Francesca turned to Andrea, who stood in the doorway, arms clutched to her breast. "I would have no way of knowing, but . . . Andrea?"

"No, signora. The night I sat outside her door I heard nothing. But . . ." She lapsed into silence, as humiliated as her mistress.

Francesca turned back to the doctor.

"Stay with her this night, signora. If only to reassure yourself that whatever plagued her cousin does not also haunt your daughter. I doubt it does. Unless you've heard other young women had the same kind of . . . dreams . . . before they met their tragic ends, I would have to say this is absolutely unrelated."

"And there's nothing else you can say, nothing else you can do?"

He shook his, almost sorrowfully. "I wish there was, signora. I wish the talent God has given me to heal could be put to use here. But I am afraid this illness may not be of the body, but of the mind."

"You mean . . . but, no! No!" Francesca did not miss the brief, swift glance between the two men. She turned to Rabbi Levan. "What?" she demanded.

"The doctor only means . . . sometimes, if there is a stressful situation, well, we've seen patients actually withdraw from life."

Something inside Francesca stilled. Slowly, she returned her attention to the doctor. "Barely a year ago Pina lost her father," she said, voice barely a whisper. "Then her cousin was murdered. And she is betrothed, but not . . . not to someone she . . . she cares about."

This time she did not mind when the men exchanged glances. Could that be it? Could that really be what was wrong with her child? She prayed it was so.

"This is what I would advise, " Dr. Mazzetti said, the timbre of his voice low, his tone gentle. "Spend the night in your daughter's chamber, if only to convince yourself your fears are unfounded. When she begins to get better, which I truly believe she will, take her to the country perhaps, some place where she can get fresh air. Where she can forget what is happening in the city, and in her life."

Without thinking, Francesca grasped the doctor's hands. Her heart brimmed with gratitude, and the symbol on his chest blurred as tears filled her eyes. "I do not know how to thank you, Dr. Mazzetti."

"Thanks are not necessary. This is my calling."

She turned to Rabbi Levan. This time, when she reached out to grasp another's hands, she knew exactly what she was doing.

"I believe, since my daughter is . . . unwell at the moment . . . that I shall have to carry on on her behalf. Please tell me what your needs are, Rabbi Levan, and I shall see to them."

"Signora Galbi, I . . ."

"You are a Godly man. I honor you. I wish to help. Please do not deny me."

Still standing in the doorway, unnoticed, Andrea felt a tear slip down her cheek.

Outside, the sun continued its journey, moving toward the night.

CHAPTER

12

For the remainder of the day, Pina could not be roused, although Francesca, with Andrea's aid, was able to force a little water between her dry lips. They sponge-bathed her and put her in a clean nightdress, changed the linens on the bed. When the lower edge of the sun's disc dipped into the sea, Andrea turned her attentions to her mistress' mother.

"You have a long night ahead, signora. Please, see to your own comfort. Let me draw you a bath and bring you something to eat."

Francesca was reluctant to leave her daughter's side, but knew she would need to be strong and refreshed for the night ahead. She couldn't risk falling asleep for a moment. She had to make certain Pina would not exhibit the same frightening behavior her cousin had.

As she went to attend to her *toilette*, however, she had a measure of peace and confidence in her heart. Everything Rabbi Levan and Dr. Mazzetti had said to her made perfect sense. Pina had, indeed, suffered mental traumas in the last year. Although Antonio was the least of them, he was still not insignificant. She would have to give the betrothal some serious thought. She didn't like the side she had seen of him.

But first she had to make it through the night. Perhaps Dr. Mazzetti was right; there was no connection between Valeria's bizarre dreams and the tragedy which had befallen her. When Pina spent a peaceful night, Francesca could be relieved of that particular fear. Then she would think about taking Pina away for awhile, away from the city where terror stalked. Whatever had caused her child to withdraw, she would discover, and rectify it. Pina would be whole again. The light in her soul would shine again. It was her mother's vow.

Francesca suffered a brief, but powerful pang of guilt, recalling the state of weakness, helplessness, into which she had withdrawn following her husband's death. She had relied on him for so long. His loss had been paralyzing. She hadn't been ready to pick up the burden he had left for her.

Then Valeria's murder. While she loved her sister, loved her niece, she realized now how she had allowed herself to be sucked back down into the morass of grief. It was so much easier to wallow in misery, indulge in tears, than to pull herself up and get on with living. Parenting.

Francesca sat forward in her tub and let Tita, her personal maid, wash her hair and scrub her back. Under Stefano's direction, Sophia prepared and brought to her a light supper with watered wine. She forced herself to eat, and allowed Tita to dress her. As the tapers were lit throughout the villa, she made her way back to her daughter's chamber.

Andrea still kept her apparently tireless vigil. But her eyelids were heavy, her head nodded as she sat beside the bed.

"Andrea."

"Signora Galbi!" Andrea leapt to her feet.

"Go to bed now, child. Sleep."

"But . . ."

"I will need you on the morrow."

Without another word, Andrea ducked her head and left. Francesca lowered herself into the chair.

Full darkness engulfed the city. The six candles in the candelabrum flickered hopefully. Though windows on either side of the chamber were open, the breeze was desultory; the candle flames barely moved. But it wasn't as hot as it had been. The evening, in fact, was pleasantly cool.

Francesca gazed lovingly at her daughter, trying to quell the fears still trying to rise up from her belly and choke her. It was as the doctor and the Rabbi said, she consoled herself. Pina was withdrawing from the trauma in her life, nothing more. She had nothing in common with her cousin but the obvious. She would begin to get better, and they would leave the city . . .

All would be well.

She was in that place again, the abyss, the black hole of sheer terror. The place where dreams should be, but were not. She was hanging, suspended, waiting for what would, should, come to her in her sleep. Every fiber of her being reached out for it, whatever *it* was, to come to her, rescue her, pull her back from the cliff.

And, finally, he came.

"Pina."

She turned her head. Opened her eyes.

He was magnificent. Feet apart, hands on his hips, arms akimbo, a smile on his lips, he beckoned to her.

"Come to me. Pina."

His shirt was open, as always. This time, however, he drew it over his head. Discarded it. She couldn't drink in the sight of his naked upper torso deeply enough. His chest swelled with power. Silken strands of sun-gold hair trailed from between his dark, masculine nipples to his navel. Disappeared into the waistband of his leggings.

Pina groaned.

She had been daydreaming, thinking about a better time, a time when her husband had been alive and her daughter carefree. Francesca jerked upright in her chair. Had she heard a sound from Pina?

"Sssshhh," Tallhart cautioned, a finger to his lips. He trailed his thumb down his midriff, hooked it in his waistband.

The heat between her thighs made it impossible to lie still. Pina shifted.

Francesca rose from the chair. She smoothed errant tendrils of hair from her daughter's forehead.

"Ssshhh, my love. Mama is here. Sleep well."

Pina stilled.

The smile slipped from Tallhart's lips. "Pina . . ."

She turned from the nebulous comfort seeming to hover about her bedside. Let her gaze caress the vision she had awaited so long.

Tallhart captured her gaze. The smile returned to his lips. The sparkle was restored to his eyes.

"My love."

Pina's lips curved in response.

Francesca let a sigh escape. She returned to her chair.

Tallhart crooked his index finger, hooked it on his waistband. With his free hand, he stroked his hip, his thigh, brought it to his groin.

Pina's tongue flicked across her lips. Her hands went to her breasts.

Something dark and cold ran through Francesca's veins.

Tallhart's grin pulled his lips back from straight, white, even teeth. He cupped his manhood. Stroked it. Straining, it jerked upright. The tip, glistening, poked out of the top of his leggings.

Pina writhed. She wanted him . . . oh, how she wanted him. Moaning, she reached for the burning spot between her legs . . .

Francesca launched herself from her seat and drew her daughter into her arms. Pina flailed against her weakly. Francesca gained a purchase on the bed and pulled Pina into her lap, into her arms. She cradled her head against her breast.

Tallhart roared.

Only Pina heard.

Her back arched. Fingers clawed at her mother's arms holding her tightly to her breast.

Francesca started to pray.

"Dear God, deliver us. Deliver us from this evil . . ."

"Cast her aside!" Tallhart bellowed. "Come to me . . . you are mine!"

Yes. Yes, she was his. She twisted, turned, fought against the restraining arms.

"Pina!"

She heard him, oh, yes. She wanted him . . . wanted to come to him.

"Cast her aside, I said!"

Something screamed inside her, shrieked. She had to make it stop, had to make the painful sound go away. She shoved at the pinioning arms, scratched . . .

"Dear Lord, hear my prayer . . . deliver us . . ." Francesca breathed, her heart clenching in her breast. "Deliver my daughter from evil . . ."

Tallhart growled, features distorting.

Pina shrank away from him, desire dimming. She felt her mother's arms.

"Begone, demon!" Francesca shouted with her final breath.

The apparition evaporated, fog in the bright light of day.

Pina's body stiffened briefly, then collapsed. Tears streamed from the corners of her eyes, but her breathing was regular, and deep.

Francesca bent over her child until she could feel her warm, even breath puffing softly against her lips. She put a hand to her chest and felt the steady beat of her heart. Emotion flowed in a tidal rush.

"Thank you," she whispered. And, Pina cradled in her arms, let the tide carry her away.

CHAPTER

13

Antonio brushed aside his valet's hand and tugged at the front of his vest. Turning his head from side to side, he examined himself in the mirror. The glimmer of a smile swiftly turned into a grimace of irritation. He whirled away from the looking glass.

"Where's the boy?" Antonio demanded with an impatient stamp of his foot. "He should be back by now."

"I'll go and see," the valet muttered quickly, and gratefully fled the room. He returned a mere instant later. "He is here, *Signore*. He has returned."

Hands on hips, Antonio glowered at the ten-year-old who entered the chamber, head bowed. "Well?"

The youngster kept his eyes on the elegant oriental carpet, struggling to control his ragged breath. He had run as hard as he could. But his heart continued to pound wildly.

His master was not going to like what he had to report.

"Speak! What's the matter with you? How goes it at Villa Galbi?"

The boy licked his lips. "They . . . the gates are locked," he stuttered, eyes still downcast. "But I . . . I climbed a wall down the alley and saw . . . saw the villa being closed . . . closed up, I think."

"Closed up? What do you mean?" Antonio's brow furrowed into a sharp V.

"The . . . the windows were being shuttered. I saw a wagon, in the courtyard, being loaded. I heard someone call for . . . for the signora's coach. I . . ."

"Get my horse!" Antonio stormed past the child, knocking into his startled valet. "Get my horse, I said!" he shouted as the man attempted to find his feet.

The boy scampered away, unnoticed. The valet fled down the corridor, trying to get ahead of his master. When he passed the man, the small hairs on the back of his neck bristled.

Villa Galbi was in chaos.

Clothing was draped over chairs and trailed from open trunks. Servants bustled about closing shutters and drawing drapes, covering furniture. Signora Galbi glided between rooms, directing the packing of the house. She paused occasionally only to press her fingers to her temples, or press a palm to the ache just behind her forehead.

"Are you all right, Signora?" Andrea's normally smooth brow was now almost permanently furrowed with concern. "Can I get you anything? Something to drink, perhaps?"

"No," Francesca replied, more sharply than she had intended. "Thank you, but I . . . I want to get away as soon as possible."

"Of course, signora."

The older woman, standing in the center of the grand salon, looked about her.

All the furniture was draped. The windows were closed and the curtains drawn. Candelabra had been lit to ward off the noonday darkness. She glanced into the room beyond, her favorite.

Only memories would dwell here, for a time. She drew in a long, shaky breath. It was hard to leave the rooms her husband had last inhabited, the corridors he had trod.

But it might be Pina's only salvation.

Signora Galbi turned back to Andrea, who continued to hover anxiously. "Do you think you and Stefano can direct the final preparations?"

Andrea's expression instantly registered shock. "You mean, stay behind?"

"Only until the villa is completely closed up. I'll have

Sophia and Tita with me."

"But, Signora Galbi, what about Pina?"

Fear lodged a splinter in her heart, but she ignored it. She had to be strong now, for her daughter. Pina was all she had left.

"Pina will be fine with me, with Sophia and Tita to help."

"Oh, signora, I didn't mean . . ."

"I know, Andrea. I know how deeply you care for my daughter. And I love you for it." Briefly, she touched the maid's cheek. "But you and Stefano are the only two I can trust to finish things in my absence in the way they must be done."

Andrea bowed her head. "Yes, signora. But . . ."

When the silence stretched, Francesca prodded gently. "Yes? What is it, Andrea?"

"What if . . . what if Signor Antonio comes back and . . .?"

"There is no 'what if'," Stefano said as he bustled into the room. "He has returned. Oh, I am so sorry, Signora," he apologized, wringing his hands. "He is at the gates, and he is most importunate. The guards have barred his entry, but he says it is his right to see *la signorina* . . . that he will call a magistrate, or . . ."

"It is all right, Stefano," the older woman said as calmly as she could. She lightly touched her steward's arm, then folded her hands at her waist and drew herself up to her fullest height. "It is my duty to speak with him. Please, bring him to me."

Andrea and Stefano exchanged swift glances before the steward hurried from the chamber. She watched him go, feeling a tightness in her chest and weakness in her knees. She avoided her mistress' eyes.

"Will you attend me, Andrea?" Francesca asked gently. "If not, I will have Stefano stay."

Andrea shook her head, silently but vehemently. Antonio terrified her. But she would not leave the mistress she adored alone with him.

"Thank you," the older woman sighed softly, and braced her shoulders as her daughter's fiance' strode into the room.

"What is the meaning of this?"

"Good day to you too, Antonio," the signora said levelly.

"I asked you, what is going on here?"

Signora Galbi took a deep, steadying breath. "As you see, I am closing the villa."

"I have eyes," Antonio snapped. "Where are you going? And why wasn't I informed?"

"You were not informed because I have not yet had time to do so. I only made the decision this morning."

Antonio's taut stance seemed to relax a bit. The tic under his eye ceased its jumping. He offered the signora a curt bow.

"My apologies, then. But you can understand, I'm sure, how shocked I was to learn . . ."

"Are you having us watched, Antonio?" Francesca was surprised the words had actually left her mouth. But her spine seemed to stiffen with the utterance and the nervous flutter in her stomach calmed. She almost smiled at the startled look on Antonio's face.

"I know much of what goes on in this city," he replied at length, tersely. "People tell me things. I have no need to have anyone . . . *watched*."

She recognized the lie with insouciance. "Is that how you knew of my daughter's 'charitable activities'? People 'told you things'?" The signora's reward came with the draining of blood from Antonio's already sallow complexion. In the next moment, however, her balloon of triumph was pricked with a sliver of fear.

Antonio's eyes narrowed and his lips thinned. His hands curled into fists at his sides. "Very well. If that is the game you wish to play, I will put the ball back in your court." A mocking smile touched his mouth. "About your daughter's . . . 'charitable activities' . . ."

"I already know." The calm returned. Along with an increasingly unpleasant realization. "I know all about the Ghetto Nuovo. I know about the Rabbi. And the doctor." She stole a glance at Andrea, who had drawn back her shoulders and lifted her chin. It took an effort of will not to smile at her. "I only wonder that you did not tell me the truth at the outset. Your veracity is very much in question, signor," she said formally. "As well as my husband's decision to pledge his daughter to you."

A second reward was delivered with Antonio's sharp intake of breath. "How dare you . . .?

"How dare *you?*" Francesca interrupted. "You have come to my home repeatedly without invitation. You have behaved most rudely. I am taking Pina to the country now, where she will be able to rest from the stresses of the city, the . . . the murders . . . and the pressures inflicted upon her by *you*. And while we are away, I will also be reconsidering some of my husband's . . . choices. Good day, Antonio."

Francesca turned to leave, then spun back on her heel. "I know you know the way to the door. And if your memory has lapsed, I will be more than happy to have the guards assist you on your way."

She could feel his eyes boring into his back, could hear the fuming sound made deep in the back of his throat. She didn't care. She felt strangely liberated, and did not even mind the words that were, inevitably, flung at her back.

"You'll be sorry. I warn you. You will *not* get away with this."

Francesca continued down the corridor. Andrea was not as lucky.

Antonio's rage momentarily stole his vision. His throat

constricted and he could feel the throb of the arteries in his neck. When the red haze dissolved from his eyes, he lunged and reached for the nearest figure, also retreating.

Andrea spun, off balance, a vice-like grip on her wrist. "Signor!"

"Shut up."

Antonio drew the girl tight up against him. His quickening erection helped to focus his anger. Lust nearly overwhelmed him as he gazed down at the girl's shining black hair.

"She won't get away with this," he hissed through clenched teeth. "She *can*not do this to me." Feeling Andrea tremble pushed his desire to the limits. He found his fingers bunching in her skirt to pull it up to her waist. His hips thrust against her.

It was more than Andrea could endure. She screamed.

Antonio pushed her abruptly away from him and, with a string of muttered curses, strode toward the door.

Sobbing, Andrea collapsed into Stefano's arms.

CHAPTER

14

The bedchamber was dark, the first room to have been shuttered. A single candle flickered softly at Pina's bedside. Francesca approached slowly, shaken both by the morning's events and her daughter's condition. Slowly, she sank into a chair.

The brief rally of her spirit had ended. When she lifted her hand to touch her daughter's arm, she saw it was shaking. She closed her eyes and willed her strength to return. But only weakness continued to flood her veins.

Her greatest fear had been realized. Pina had struggled in the night with the same symptoms her cousin had displayed. She had felt the presence of some unseen demon. It wanted Pina. Her daughter would be its next victim. She would not allow it.

The well, empty of her courage, began to refill. Signora

Galbi gazed at her daughter's face.

"When she begins to get better, which I truly believe she will, take her to the country perhaps, some place where she can get fresh air," Dr. Mazzetti had advised. *"Where she can forget what is happening in the city, and in her life."*

Francesca sat back, one hand still resting on her daughter's arm. Dr. Mazzetti had been wrong about the most important thing: Pina was not going to get better. Not unless she could get her daughter away from whatever fiend pursued her, the demon that had murdered Valeria and haunted the Venice streets. If they were safely away from the city, maybe there was a chance the monster wouldn't — couldn't — follow. It was her prayer, her only hope.

Secondarily, it would get Pina away from other pressures, as the Jewish doctor had suggested. Pina would be away from reminders of her cousin and the other murders. She would be away from Antonio as well. Francesca sighed.

Her beloved husband had known Antonio's family well, but not the man himself. The family's heritage was impeccable, their wealth vast, their business well entrenched. The match had seemed ideal.

Francesca, however, could no longer deny her husband might have made a terrible mistake. She recalled Andrea's hysterical weeping, her description of the lewd manhandling, and the threat against herself. Was there more than one monster in pursuit of her child?

She did not want to doubt Antonio, to go against her husband's last wish and final arrangements. Giving Antonio the benefit of the doubt, she wondered if the stress of events had clouded his judgment and weakened control of his temper, taking its toll on him as well as everyone else. It was possible, she supposed.

Francesca knew for certain that time away, in the country, would give her a chance to mull the dilemma over. And, perhaps, pray to God, save Pina's life. That was first and foremost. She must flee with her child. She could think about Antonio later. Rising, Francesca leaned over the bed and gently shook her daughter's shoulder.

"Pina? Pina, my dearest, it's time to get up. I must get you dressed. It's time to go . . ."

Once again, it was like climbing up from a deep pit. But she would do anything for her mother. Pina struggled upward. Her eyes opened fractionally.

"That's it, darling. Let me help you sit up." Francesca inwardly flinched at the pallor of her daughter's flesh. Even her golden hair appeared dull and lusterless. Spread across the pillow, it framed a face pinched with pain. The smudges beneath Pina's eyes looked as if they might have been drawn with charcoal. Francesca gripped her child's shoulders to help her sit up.

"That's it, my love. It's time to go. I'll help you dress."

Pina's head lolled. Her gaze searched the room. "Where . . . where's Andrea?"

"She's helping Stefano close up the house."

"Close up the house?"

Francesca caught the inside of her cheek with her teeth. "Yes, dear. Yes. We . . . we're going to the country for awhile. Remember? I told you this morning when you first awakened. We're going to the lodge."

Pina offered a faint smile. "I love it there. I love the lodge." In the next moment, however, her smile faded.

What if he couldn't find her there? What if she never saw him again? Pina's gaze flicked to her mother.

She was trying to keep them apart. Something ugly rose in Pina's breast.

Francesca drew back, subtly aware of something malignant issuing from her child. But as quickly as it had come, it evaporated. Pina looked up at her with clear eyes.

What had that unpleasant feeling been, Pina wondered, and where had it gone? No matter. She allowed her mother to assist her from the bed and into her clothes.

"You haven't dressed me in a very long time, Mother." Pina smiled vaguely. "Not since I was a little girl."

"You're still my little girl," Francesca said fiercely. Finishing the last button at the back of Pina's gown, she turned her in her arms.

"What's wrong, Mother? And why . . . why do I feel so weak?"

Francesca fought the urge to burst into tears. "You've been ill, my darling. But I'm going to take care of you. Come now. Come along. The carriage is waiting."

Although walking from the darkened house out into the sunshine had been painful at first, Pina soon felt the warmth of the buttery light invade her very bones. She hadn't realized she'd been so cold. So cold. Even Andrea's arms around her, when they said their good-byes, lent warmth. What had brought such a chill to her flesh?

Gratefully, Pina sank onto the upholstered bench inside the coach. Why was she so tired all the time? Tired. Cold.

Her mother told her she'd been ill. Why couldn't she remember?

Brow creased, Pina watched her mother climb into the carriage and take a seat beside her. The carriage tilted as Sophia and Tita climbed up to ride behind the coachman. Then Andrea closed the door. A whicker and a whinny, the stamping of an impatient hoof, and they were away.

"You're not sad to be leaving, are you, my dearest?"

Francesca inquired gently.

Pina shook her head, then hesitated. "I . . . I'll miss Andrea."

"She and Stefano will follow in a few days, once the villa is secured."

Pina watched the familiar sights of the city roll by, still reveling in her newfound warmth. Some of the strange lethargy seemed to leave her. Her thoughts cleared. She looked at her mother sharply.

"What about . . . what about Antonio? Does he . . .?"

"Know we're leaving?" Francesca finished for her. "Yes. I spoke with him briefly this morning."

"And he . . . he's not angry?"

Signora Galbi patted her daughter's knee. "Don't worry about Antonio, my darling. Don't worry about anything. We're going to the country to rest, relax, and allow you to regain your health. Think only of how much you love the lodge, and the many happy memories that await us there."

Pina sat up a little straighter. "Mother, will I see Erta? Will she be there?"

Oh, yes, Erta would be there. Francesca had sent a message ahead of them. She nodded.

"Of course you'll see her. Are you glad?"

Pina's smile felt rusty, unused, but she relished it. "Yes. Yes, I can't wait. It's been so long."

Was there a change in her daughter already? Francesca hardly dared to hope.

Eventually the coach left the city behind and rolled out into the countryside. Pina let her weight fall against her mother's shoulder as the view of cypress trees standing sentinel along the sides of the road became monotonous. Soon the rolling green hills beyond became a blur, and only the rutted road kept her from slipping back into sleep. But her tiredness was pleasant, rather than exhausted. Pina felt as if some kind of weight had been lifted from her back, and she might rest from her labors. She let her thoughts drift to the lodge.

The dwelling was very different from the villa, built of wood rather than stone and marble. It was comfortable rather than opulent and, most of all, a place where she felt close to her father. The house would welcome her.

Unaware she had slipped the bonds of consciousness, Pina dozed. In the half-sleep, she felt a shadow fall across her mind, chilling her. An unwelcome thought penetrated:

Would he find her? Would she see him again?

With a choking gasp, Pina's eyes flew open and she sat up straight.

"Pina, what is it?" her mother asked, alarmed. "What's wrong?"

"I . . . I don't know." Pina shook her head and pressed her fingers to her temples. "A dream maybe . . . I don't know."

Francesca put her arms around her daughter and pulled her close again. "It's all right," she crooned. "You're fine. You're with me, and I will never let anything harm you."

"Even my dreams?" Pina tried to smile, making light of it. But her mother's expression sobered her. With a shiver, she relaxed into her parent's embrace and returned her attention to the scenery. Familiar sights buoyed her immediately, chasing away the last lingering shadows of the dream she could not quite recall.

Early dusk fell about them as they entered the woods. Giant elms shaded the winding road to the lodge. Beyond stood acres of poplar and alder. Through a break in the trees, Pina saw the little lake where she had learned to swim as a child. The willow in whose shadow she had napped still stood by the water, branches trailing on the still surface. Three does, who had come to the water to drink, raised their heads, muzzles dripping. In an instant, they were gone.

"The deer, Mother. Did you see them?"

"What, my dear? I didn't hear you."

Pina's gaze remained fixed on the clearing. A mysterious fog rolled in, clouding her vision. "Tallhart," she murmured.

"Speak up, my darling. What did you say?"

"Nothing, Mother. Nothing." It was the truth. She did not even remember speaking.

A final bend in the road and the forest opened, revealing the low, sprawling lodge, its mass visible despite the failing light. A servant came from the doorway, lantern in hand. The sight was familiar, welcoming. Pina took a great, deep breath.

The scent of the woodlands came to her. Pine trees and fecund earth. Some kind of small mammal chattered in the darkness of the surrounding trees. The fog that seemed to cloud her mind dissipated completely, blown away in a stirring night wind. She felt refreshed, almost . . . light.

Francesca watched her daughter sit forward on the seat and press her face to the window; watched the smile curve her lips.

Yes. She had done the right thing.

CHAPTER

15

The small staff that maintained the lodge had put forth their best efforts to welcome the signora and signorina. Francesca felt a bit guilty that she had not visited the lodge since her husband's death. She had also feared being assailed by memories that might bruise her still-healing heart. But quite the opposite happened.

Almost every room had been filled with fresh flowers, some wild, some from the gardens at the back of the house, still others from the tubs lining the garden pathways. Windows had been opened wide to the enchantment of the star-filled, fragrant night, and one of the family's favorite meals had been prepared.

"Where on earth did you get venison," Francesca exclaimed, taking her seat at the head of the table.

"It is plentiful," Ramona, both cook and housekeeper,

replied, a blush staining her pale, narrow face. "And my husband, Vigo, is . . ." she faltered.

"An excellent marksman," Francesca supplied. "I remember well. My husband so enjoyed hunting with him."

Ramona heaved an audible sigh. Francesca smiled.

There. It was done. They were past it. She was going to be all right. And so was Pina.

The spring evening in the country was cool, and a fire glowed and crackled in the hearth at one end of the long room. Candlesticks cluttered the center of the dining table, artfully arranged among bowls of flowers. The flickering lights revealed the color returning to Pina's cheeks, and the return of her appetite. She made short work of the saddle of venison and accompanying garden fresh vegetables, and had two glasses of a fine red wine from her father's cellar. Tears suddenly welled in Francesca's eyes.

Was it truly possible they had escaped, both of them? She from a grief so profound she had almost forgotten how to live, and her daughter from a murderous terror that came in the night? Francesca resisted the shudder that tried to crawl across her flesh.

The previous evening seemed very far away. It was even becoming difficult to recall the horror of her struggle. Had it really happened?

Yes, Francesca told herself firmly. It had happened. She must not let the peace of the countryside, and the balm of happy memory lull her into complacency. She had fought for her daughter's soul. It had been real.

But it was also behind them. They had left it behind in Venice, Francesca was sure of it. How could she doubt, looking at her daughter as she was now?

"Oh, Mother, how could you let me eat so much. I'm going to pop."

"It's good to see you've regained your appetite. You had us all very worried."

Pina frowned. "You know, it's funny I can't even remember being ill."

"It could be a blessing."

"Yes. Maybe it is." Pina smiled. "Thank you for bringing me here. I had forgotten how much I love it." She sat forward in her chair. "Can I see Erta tomorrow?"

"I see no reason why not."

Pina smothered a yawn and Francesca felt a prick of fear. "What's the matter, dear? Don't tell me you feel tired already?"

"In a good way, Mother. Sleepy, not tired. There's a difference."

"It was a rather long trip," Francesca conceded.

"And I made a pig of myself. Just eating that much is enough to make a body sleepy."

The prick subsided. "Retire to your room if you wish, my dearest. I'll be along shortly."

Pina excused herself and left the table, her sense of well-being expanding. Not being able to recall the illness her mother said she had suffered last night frustrated her — she remembered being tired before that, though not knowing why — and a lingering lethargy had plagued her throughout the day. But she felt fine now. Whatever had been wrong with her was probably, as her mother had said, a result of the combination of events: her father's death; Valeria's murder, among so many others; and her betrothal to Antonio.

Antonio.

Pina stopped still in the dimly lit corridor that led to the family sleeping chambers.

Her mother had said not to worry about him, not even to think about him. Was she coming around to Pina's way of thinking? She recalled the time — had it only been a day or two ago? — Antonio had arrived on Dr. Malmo's heels. Her mother said he had treated her rudely. Was it possible her mother was seeing the real Antonio? Was it possible she might relent and release her from the betrothal?

Pina's spirit soared. It was certainly a possibility. She and her mother had grown closer than ever. They talked about everything. She had actually listened to her complaints about Antonio.

Could good things be emerging from bad?

She could not doubt it. Light of step, Pina continued

to her room.

Francesca moved slowly, walking the familiar corridors, enjoying the familiar, musty scents of the aging wooden lodge. Sconces were few and far between and she carried a candle, shielding the flame with her hand. There was one final test.

Eduardo's clean male fragrance still clung to the study where he had spent so many hours. Aromas of tobacco, fine wines and liquors, the yellowing pages of the many books, and the smooth, distinct smell of good leather combined to make her head swim. Francesca entered the room and remained still for a moment, letting her heartbeat return to normal.

His ghost was benign. He did not haunt her with sadness. Their time together had been good; they had loved deeply. The tears she shed were cleansing.

Someone had lit a candelabrum on the desk, no doubt anticipating she would have to make this journey. She silently blessed whichever thoughtful, loyal servant had done so, and placed her single candlestick on the opposite side. Letting the memories caress her, Francesca lowered herself into her husband's chair.

She wasn't certain how long she had been in the study,

lost in her thoughts, when Tita, round face etched with concern, came through the door.

"I'm so sorry, signora. *'Scusi.'*"

"What is it, Tita?"

"A visitor."

"So late?"

"It's the old woman, signora. She said you sent a message of your arrival."

"Ah, yes." Francesca nodded. "But I though she'd wait until the morrow."

"Shall I tell her to return in the morning?"

Francesca shook her head and sighed. "No. It's all right. I'll see her now."

"*Si*, signora. I'll show her in."

"Thank you, Tita."

Entering Eduardo's study had not been the final test after all. Francesca squared her shoulders.

She believed in God, the Holy Trinity, her Catholic faith. She believed in Hell and the Devil. Last night she had learned to believe in the Devil's minions. Because she would go to any length to save, to protect, her child, it seemed she might have to learn to believe in magic as well.

Francesca heard the footsteps first; Tita's brisk waddle; then a slower shuffling. Tita's round form entered the room and quickly stepped aside. The old woman hobbled into the study.

"Signora Galbi." The impossibly old woman smiled, revealing pink gums, but not a single tooth. "It has been a long, long time."

Francesca nodded her permission for Tita to leave and gestured at a carved wooden chair with a comfortably upholstered cushion. "Please, sit down, Erta. It's good to see you. Thank you for coming."

The old woman remained motionless. "Your housekeeper gave me soup. She told me you would give me a silver." Surprisingly, she uttered a cackling laugh.

Francesca willed her features to remain impassive. "I will give you anything you want if you tell me what's wrong with my daughter."

The crone seemed to consider. Gathering the folds of her shapeless, colorless garment, she settled at last in the offered chair.

"You have changed a great deal, signora," Erta said at length.

"I am older, certainly," Francesca replied somewhat stiffly.

The cackle sounded again. "Your hair is white, yes, but your beauty has not aged. No. Time has nothing to do with this."

"The passage of time has everything to do with it."

Erta nodded slowly. Then she stilled and regarded Francesca for a long moment. "Your heart was always open, if guarded. Now, your mind is open as well. What do you want of me?"

"I want you to help my daughter," Francesca replied immediately.

"I reared your daughter. Much to your chagrin." The old woman laughed once again.

Francesca straightened, pulling her shoulders back, and clasped her hands on the desk in front of her. "I trusted my husband. Eduardo trusted you."

"Ah, yes. And Pina loved me." The steely gray eyes darkened to storm clouds. The smile on her lips seemed incongruous. "She loved me . . . and adored *you*."

For the first time since the old woman had entered the room, Francesca relaxed. Her shoulders sagged and her expression softened.

"Yes. And I would do anything . . . *anything* . . . to protect her well-being."

Again, the old woman nodded. "Then, you must talk to me," she said softly.

"I . . . it's difficult. Very difficult. It's . . ."

"It's in my realm, not yours, eh?" Erta continued to nod. "I admire your courage, signora. Now . . . tell me what has happened."

Francesca took a deep breath.

CHAPTER

16

The fire needed to be tended; only a feeble glow came from the charred remains of the fuel. Candles had melted into grotesque parodies of themselves. A second candelabrum had been called for, and supplied. Shadow and light danced together on the book-lined walls.

Francesca had found it amazingly easy to fill the old woman in on the more intimate details of Pina's "illness". Undoubtedly because Erta was so connected to the elemental nature of all things. When she had finished her tale, she sat back, hands limp in her lap.

Erta remained silent for several long moments. Gnarled fingers stroked the coarse material of her shapeless garment. She nodded to herself.

"So," she said at length, "she worsened each day, and became harder to wake?"

"Yes." Francesca's voice was barely a whisper.

"A night stalker," Erta mumbled, as if to herself. Then she looked up sharply. "Yet, you say *il doctore* found no mark upon her?"

Francesca shook her head. "None. Dr. Malmo found nothing."

"Probably didn't look in all the right places, though," Erta muttered.

Francesca felt her blood chill. "He . . . he was very thorough," she said defensively.

Erta merely raised her brows and Francesca sagged. Embarrassed, she averted her eyes.

"You're right," she admitted.

"And the second doctor?"

"He suggested her . . . wasting . . . might be an illness of the soul, rather than the body." Francesca was finding it a little easier to breathe. But in the next moment, her chest clogged again. "He suggested I stay with her through the night to prove to myself that she wasn't having those . . . those dreams . . . like her cousin."

Erta compressed her lips so tightly over her toothless gums her chin nearly met her nose. For several seconds she mumbled incoherently to herself. Then:

"You felt the evil. I believe you. Pina is being stalked."

"But by *what*?" Francesca slammed her hands, palms down, on the desk top. "And *why*?"

"Why? Why does anyone become a victim? As for the what . . . I must see Pina. Examine her."

"Of course. Of course." Francesca's words were tinged with desperation. "But first you must tell me what you fear."

"The devil that comes by night," Erta answered without hesitation. "The blood drinker."

Francesca could feel the color drain from her face. Nausea swirled in her stomach.

"A . . . a blood drinker?"

"Yes. A soul stealer. A killer."

Francesca moaned.

"But, I must look at her first. Take me to her."

Mute, Francesca nodded.

It surprised Francesca, when she rose from her chair, to see definition beyond the study window. The first pale light of dawn had crept above the rim of the world. She saw the vast stretch of verdant lawn, patchwork gardens, and meandering paths. The edge of the forest. Life. Normality. She took a deep breath of it before turning back to the old woman.

"Come. I'll take you to her room."

The lodge had been built over the years with many additions. The women made their way through a series of corridors to the wing housing the sleeping chambers. Francesca knocked softly on a door near the end of a long hallway and, when she received no response, quietly opened it.

Pina's slumbering form lay curled under a thick duvet, the cover pulled up around her head. Chill morning air filled the room from the wide open double doors that led onto a square of lawn. The perimeter was lined with a spring bounty of blooms, petals now dew-laden, and tubs of fragrant lemon trees. A songbird trilled the day's first melody. Francesca tip-toed to the bedside.

"Pina?" She pulled the cover away from her daughter's cheek. It bloomed the color of the roses outside her doors. Shining golden hair fanned across the pillow. Francesca touched it. "Pina?" She felt Erta's earthy presence close in behind her.

"Her sleep is healthy. And deep. Nothing has visited her this night. But you tempt fate with those doors."

Guilt nipped at her heart. "I . . . I never told her good night, or left instructions with the servants."

"No harm done. Yet. Let me see her."

Francesca stepped aside. Pina stirred as Erta leaned over her. Long, dark lashes fluttered against porcelain flesh, then opened in a flash of blue.

"Erta?"

"Yes, child. 'Tis I. Your old nurse."

"Erta!" Something joyous flooded Pina's heart. She

128

sat up and threw her arms around the old woman's neck. "Oh, Erta, I'm so glad to see you. Let me look at you." Pina released her and held her at arms' length. Her hands flew to her cheeks. "What happened to your teeth?"

"Pina!" Francesca hissed.

Erta cackled. "Your mother always told me if I continued to eat so many nuts and roots I would lose all my teeth. She was right."

Pina looked over at her mother, overjoyed to waken to the sight of the two people she loved most in the world. But she sobered immediately with Erta's words, and the solemn expression that fell across her features.

"Your mother tells me you have been ill."

It was almost impossible to believe, at the moment, she had been sick. With the warming morning light, garden perfumes, and birdsong, it was difficult to recall the exhaustion and lethargy she had experienced. Pina offered only the slightest of nods in reply.

"Pina, child, would you let your old nurse look you over?" Erta asked softly.

Pina's gaze flicked to her mother and back to the old woman. Again, she gave the faintest of nods, although she pulled the coverlet up under her chin in an unconscious gesture of modesty.

Erta stroked her flaxen hair. "Lie back, child. Lie back and close your eyes."

Pina couldn't have opened them if she wanted to; her humiliation was nearly overwhelming. While her mother held her hand, tightly, Erta went over every inch of her body, even the sacred, secret spot between her thighs. Hot tears managed to squeeze from beneath her lids.

"There. All done. I am sorry, child."

Clutching the duvet to her chin once more, Pina opened her eyes. The tears were able to flow freely.

"I'm sorry," Erta repeated. She turned to Francesca. "There is nothing. No mark. Anywhere. It is not as I feared."

Once again Pina's gaze flickered between the two women.

"What? What did you fear?" she demanded.

Pina watched her mother give Erta an uncertain nod.

"I feared the blood drinker, the evil one who comes by night, had claimed you as victim. I was wrong. I did not see his mark anywhere upon you."

Pina felt weak all of a sudden. "You . . . you actually believe such a creature exists?" she asked. "Couldn't I simply have been sick?"

"Was your cousin 'simply sick'?" Erta tossed back at her.

Pina watched her mother visibly pale.

"I have seen some who gave their souls up to the blood drinker," Erta said to Francesca as if Pina had not spoken. "Her symptoms are so like one of them I cannot believe I saw no mark."

"Then what can explain . . .?

130

"Close those doors," the old woman ordered. "Lock them. Lock all the doors and windows."

"But, last night . . . I mean, she's fine this morning. Why . . .?:

"Do as I say. I do not know the enemy yet, but I fear last night was a mere battle won, not the war. If she is stalked, it will find her. It must."

Francesca did not hesitate another moment. She went to the doors herself, pulled them closed and locked them. Then she turned her back to them, hands still clutching the door latches. The unspoken question shone in her eyes, accented by the arch of her elegant brows.

"This is more than illness," Erta said tiredly. "It is evil, evil that comes in the night. I do not know, exactly, what form it takes, or how it steals away her vitality. I do not know how to ward against it." The old woman appeared uncomfortable. She backed away from Pina's bed. "Guard her. It is all I can tell you. Her last bastion will be her own strength of mind and spirit."

"Erta!" Francesca called as the old woman shuffled from the room.

She paused, briefly.

"I wish I could help you. I cannot."

CHAPTER

17

The villa looked as if it was inhabited by ghosts. Pale linen drapes covered every piece of furniture. Silver candelabra weighted table coverings which fluttered in the occasional breeze of an opened door. Andrea hated it.

More than she hated the dim and darkened halls, however, and the ghostly drapings, she loathed the sound her footsteps made on the polished marble floors. They echoed like mocking laughter, reminding her of better times, happier times — times she might never know again.

Wiping away a tear, Andrea glanced around the small chamber that had been her home for so long. Would she ever see it again, she wondered? Would she ever even return to Venice?

A shiver worked its way down Andrea's spine. Her world had been so wonderful. How had it gone so wrong so quickly? She recalled hearing about the first of the murdered girls, speaking to Pina about it, shuddering over the horror. But never, ever did she think the terror would reach inside the walls of this villa and touch them all with cold, dread fingers. Never did she think a member of Pina's family would be victimized.

And what was happening to Pina herself?

Andrea stared at the bag she had packed without seeing it. What was wrong with her mistress? Why had she looked so pale and wan the last few days? What illness did Pina suffer the doctors could not diagnose? And why had the signora left so suddenly for the country?

Andrea tried to tell herself it was simply the stress of all the events, not the least of which was Pina's betrothal to a man like Antonio. But in her heart of hearts Andrea feared there was something much more sinister going on. The servants whispered, oh yes, and the tales they told belonged hidden in the dark of night from whence they had come.

With a shake of her head, as if to dispel her dark thoughts, Andrea picked up her bag and hurried from the room. Stefano awaited.

"Is this everything?"

Andrea nodded at the steward and watched him toss her bag up to the guard securing luggage atop the coach.

"Would you rather ride in, or out?"

Andrea looked inside the coach. She remembered the villa's dim, silent corridors.

"I'll ride on top."

When she was settled on the bench seat behind the driver, Andrea once more took stock of her situation.

They were all, but for a few guards, leaving Villa Galbi behind. And not, as before, on a light-hearted vacation to the countryside. They were fleeing something, although Andrea was not sure just what. They were moving, inevitably, into the future, but a future now obscured by clouds.

As if to underscore her thoughts, the sun's brightness winked out, and Andrea looked up into a sky of oncoming gray. She looked down again as the carriage passed through the gates. And froze.

There were six of them, Antonio at their head. Their horses were arrayed across the road leading away from the villa.

The coachman hauled on the reins and the team came to a halt. Andrea watched Stefano, sitting beside the driver right in front of her, stiffen his spine.

"Good day, signore," he called in a level tone.

"Ah, yes, it is a good day. A good day for a ride to the country. I think I shall accompany you. Gentlemen?"

Antonio gestured to the less than savory individuals surrounding him and they moved their horses aside. "Wait," he ordered suddenly.

Sweat broke out under Andrea's arms when Antonio looked up at her, pale blue eyes unblinking. Wisps of light hair blew across his face with the freshening wind and he brushed them aside with obvious irritation.

"It looks like we might have some weather moving in. I think I'll ride in the coach for a way. Someone take my horse."

Antonio dismounted and handed his reins to one of the riders. He smiled up at Andrea.

"Why don't you join me inside, my dear? I'd hate to see you get a soaking."

"Stefano," she whispered desperately. But there was nothing he could do; she knew it. Antonio knew it. Slowly, heart pounding, Andrea climbed down.

It was a nightmare, it had to be. The sky continued to darken and Antonio sat across from her, a leering smile on his face as the carriage rolled through the Venice streets. Leisurely, he crossed his legs, then braced his hands on either side of him.

"So," he said at last. "We meet again, pretty little thing."

Andrea swallowed, keeping her eyes on the hands folded tightly in her lap.

"The circumstances are a little more auspicious, wouldn't

you say? This time you're not sneaking around with your purloined . . . goodies. It's so much nicer for us now. Isn't it?"

She didn't dare look at him, not even for an instant. Her very insides trembled. The silence stretched and she heard a distant rumble of thunder. The light continued to fade, darkness growing, constricting her within the confines of the coach.

"One of the benefits of my being married to your mistress," Antonio said at last, "would be our ability to see each other when and where we chose. Don't you agree?"

Was he mad? Andrea squeezed her eyes shut.

"You really must help me promote this wedding, you know," Antonio continued. "It would be in all of our best interests. I know you agree. Don't you?"

He took her so thoroughly by surprise, the air *whooshed* from Andrea's lungs. One moment she was alone in her own seat, eyes closed. In the next he was all over and around her, body pressing, arms tightening. She felt the slime of his tongue lick the side of her neck. She would swear, to her dying day, his tongue felt forked. A low moan issued from somewhere deep inside her.

"Yes, oh yes, that's it," Antonio crooned in Andrea's ear. "You want me. I know you do."

She was going to die. Her heart would simply cease to beat and she would die. Please, God, let her die.

Long, pale, strong fingers were suddenly about her

throat, cutting off her air. Antonio forced her head back.

"Open your eyes," he commanded in a hard, cold voice. "Open your eyes and look at me. Ah, better. Yes." The glimmer of a smile disappeared instantly. "Give your mistress a message for me. Tell her it will do her no good to hide. Distance will not shield her. Or the pretense of illness. I will come for her. Tell her."

Antonio gave Andrea a little shake as if for emphasis.

"Tell her. And know this as well."

Lips came down on hers. Fetid breath filled her nostrils. The devil's tongue raked her mouth, then withdraw.

"I will come for you, too. And I will make you beg for more."

There they were again, those words, bringing the onset of nausea, making her head spin. Andrea was only vaguely aware of the carriage halting and Antonio exiting. When she felt motion once again, she curled into a fetal position on the seat and let the flood of tears carry her away.

CHAPTER

18

Pina woke to darkness so total it scared her. Unable to get her bearings, even to remember where she was, she rolled over and clutched her pillow to her breast. Then she saw light seeping in from around a double-door frame. Air left her lungs in a sigh of relief.

Stubbing her toes only once on her way toward the light, Pina flung wide the doors. Sunlight flooded the room, wrapping her in its warm embrace. The myriad melodies of birds rode in on a breeze and the fragrances of forest and garden filled her soul. The world was soft and new and alive. Pina opened her arms to it.

With reluctance, she turned to the knock at her interior door. "Enter."

With surprise she watched her mother enter just ahead of Tita's short, round form. Francesca nodded at her maid.

"Thank you, Tita. Get yourself some breakfast now, and some sleep. Andrea should arrive today and will take your place tonight."

The maid disappeared down the corridor and Pina raised her brows. Her mother closed the door.

"Andrea will take her place doing what?"

"Watching over you." Francesca strode briskly to the garden doors and started to pull them closed.

"Mother, wait. What are you doing? It's a beautiful day."

"Don't you remember?" Francesca pulled the doors shut and the room was once again plunged into darkness. She opened the pale yellow drapes at the windows, and the light returned.

"Remember wh . . .?" Something cold and unpleasant slithered through Pina's body. "Erta was here . . . last night."

Francesca remained silent, lips compressed.

"She examined me." The cold turned into a flush of heat. "She thinks I'm being stalked by something evil . . . the thing that killed Valeria . . ."

Pina's knees felt suddenly weak. She sank down on the edge of her bed. Her mother came to her and wrapped her in a tight embrace.

"Do not fear, my darling. You're better already. I can see it, feel it. Whatever it is, it has not followed us."

Pina clung to her mother, shaking. She remembered being too tired even to fear last night; Erta's words were almost unreal. She had fallen into a deep, apparently healing slumber. And now . . .

Pushing her mother gently away, Pina rose and crossed to the double doors, throwing them wide.

"Pina!"

"It didn't follow us, I'm better, you just said so. But I'll waste away if you keep me locked up in darkness. Look, look how beautiful that is." Pina whirled, acknowledging the world beyond her windows with both arms, then returned her attention to her mother. "Close the house up at night, lock it, put a guard at my door. Erta said the thing, whatever it is, comes at night. But, please, please, don't lock me in during the day."

"Pina, I . . ."

But having started, Pina found she could not stop. "Antonio tried to make me a prisoner. Remember, Mother?"

"I do not wish to defend him, but he was correct, Pina. The city was — is — dangerous. It wasn't safe for you to be out on the streets."

Pina waved the statement away with a flick of her hand.

"Even were it not for events, he would try to . . ."

"Pina, please. Stop." Thoroughly uncomfortable with the subject of Antonio, Francesca placed her hands on her daughter's shoulders and tried to still her. "That's behind us now."

"Is it, Mother. Is it?"

"Antonio . . ."

Pina pulled from her mother's grip. "Antonio is not behind us. But he should be. You think something evil stalks me, and it does. My *fiancé*."

Francesca flinched. She dropped her chin to her chest, and Pina was immediately overwhelmed with guilt.

"I'm sorry, Mother. I didn't mean to be so harsh."

"I know," Francesca said quietly. "I know. I also know we must finish this conversation. But later. Later, when there is not such a beautiful day awaiting us." She straightened and let a smile lift her mouth. "For now, have some breakfast, get dressed, and join me for a walk in the gardens." Francesca started for the door, then turned.

"You're right, my darling. A lovely world awaits. There are many hours to fill before the darkness. We must not waste them."

The day had been almost too warm. Andrea had stifled inside the coach, but when she returned to her seat on top the sun, which had re-emerged just outside the city, beat down on her relentlessly. As had Stefano's questions, no matter how kindly intended. She had returned inside.

Now, however, as shadows lengthened and the sun dipped below the level of the surrounding trees, Andrea felt a chill. She hugged herself and watched out the window for familiar landmarks. They were getting close. When the forest thinned, she knew she would soon see the lodge around a bend in the road. A nervous thrill soured her stomach.

What was she going to do? What was she going to say to Pina and *la signora?* They had already been through so much. They were trying to escape to the country; escape the madness, the sadness, and whatever strange illness plagued her mistress. How could she bring more drama and fear to them in their sanctuary?

Then again, how could she not?

Should Pina become Antonio's bride, her life would not be worth living. He was a cruel, brutal man who had not even the slightest intention of remaining faithful to his wife. He was a user and a destroyer, perhaps slightly mad. Andrea shuddered with revulsion, remembering his hands on her, his vile tongue on her lips.

No, the sweetest woman on earth could not face such a fate. Andrea knew she would have to do whatever she could to prevent it. Besides, there was something she wasn't recalling, something that tickled the edges of memory, something that set off a new set of alarm bells, as if there wasn't plenty of warning from Antonio himself. The fog-bound recollection tugged at her, tantalizing her, and was abruptly forgotten when the lodge came into view.

She would think about it later. And in the meantime, she would deliver Antonio's chilling message.

Pina and her mother greeted their servants in the wood-planked entranceway, Pina overjoyed to see her petite, dark-haired maid, lifetime companion, but dismayed by the expression on her smooth, round face.

"Andrea, what's wrong? Did something go amiss on your journey?"

"We had an . . . encounter, signorina," Stefano offered before Andrea could speak.

Mother and daughter exchanged knowing glances.

"Go ahead," Stefano prompted. "You were alone with him in the coach. I . . ."

"You were alone with him?" Pina exclaimed. "Oh, Andrea. No. What happened?"

"Perhaps you'd like to speak with us privately," Francesca wisely interjected. "Stefano, please see Andrea's things are taken to her quarters. Andrea, come with me."

The three women entered the library to find Ramona laying a fire. Candles and lamps had already been lit. The last bit of light was fading outside the windows.

"Sit down, Andrea dear," Francesca said, and waited for Ramona to leave the room. "Now, tell us what occurred."

It was difficult for Pina to imagine that her cousin had been murdered by some kind of a monster, a demon, a night stalker. It was inconceivable such things could exist, although if the Church said there was a Hell as well as a Heaven, it must surely be inhabited by demons of all sorts. Harder to believe was that the creature might be stalking *her*. Just because Erta said it, didn't make it so. And she could recall nothing herself; only the terrible lethargy and exhaustion. That kind of terror was just too much to believe in, especially after such a beautiful day. But it was easy to believe in the monster called Antonio.

Pina listened to Andrea's recitation of the confrontation as the coach left the villa. She listened, her flesh growing cold, to the message Antonio had sent for her, and exchanged another glance with her mother.

When Andrea's tears overflowed to run down her cheeks, Francesca took both her hands.

"Oh, my dear, I'm so sorry," she said. Brow contracted over her aquiline nose, she looked at her daughter. "It seems we're going to have that conversation sooner than I anticipated, Pina. As for you, Andrea, let's get you a cup of tea and get you settled in your quarters. And, please, do not fret over this any more, my dear. Signor Fontini can threaten all he likes. And he can *try* and come for my daughter . . ."

Tita was not, after all, relieved by Andrea that night. A chair, not too comfortable, was placed outside Pina's door to maintain vigil. Then, as Ramona and her husband prepared to set dinner on the table, Francesca and Stefano went about the lodge closing all the windows and shuttering them, locking doors, checking and rechecking them.

Pina listened to the sound of slamming, over and over again, reverberating throughout the lodge. On Erta's advice, her mother was protecting her against the thing which might come in the night to steal away her soul. But it was not a demon she pictured waiting in the darkness for her. It was Antonio.

Slam. Slam. Slam.

Shutting out the devil.

CHAPTER

19

For three days, each dawn was perfection. The sky lightened and the darkness melted away into striations of lavender and pink, the brightness of the day another blessing, another deliverance from the night and the terrors it might hold.

And despite the lodge was closed and locked tight every night against their fears, and a guard was set at her door, it became ever more difficult for Pina to recall the reason for their flight to the country. The shock and pain of Valeria's loss had eased, and the ever-present grief over her father's death had lessened. She didn't even need to have the "conversation" with her mother. Although Andrea's experience with Antonio had been terrible, it had ultimately served a valuable service, and it was as if by mute agreement mother and daughter had settled the matter of the betrothal. The only thing to be done now was a formal letter from her mother to Antonio's father. The terrible burden would be lifted and she would be free once more to follow the dream of her heart, the dream her engagement to Antonio had stolen away — to find a man she could love who loved her in return, whose children she could bear in joy. There was only one cloud on her otherwise clear horizon.

Pina closed the book she had long ago ceased to read, set it on the table by her right hand, and crossed to the study window. While she had a small privacy garden outside her bed chamber, her father had preferred open spaces, and the area outside this portion of the lodge had been cleared and planted with grass. Pina gazed out over the verdant landscape to the wood beyond.

As a child, the forest had been her playground. She certainly had nothing like it in Venice, and the times they spent at the lodge were times Pina spent wandering the woods. It had worried her mother, she knew, but not her father. Eduardo knew he had found his child the best teacher of all things natural — Erta.

Pina turned from the window to gaze at the sunlight pouring over the carved wooden chair where her father had liked to sit. The long mahogany library table was still strewn with his books and papers. Pina gazed up at the shelves that held hundreds of other volumes.

So much knowledge, collected over a lifetime. The

sources her father had drawn from to rise through the Venetian Council to become its most respected and powerful member. Knowledge, not money or cunning. He had been a thinker and a doer. "Know your facts, keep your wits about you, and you can take charge of any situation in which you find yourself." Pina sighed. She missed him. Yet, in many ways, he remained with her. The things he had taught her, the gifts he had given her, were useful still. She had only to remember, and employ them. Pina returned her gaze to the window, and her gaze became unfocused, as if she could see through the trees to the old woman's woodland hut.

Her mother had never been entirely happy with Erta. She had always known it, on some level. Francesca hadn't thought Erta polished enough to rear the daughter of such an important man. But her father, Pina knew, thought Erta the perfect balance in her life. He had been right. He had been right then . . . and now.

Abandoning her book altogether, she left the study.

Francesca looked up from her ledger when Pina entered the small room off the master chamber. She put her pen aside and sat erect in the straight-backed chair.

"Is it time for lunch already, my dear?"

"No, Mother." Pina laughed lightly. "You just had breakfast."

Francesca relaxed. She had been totally focused on her correspondence, catching up, getting into life again.

"Thank goodness. So, what are you up to, my darling? Besides trying to make me believe my memory ails."

Pina clasped her hands behind her back and turned her attention to the single window overlooking the herb garden. She saw Vigo, back bent, harvesting basil and oregano, undoubtedly for his wife's stewpot.

"Are you comfortable yet, Mother? Do you feel safe?"

Francesca regarded her daughter thoughtfully for a moment. "I am . . . content. Happy to see you thrive. But, as a mother, cautious still."

Pina smiled. "Do you remember when I was . . . six? You and Father brought me here for my birthday."

"Of course." Francesca's expression remained fixed. "Yes, of course I remember."

Pina's brows arched slightly. Her mother did not look in her direction. It did not seem she needed to.

"It was the first time I let you go into the woods alone."

"I wasn't alone."

Francesca's gaze never wavered. She stared straight ahead. "No, you weren't."

Pina let the silence stretch a moment. Then: "I miss Erta, Mother. I was so happy to see her. I want to see her again. I want to visit with her, talk with her."

"Yes. Of course." Francesca turned slowly in her daughter's direction. "I'll send for her again if you want to see her."

"It's not the same, Mother, and you know it. I want to get *out*."

"I . . . I just don't think it's wise, Pina. We don't know what might be in the woods."

Impulsively, Pina threw her arms around her mother. "Then let Vigo walk with me. He can come right back. And I'll be safe with Erta."

"Oh, Pina . . . I don't know . . ."

"Please, Mother."

"Don't push me, Pina. Be happy I've given leave for the windows to be unshuttered each morning, the doors unlocked."

"I am," Pina replied quickly. "I'm grateful, Mother. I'm also grateful nothing's happened during the night. I am, as you see, perfectly well."

"Yes. And you are well, perhaps, because I *do* lock this house up at night."

There was no reply to that. Pina straightened with a sigh, though she wasn't finished yet.

"But the house is wide open all day. And nothing has happened."

It was Francesca's turn to sigh. "We'll see," she relented.

"We'll wait till the end of the week. I'll have Vigo scour the perimeter woodlands in the meantime. Then, maybe . . ."

"I love you, Mother." Pina hugged her once again and kissed her pale, parchment cheek. "Thank you."

With hope in her heart for the end of the week, Pina settled for the bench in the garden outside her chamber and let her eyes roam the distant forest. She had long thought of the lodge as a place of peace. The activity associated with it, hunting, had never seemed to intrude upon its serenity. Even the deer apparently felt safe in the vicinity of the dwelling. Or, because they had not been vigorously hunted in so long they had lost their fear. Whatever the reason, Pina thought she saw them moving in the trees at the edge of the lawn. She stood and walked to the edge of her garden to get a better look.

A light breeze whispered past her cheeks. It lifted the hair from her shoulders and shivered through the leaves of the surrounding forest. A cloud passed over the sun. In spite of the warmth of the day, Pina felt a chill. She hugged her arms to her breast.

The cloud scudded away and sunlight returned, but only for an instant. The sky was crowded and shadows moved swiftly over the wide stretch of green. It was an eerie effect. Even the far trees appeared to flicker. Dizzy for an instant, Pina pressed a hand over her eyes.

When she looked again, the scene before her steadied. But something still moved, tantalizingly, in the trees. Was it deer, as she had thought? It had to be. The breeze stirred again, and the scents of coming summer filled her nostrils: grass and flowers, the pungent and mysterious perfume of the forest. How she longed to walk its paths as she had done as a child.

At the end of the week, Pina consoled herself.

At the end of the week . . .

CHAPTER

20

Vigo stood in the dining room, near the kitchen door, nervously turning his battered straw hat in his hands. His deeply lined face was tanned so darkly it was nearly the color of the garden soil permanently packed beneath his fingernails.

Francesca neatly aligned her knife and fork on her breakfast plate. "Thank you, Vigo. You're absolutely certain?"

While Pina held her breath, Vigo nodded. "Yes, signora, as certain as I can be. For the last five days I have seen only birds and squirrels, a few deer. No sign of anything else, not even pigs, wolves. No tracks, nothing."

"Very well. I appreciate your efforts, Vigo. You may go."

Pina hardly dared look at her mother. She glanced quickly at Andrea, who was clearing the sideboard and trying hard not to smile, then opened her mouth to speak, inhaling a breath for her question to ride out on. But Francesca was too quick.

"I still don't know, Pina. I simply don't like the thought of you walking through those woods."

"Then send Vigo with me. Please."

Francesca heaved a great sigh. "Oh, all right. All right, Pina. Find Vigo and tell him I'd like him to accompany you to Erta's."

Pina was already halfway across the dining room.

"And be back by lunch," Francesca called. "Do you hear me?"

Pina turned on her heel, ran back to her mother, and hugged her. "I hear you, Mother. I'll back by lunch. Promise."

Pina left by the front door and took the path to the left that would lead her to the herb garden where she expected to find Vigo. Although she'd walked through the gardens several times with her mother, the air smelled somehow cleaner today, fresher. Maybe because of her mood, and the time already spent in the country. She felt so cleansed she could barely even recall the heavy smells that hung over Venice like a pall, from the canals and filthy, crowded streets; the mingled fragrances of the market, unwashed bodies, and the offal left by animals. Although it was her home, and she had lived there all her life apart from visits to the hunting lodge, she had always thought Venice had a slightly sinister atmosphere.

Here, however, nothing bad could happen. Nothing bad *had* happened. Her mother had been right to bring her here, both to recover her health and to escape whatever madness was taking young girls in the city. She had nothing to be afraid of. Nothing.

Vigo was not tending his herbs. Pina wandered down another path. Lost in her thoughts, she was startled to see movement out of the corner of her eye. She turned her head so quickly she heard her neck crack, and was in time to see a lean, brown shape move away from her into the shadowed depths of the woods.

She did it without thinking. It had been a game as a child, to chase a squirrel into the woods, or try and follow the flight of a colorful bird. Pina darted toward the trees.

The animal, whatever it was, had moved out of sight. Pina heard the sound of its progress. It was a big animal, heavy, and moved noisily through the underbrush. She hesitated briefly, realizing it might be something dangerous, but remembered what Vigo had said. Squirrels, birds, a few deer. Nothing that might wish to make a meal of her. She was hoping it was a doe; at this time of year they usually had fawns at their sides. Only slightly guilty she was leaving Vigo behind, Pina started to run.

Twigs and branches caught at her clothing. The dress was old, however, a simple, high-waisted white linen, and the thrill of the run, the chase, drove her onward. She heard a strange sound and realized it was her own laughter. Seized by a kind of mysterious ecstasy, Pina ran on.

The light appeared strong just up ahead; the trees were thinning. A moment later Pina burst into a sunny clearing. She stopped and put a hand to her breast, trying to catch her breath. A smile tipped up the corners of her mouth. The place was familiar.

When she had finally reached the age when she no longer needed a nurse, her father had generously granted Erta any boon she might ask upon her departure from service. The old woman had wanted little, preferring to shun the company of men and live among the forest creatures she had always loved. Erta had found this sunlit glade in the heart of the woods, and Signor Galbi had built the modest hut she had requested.

Smoke curled from the rudimentary chimney in the wooden roof. The door was ajar. Pina tip-toed inside.

The old woman stirred a pot hanging over the flame in her tiny hearth. Aromatic steam rose upward in lazy spirals.

Pina took a deep breath of it.

"That smells wonderful, Erta."

The old woman turned with a swiftness that belied her age. "What are you doing here?" she asked sharply.

Pina's smile faded. "I thought you'd be glad to see me."

"I asked you . . . what are you doing here?"

"I . . . I was walking. Near the lodge. I saw something in the woods. I chased it, I . . . I found myself here."

"Did your mother not warn you not to go out alone? Does she not have someone watch over you?"

Pina clasped her hands behind her back. Her chin dropped. "Andrea sleeps on a pallet in my room at night, but by day . . ." Erta's glare stayed her next words. "I was supposed to have Vigo escort me here," she continued instead, "but I . . . I saw whatever it was and just . . . took off running."

The old woman's gnarled and deeply etched features softened. "You are willful and disobedient. Also full of life, thank the heavens." Erta returned to her stirring. "Well, you are safe with me, anyway. You may stay."

Pina took a tentative step into the hut. "Thank you for coming to see me the night we arrived. And what are you cooking?"

"You had been in a bad way, according to your mother," Erta replied, ignoring the second half of the question. "Certainly I would come to see you."

"Thank you," Pina said simply. "I was so very glad to see you again."

Erta turned around on a sigh. "I, too, child am happy to see you. Especially in fine health. Whatever it was . . ." The old woman apparently thought better of what she was going to say. "Never mind. I'm simply glad to see you as you are," she finished.

Pina's smile returned. "So, now will you tell me what you're cooking?"

"You are too curious by half, child. I cook nothing. It is a potion."

Pina took another step nearer the fire. "What kind of potion?"

"An aromatic potion."

"Why? For who?"

The old woman made a small sound that might have been a laugh. "The sickness has turned you into a child again. One of the reasons I chose to live alone in the forest is because you plagued me with so many questions."

"Just one more won't hurt."

The toothless gums were briefly revealed. "Come. I'll show you."

Pina watched Erta wrap a rag around the pot handle and lift it off the fire. The fragrant steam wafted more strongly through the small room. She walked around Pina and out the door. Pina followed.

She did feel like a child again. She had followed Erta around exactly like this on their excursions to the forest, where she had learned many things she had not been able to read in a book. Silently, Pina named the plants she saw as they passed, and looked for the tiny forest creatures she had been taught to see. Suddenly, Erta halted and pressed a finger to her lips.

They advanced slowly, cautiously, through the thinning trees to a small glade similar to the one where Erta's hut stood. Pina caught her breath.

The stag must once have been magnificent, but now it appeared sick and weak. Its hide was dull, ribs showed, and it hung its head under a heavy rack of antlers.

"What's wrong with it?" Pina whispered.

"I do not know. It will accept no food. This is the last remedy I can think to try. "

The hart lifted its head slightly when the old woman approached, and flinched backward when she swung the pot. Pina saw its nostrils twitch. It stared straight at her with its large, brown eye. She noticed, oddly, the eye was flecked with gold.

"Poor thing," Pina murmured, overcome with sympathy for the animal. "Poor, sweet thing."

"Don't go any closer, child. It's still a wild animal. And deer are fiercer than you might imagine."

But Pina was drawn in spite of herself. She moved

closer to the beast, and when it did not shy away from her she extended her hand.

"Pina . . ."

Ignoring the old woman, she touched the stag's cheek.

A tingling sensation she had never felt before shocked her fingers and traveled up her arm. She snatched her hand away. The deer's eye never left her.

"Move away, child," Erta said. "Slowly."

Pina obeyed.

"I never would have believed he would let you touch him. Perhaps he is too sick to be frightened."

"Or your potion has worked some magic."

The old woman continued to swing the pot, and the fragrant steam swirled about the stag. His unblinking eye remained fixed on Pina.

"We've done what we can," Erta said at length. "On the morrow we'll return and see what we find."

Reluctantly, Pina followed the old woman from the glade.

Pina made it back to the lodge in time for lunch, cheeks so pink her mother was unable to tell if she was flushed with pleasure, or kissed by the sun. A little of both, no doubt. It had been difficult to remonstrate with her about leaving

Vigo behind. Her trek to the hut had been successful, after all. Nothing amiss had occurred. Francesca began to hope they had left the terror, whatever it was, well and truly behind them. When she kissed her daughter good night, it was with swelling happiness she had not felt in a very long time.

"Good night, dearest. Sleep well."

"I love you, Mother."

Francesca touched her fingers to her lips, then to her daughter's. Carrying a single candlestick with her, the only light in the room, she exited, closing the door behind her.

Pina watched her mother until darkness enfolded her. Glad Andrea had been released to spend the night in her own chamber, she pulled the coverlet up to her breast and closed her eyes.

It had been a good day, a very good day. Time spent with Erta was gratifying, the encounter with the stag fascinating. Her mother hadn't been angry and had, in fact, seemed to relax about the entire situation. Hence, Andrea's release. Doors were still locked and windows shuttered, of course. But they would be thrown wide to the morning. And Pina would be allowed to visit Erta again. Unaccompanied.

A very good day, indeed. On a rolling wave of contentment, Pina drifted away.

Pina woke abruptly, terrified. In the total darkness, she felt as if she were at the bottom of a black well, drowning.

Heart pounding, she struggled to control her panic. She forced herself to remember every detail of the room she knew so well; the pale green armoire painted with its birds and flowers on the end wall with the dressing table opposite; the table by the bed and the trunk at its foot; the expanse of green and yellow oriental carpet in the center of the room. When she was able to catch her breath, she edged out of bed and groped her way to the dressing table. Her hands shook so badly it was over a minute before she was able to light the candelabrum.

Feeble light flickered in the darkness, but did not dispel the shadows. Pina looked around her wildly, as if she might see the demons lurking in the corners.

But there were no demons. The terror had been in her dreams. Or, rather, her *lack* of dreams.

One hand braced on the dresser top, Pina tried to remember why she had been filled with such horror. And why it seemed somehow familiar. As she had groped in the darkness, Pina groped in her mind.

She had been in the *place* of dreams. But that *place* had been empty. Empty and cold. She had been alone, stripped of the familiar contours and comforts of her unconscious mind. She did not think she had ever felt so frightened.

After a time, Pina went around her room and lit every candle. She held the darkness at bay, though not the fear.

She did not sleep again that night.

CHAPTER

21

Dawn's fingers drew a welcome silhouette around Pina's garden doors. Clutching her coverlet around her shoulders, dragging it with her, she crossed the room to let in the light. Her hand hesitated, however, hovering above the door latch.

Was there something out there?

No, she told herself firmly. It had been only a dream. A bad dream.

Even as she said the words in her head, something bothered Pina. Though fear cloaked the memory, partially obscuring it, she remembered that whatever frightened her hadn't been dream-like at all.

But what else could it have been?

Nothing. There was nothing else it could have been.

Pina opened the doors and swung them wide.

Fog misted her garden. She could see nothing beyond the tubs of ornamental lemon trees. Yet the sky continued to lighten. She watched until the fog began to lift and the daylight fully invaded her chamber. Gathering up the folds of the coverlet, she went to her dressing table and sat down.

Pina blinked at her reflection. Her stomach tightened into a knot.

Her complexion seemed paler than normal. And were those dark circles beneath her eyes, or merely a trick of light?

Was she ill again? Was there a chance that the creature Erta feared . . .?

No. She wouldn't even allow herself to think it. It wasn't possible. The lodge was locked up tight all night. It couldn't happen. Sleeplessness had caused the slight pallor, nothing more.

Ordinarily, Pina did not use makeup of any kind. Now, however, she was glad Andrea had insisted a lady always keep a few basic items at her dressing table. It would not do to let her mother see her looking even slightly unwell, and reawaken her fears.

At the breakfast table, Pina found her appetite a bit depressed as well. To appease her mother, she forced a smile to her lips and chatted amiably while she picked apart of slice of bread and sipped at a cup of tea. Eventually, her mother dabbed a napkin to her lips and looked as if she was ready to rise from the table.

"What are your plans for the day, my dear?"

The mere thought of what she wanted to do made Pina feel better. "I'm going to visit Erta . . . if that's all right."

Francesca nodded slowly, as if distracted.

"Is it? All right, I mean?"

Francesca seemed to come awake suddenly. She focused her attention on her daughter.

"Why, yes. I don't see why not. Everything seems to be . . . fine. Doesn't it?"

"Yes, of course," Pina answered quickly, with only the faintest twinge of guilt. "And I'd like to spend the whole day with Erta, if that's all right as well."

"Yes, I . . . I suppose it is. I have a busy day myself. I intend to finish catching up on my correspondence. And, Pina, I . . . I'm going to go ahead and write to Antonio's father."

Her heart stuttered. "Oh, Mother, you are? Really?"

"I've been thinking about it. You know how torn I am, because of your father. But as time went by, I realized Antonio might show up here, at the lodge. And I knew I didn't want that to happen. If I fear a confrontation with him, how could I possibly abide him as a son-in-law? And then there's poor Andrea . . ." Francesca stopped and shook her head. "No, no, I can't allow this sham of a betrothal to continue. I'm going to write the letter this morning and send it off to Venice at once."

Pina reached across the table and grasped her mother's hand. "Thank you," she whispered.

Francesca squeezed back. "I'm your mother, Pina. It's what I'm supposed to do . . . protect you." She pushed her chair back and rose. "Now run along and enjoy your day with Erta."

A few tendrils of fog still clung to tree boles when Pina made her way through the forest. The effect was eerie and Pina hurried her steps. She was relieved and out of breath when she reached Erta's clearing.

"You're here early," the old woman said when Pina entered the hut.

"And I have Mother's leave to spend the entire day."

Erta rolled her eyes in mock sarcasm.

"Are we going to try and find the stag, see if he's better?"

"Yes, I had planned to do that. Have you had breakfast?"

Erta was once more stirring her pot, but this time whatever it contained smelled suspiciously like gruel. Pina bit her lower lip as her stomach roiled.

"What's wrong, child?" Erta's still sharp eyes flicked over Pina's face. "And since when have you been wearing makeup?"

Pina flinched inwardly, praying her outward expression remained impassive. "Since I had a little trouble sleeping last night," she replied evenly.

"That's the whole of it?" Erta inquired, never taking her eyes from Pina's.

"What else could there be? Besides I hate gruel and the smell of it is sickening." Unable to hold the pose any longer, Pina threw up her arms and crossed to the hut's single, small window. She sat in one of the only two chairs and gazed out at a blue jay scolding a squirrel. "I'm just fine, you know. And tired of people constantly worrying about me."

Her only reply was a guttural grunt. She kept her eyes on the jay, trying to shut out the sounds of the old woman noisily slurping her breakfast. It seemed an eternity before Erta was finally ready to go.

"Well, it's time to see what we will see. Hopefully, it will be nothing at all."

"Oh, but I want to see him, Erta."

"Yes, he is a magnificent creature. One I hope is healthy enough now to have run off into the woods."

They made their way in silence through the woodlands, picking their way through undergrowth where the trees thinned, stepping over fallen logs where the forest shadows were dense and the air cool. They came at length to the clearing, and Pina's heart leapt in her breast.

There the creature stood, head lifted, eyes regarding their arrival. But there had been a very great change in him.

"Erta, he looks so much better. It's amazing . . . a miracle."

The old woman nodded slowly. "Yes. So it appears. Yet, I like it not."

Pina looked at Erta sharply. "Why?"

"Look at him." Erta indicated the stag with the tip of her chin. "Yesterday you could count his ribs. Today you can barely see their outline."

"But, that's a good thing, isn't it? You should be happy." Pina looked askance at the old woman. "Whatever that concoction was you made, it apparently worked."

"Did it?" Erta muttered, as if to herself. "Or was it something else?"

Pina paid no attention. All her focus was on the stag. He was incredible, standing tall and strong, carrying his spreading rack as if it had no weight at all. And the way he looked at her with those great, gold-flecked eyes sent a shiver down her spine. Pina was sure now, certain, although she could not have explained why, that it was the stag she had glimpsed in the wood, the stag she had chased. Without realizing it, she took a step closer to the hart.

"Pina, go no closer," the old woman ordered.

She stopped in her tracks. But she was not frightened of the deer, wild and well defended as he was. Quite the opposite, in fact. She stretched out her hand.

The stag extended its neck. Its cool, brown muzzle touched Pina's fingers. Once again she felt a tingling. It was surprising, but not unpleasant.

"Pina, get away," Erta hissed. "This is not right."

Slowly, she dropped her hand. The old woman grabbed her elbow. Pina was hauled backward. The stag followed.

"Turn around and walk with me, Pina," Erta whispered. "Do not look back."

The old woman's concern and the tone of her voice had an effect on Pina. She did as she was told, although the desire to look behind her was almost overwhelming. Side by side, Erta and Pina returned to the hut and went inside. Erta shut the door and pulled the bar down to secure it. Pina went to the window.

"He followed us," she said simply.

"Close the shutter."

Pina took a long, last look at the hart. She did not wish to shut away the sight of him, but she was too used to following Erta's directions.

The tiny room was bathed in darkness when Pina closed the shutter. Erta lit a candle and stoked the fire in her hearth. The room was soon stifling hot.

"Erta, what's the matter?" Pina asked finally. "Please, tell me what's wrong, what you fear."

"I've never seen anything like this," the old woman said. "I grew up near here, I played in this forest. I know the animals, their nature. Since I left your father's employ, I have spent all my time among them, learning constantly of their ways, helping them when I can. This is not right, not natural. There is some magic at work here. I do not like it."

Pina's face was beaded with moisture. A trickle of sweat tracked a course down her spine. "Erta, please let me open the shutter," she begged. "Even if this be magic, I sensed no harm."

The old woman narrowed her eyes as she regarded Pina. "Very well," she allowed. "But open it slowly."

Pina did as she was bid. She looked through the crack and saw nothing. Strangely disappointed, she threw the shutter wide. Erta crossed to her side and looked through the window herself.

"Now I will take you home," she announced abruptly. "You will go into your father's house and stay there."

"Erta, what . . .?"

"Come. And ask no more questions."

CHAPTER

22

Silent, Erta had walked with Pina to the edge of the forest where the vast lawns surrounding the lodge began. Still, she had said nothing, just waved Pina on, and stood watching until she had walked around the dwelling's sprawl to the front door. When Pina looked back, just before rounding the corner, the old woman was gone.

Erta's reaction to the stag's behavior was unsettling. Could there truly be magic at work? Or was there a simpler, more natural explanation? Erta certainly didn't seem to think so, but Pina wasn't so sure. Mightn't it be she had some kind of connection with the animal? Though she herself had never been allowed to have a house pet, she had spent plenty of time with the various small creatures the servants smuggled into their quarters. She had always seemed to have a way with them. Couldn't that be the case now, even with a feral animal?

The question continued to plague her throughout the day, though she tried to distract herself with an assortment of activities. After explaining, somewhat vaguely, to her mother that Erta was busy with "boring things" for awhile, she straightened her jewelry box, worked on a piece of embroidery, rearranged the clothes in her armoire and trunk, and puttered in her garden. Thankfully, by dinnertime, she had worked up enough of an appetite to escape her mother's unwanted attention to her health.

As night fell, however, tiny, nervous butterflies fluttered into life in the pit of her belly. Pina was relieved when Andrea came to brush out her hair and braid it.

"Did you get your embroidery done?" Andrea asked conversationally as she pulled the brush over and over through Pina's long, sun-touched hair. "I saw you prick your finger more than once."

"I'm hopeless. No, I didn't get it done. You wouldn't want to finish it for me, would you?" she asked jokingly.

Andrea stopped brushing. "I'd do anything for you, Miss Pina," she replied seriously.

Their gazes locked for a moment in the mirror, dark head and light, sun and moon. Pina reached up and briefly squeezed Andrea's hand holding the brush.

"I know you would. And I hope you know how much I appreciate it."

Andrea cleared her throat, laid the brush on the table top, and took a step back. "Is there anything more I can do for you now?"

Pina glanced about the room. "Actually, Andrea . . . would you mind bringing me two or three more candles?"

Andrea's brows flicked upward, but she said only, "Yes, Miss. I'll be right back."

Pina gauged the candelabrum on the side table she had recently lit. The candles were fresh and would last long into the night.

"Thank you," she said to Andrea when the maid returned. "Put two on the dressing table, would you? And one more here, near me."

"Shall I light them?"

"P . . . please." Pina avoided Andrea's gaze while she was moving about the room, placing and lighting the tapers.

"Anything else, Miss Pina?" she asked when she was done. "Would you like me to move back into . . .?"

"No." Pina shook her head. "No, not at all. I'm fine, really. I just thought I might read for awhile, that's all."

The lie was obvious. Pina knew Andrea hadn't seen a single book in her chamber. But it was too late. She held her breath, only releasing it when Andrea left the room without another word.

What was she afraid of?

Sleep. Pina couldn't deny it. She was afraid to go

to sleep, afraid to visit the place, whatever it was, she had gone to last night.

Realistically, Pina knew must eventually drift off, but prayed that maybe, just maybe, the light would keep the "bad thing" away.

But sleep didn't come. Hours passed, and still the thudding of Pina's heart kept her awake. The candles burned lower. Three hours before dawn, just as they guttered, Pina's eyelids closed. Her breathing deepened.

She was in the forest. Overhead the sunlight was brilliant, but it was dim beneath the canopy of leaves. Only occasional shafts of light penetrated the dense foliage. Pina could see dust motes riding on them. She saw nothing else.

Then there was a rustling of leaves. The sound of twigs breaking. Pina's flesh tingled. Soon her eyes made out a magnificent rack of antlers, partially camouflaged by the intermittent light and shadow. The animal moved again. Stood before her.

Its gold-flecked gaze was unblinking. It briefly bowed its head, acknowledging her. Pina blinked.

The stag right before her became indistinct. A trick of light and shadow? Then the antlers dissolved into nothingness right before her very eyes. The beast's muzzle foreshortened, drew in upon itself. It raised up on its hind legs, tall, and taller. Its front legs were suddenly gone; they had become arms. The animal's torso became a man's. Its hide became lightly tanned flesh. Features molded.

The metamorphosis stunned Pina. She stood looking at the most handsome man she had ever seen. And he wore not a shred of clothing. Unable to stop her hungry gaze, it traveled downward.

His chest was muscular, smooth, with only a faint line of shadow, the finest of hair, running from his throat to his firm, flat abdomen. The shadow widened, encasing his manhood, paler than the rest of him, arresting. Pina thought she heard herself gasp. Her gaze returned to his face.

Thick, wavy brown hair framed it. His lips were generous, features regular. His brown eyes were flecked with gold.

Molten lava replaced the blood in Pina's veins. Desire filled her breast until she could scarcely breathe. She reached out to touch him. She couldn't help herself.

He vanished.

Francesca was alarmed at first when Pina did not appear at breakfast. Andrea, arranging bread on the sideboard, reassured her.

"She slept late, signora. I'm going to the kitchen now to prepare something to bring to her in her room."

Francesca nodded, somewhat absently. She herself hadn't slept all that well. Despite the serenity she always experienced in the country, and although Pina's health and vigor seemed to increase daily, with no terrors in the night, she had had nightmares that something was coming for her child, chasing her. It was faceless, but frightening nonetheless in her dreams.

Suddenly remembering Andrea, Francesca looked up. But the little maid had gone. Pushing from the table, she rose and headed for the small room where she liked to do her correspondence. A pounding on the front door halted Francesca in her tracks.

Ramona, arms laden with fresh-cut flowers, was just crossing the foyer on her way to place her blooms in the reception rooms. Transferring her burden to one arm, she opened the door.

Francesca captured her indrawn hiss of breath in time to render it inaudible. She froze her expression in place and glided elegantly toward the visitor who stood silhouetted in the doorway. She extended a slender hand.

"Signor Fontini."

The tall, thin man in the immaculate *camicia* bowed low over her hand and touched it ceremonially to his lips. "Signora Galbi. You are as lovely as ever."

"And you are as smooth tongued." Francesca watched the man's eyebrows, as snow-white as his hair, rise almost imperceptibly. She was a bit surprised herself. As recently as a month ago, she would not have dreamed of saying such a thing to the man who had been a friend and colleague of her husband.

"Is this a social visit?" Francesca inquired lightly, though she knew it was not. Having learned from Eduardo, she could play a game as well as anyone. She merely hadn't tried before. "If so, you've come a long way."

"Yes, I have come a long way. And no, this is not a social visit. As you well know."

Francesca inclined her head ever so slightly. "If you'll follow me?" She heard his steps following her as she headed for the large, airy room where she and Eduardo had entertained guests.

Ramona had gone ahead and placed the flowers, Francesca noted; periwinkles to match the velvet drapes at the long row of windows, looking over the gardens. She selected a dainty chair Eduardo had once given her as a gift; flowers were carved into its legs and the arms were upholstered in pale green silk. She gripped them and smiled as Signor Fontini took a seat across from her.

"May I offer you refreshment? You must have traveled all night to arrive here so early in the morning."

"I spent the night at a nearby inn, and I just broke my fast. Now, may we get to the point?"

Francesca's abdomen tightened. She smiled graciously. "Of course. Please, go right ahead."

"He *what*?"

"He came to the door, bold as you please," Andrea said.

"What did my mother do?"

"Well, what could she do? She invited him in."

Uttering an unladylike oath, Pina flung the covers away and swung her legs over the edge of the bed. The lingering effects of a near-sleepless night — and the excitement of her strange dream — were temporarily forgotten.

"Help me dress, Andrea. Please. Quickly."

Dread tainted her blood and was carried to every part of her body, weakening her. It did not stop her from carefully choosing her attire, however. A beautiful woman beautifully dressed could be as formidable as a knight in armor, her father had told her more than once.

Pina chose a simple off-white gown which fell to the floor in straight, soft folds from beneath the satin ribbon tied under breast. Egg-shell white lace covered, but barely concealed, her cleavage. She had Andrea catch her hair up in pins, artfully arranging a few stray curls to fall to her shoulders.

Andrea stepped back, admiring her handiwork. "You are perfect, Miss Pina. In every way."

Pina turned her head slightly, evaluating her complexion

in the mirror. Did she need makeup? It didn't seem so, and there wasn't time anyway.

"Let's hope so," she said at length in reply to Andrea's compliment. Pina kissed her maid's cheek. "Let's hope."

Claudio Fontini had wasted no time. He'd launched right into her.

"I'm amazed at your effrontery in sending me this letter, Francesca," he said, dropping all pretense of politeness. For effect, he produced the offending missive and waved it at her. "How dare you suggest the union your husband pledged be put aside so casually?"

"My decision was hardly casual, Claudio. I made it after much soul searching and deliberation."

He made a rude sound in the back of his throat. "You made nothing but a spineless concession to a spoiled child."

This time Francesca didn't try to hide her hiss of displeasure. She compressed her lips to a thin, white line and sat erect in her chair.

"If my husband were alive," she said stiffly, "he would throttle you where you sit for speaking to me in such a manner."

"But he's not alive, is he, Francesca?" A cruel smile twisted Fontini's mouth. "He's gone, and but for Pina, you're alone in the world."

"I have my sister," Francesca bit out defensively, in spite of herself.

"A mindless wreck since the death of her child," Claudio replied dismissively.

Francesca had to take a moment to gather her wits; the naked spite and brutality of Claudio's words had pierced her heart, as he had intended. But watching him gloat over her discomfiture made it easy to pull herself back together.

"It's not difficult to see," Francesca began slowly, "where Antonio learned his manners. And his attitude toward women."

"I couldn't agree more, Mother."

"Ah," Claudio said on an exhalation of air as he pushed to his feet. "The she-wolf's whelp."

Something burned in Pina's breast. With tremendous effort, she willed her blood to cool.

"Good morning to you, too, sir," she said icily. "How fares your . . . son?"

"He is bereft at the loss of the company of his fiancé', as you might imagine," Claudio said smoothly, "since your . . . vacation . . . to the country."

"This is no vacation, and I am not your son's fiancé'."

With arched brows, Claudio turned his attention back to Francesca. "And you mention my *son's* manners?"

Francesca rose and moved to her daughter's side. "This is not, ultimately, about deportment," she said with quiet dignity. "It's about a mistake . . . a simple mistake."

Pina watched Antonio's father subtly relax. She watched her mother move in for the kill.

"My husband mistakenly thought you were a gentleman and that, by association, your son was as well. He couldn't have been more wrong. The betrothal is broken. Neither you nor your son are welcome in my home. Now, please, leave."

A helpless sputter was all the unmanned Fontini could manage. He spun on his heel and strode toward the door, Pina, Francesca, and now Andrea in his wake. Andrea sprinted ahead to open the door.

Claudio walked through it without hesitation. Once outside he turned, prepared to deliver his final volley.

Andrea slammed the door.

CHAPTER

23

With a hand to the small of her aching back, Erta bent to retrieve a stick of kindling that had fallen from the bundle nestled in the crook of her left arm. Straightening, she grunted and turned back in the direction of her hut. She had barely taken a step when she heard a rustling in the undergrowth. Erta froze.

There was no fear in her. Having lived in the woodlands for so long, she could identify and translate every sound. It was no animal that approached, but a human. A human making absolutely no effort at stealth.

Pina.

Even had she not known the cadence of her step, Erta would have sensed her. She frowned, however. Two things were very wrong.

One, she had bidden Pina to remain in her father's

house. Hadn't she expressed her urgency? Something was not right, not aligned with the natural magic of the forest.

Two, Pina was not running as if she had a destination. Her steps suddenly slowed, faltered, then resumed. Erta heard the snapping of twigs and the protest of the underbrush when Pina abruptly changed course and put on a burst of speed.

A feeling of alarm built in the old woman. Abandoning her sticks, Erta moved quickly toward the sounds of Pina's erratic passage.

Pina flung herself headlong down the faint deerpath. Had she lost him? Had she really seen him at all? She slowed, eyes darting about her, scanning the play of light and shadow beneath the woodland canopy. Had the vision been only an illusion?

No! There it was again, a flash of movement passing between some distant poplar boles. Pina sprinted in that direction.

Somewhere in the back of her mind was a niggling doubt, a pinprick of fear. What was she doing after all, chasing some unknown creature, or person, all alone in the forest? Before reality and good sense could intrude and redirect her steps back to the relative safety of the lodge, or

Erta's hut in the clearing, however, the strange compulsion to follow the elusive . . . whatever it was . . . overcame her once more, strongly. Pina ran on.

A flock of startled birds rose noisily from a forest giant just ahead. Pina didn't think she had been close enough to startle them herself. Her heart increased its beat and her footsteps quickened.

Another brief glimpse . . . was it a man? Yes, it had to be! It was upright; an abundance of long, thick hair streamed behind when he swiftly turned and darted away in the opposite direction.

Pina found herself laughing. It was as if they played a game. She sensed absolutely no harm, only an inexplicable . . . joy. There was no other word for it. With another bubble of laughter, Pina raised her skirt a little higher and lengthened her stride.

Erta's unease became distinctly uncomfortable when she heard the sound of Pina's laughter. What was going on?

A flicker of memory passed before the old woman's mind's eye: Pina pulling free of her grip, stumbling away on chubby legs, regaining her balance, laughing. Chasing after the brilliant butterfly, arms outstretched.

Pina, skipping ahead of Erta beneath the forest

shadows, supposedly intent on the mushrooms she was seeking. A flash of blue, a jay's sharp scold, and all was forgotten; she was off. The chase was on.

Erta's heart faltered. Pina was after something. But she was a young woman; she had put childish flights of fancy aside. And she had been warned . . .

The feeling that something was not quite right deepened. Though the stag had been gone when Erta went to look for it, she knew it had not left the vicinity entirely. And she knew it never should have reacted to Pina in the way it had.

Running in her hobbling gait, Erta cried out: "Pina! Pina, child . . . wait for me! I'm over here! Please, come to me."

The familiar voice instantly penetrated Pina's concentration. She hesitated, tripped over her own feet, and spun in the direction of the old woman's voice. She shook her head.

What had she been up to? What was she doing running through the forest unaccompanied? Her mother would be furious. And Erta . . .

"Over here, child," the old woman called again. "I'm over here." A moment later Erta saw her emerging from the trees, picking a bit of twig from her hair.

"Erta! I was looking for you."

"Were you, now?"

"Yes. Yes, of course, I . . ." Pina paused, suddenly

confused. She *had* been looking for Erta, hadn't she? There was so much to tell her; so much had happened only this morning. After the unpleasant, yet satisfying confrontation with the elder Fontini, she had set off to see Erta with her mother's blessing. She had been headed for the clearing, but then . . .

Something had moved through the trees, tantalizing her, tantalizing her memory now. What was it?

"Pina," Erta said briskly. "What were you doing alone in the woods when I told you to go to your father's house and stay there?"

It all came back to her in a rush: the stag; Erta's uneasiness; the dream. The dream!

"Don't be angry, Erta. Please. So much has happened since I saw you yesterday. I have to tell you everything." Pina pressed a hand to her chest as if to help her catch her breath. "The most amazing thing has happened . . ."

"Wait, child. Wait." Erta glanced about her, unaccountably nervous in her familiar, beloved surroundings. "Come to the cottage. We'll speak there."

Erta took off at once and Pina had no choice but to follow. She trotted along behind the slight, hurrying figure until they reached the clearing and entered the simple dwelling.

Erta slammed the door behind them. "Now, tell," she said without delay. "Tell me what's so important you had to go running through the woods when you've been warned . . ."

"Signor Fontini came to the lodge this morning," Pina interrupted breathlessly, pushing Erta's, and her mother's fears aside.

With a sigh, Erta allowed her to go on. "And Signor Fontini is who?"

"The father of my fiance', Antonio. Only, he's no longer my fiance'." Beaming, Pina grasped the old woman's hands. "Mother has stood up to the Fontinis. She's broken the engagement. I don't have to marry that . . . that worm."

Erta could not help but be infected by her former charge's buoyant spirits. "Worms are really quite useful creatures," she countered.

"Oh, I'm sorry, Erta," Pina apologized with mock solemnity. "I didn't mean to malign one of your forest friends." She pressed her fingers to her lips to stifle a giggle. It wasn't funny. Not really. Antonio and his father were less than savory human beings who had caused her and her family, Andrea included, heartache and distress. But being rid of them, finally . . .

"If only you knew how happy I am." Pina threw her arms around the old woman and hugged until she protested.

"There, there . . . enough." Erta pushed Pina away, but she was grinning her toothless grin. "I can see how happy you are. You don't have to show me any more."

Pina laughed, and Erta saw at once that there was more than one reason for her lightness of being.

"Come, child. Tell me what else is on your mind and in your heart. I see there is more."

Pina felt a twinge of nerves at last. She had been excited since she had awakened to tell Erta about her dream. She would know what it meant. But now that the moment had actually arrived, she experienced a strange reluctance.

"What is it, child?" Erta pressed. "Talk to me. Talk to your old Erta."

"I had a dream." The statement came out as barely a whisper. Pina sank into the chair by the window. Her gaze unfocused.

"I had a dream, Erta. I saw the stag again, in the forest. But as I watched, he . . . he transformed into a man."

Icy fingers wrapped around Erta's chest, squeezing the breath from her lungs.

"He was handsome, so handsome. With gold in his eyes, and . . ."

"Enough!" Erta rasped.

Pina looked up sharply, rudely startled from her reverie. "What is it, Erta? What's wrong?"

The old woman shook her head, mumbling to herself.

"Erta!" Pina jumped to her feet, the hair on the back of her arms prickling with alarm.

The old woman looked her right in the eye. "Magic. Magic is what's wrong. Dark magic."

"But, it was only a dream!"

"And the stag was only a stag? No, I don't think so. There is something afoot here. Something evil."

"No!" This time it was Pina who shook her head. "Don't say that, Erta. You're scaring me. It wasn't evil, it couldn't be."

"How do you know?" Erta demanded in a hard voice.

"Because, I . . . I . . . I just know. I . . ."

"You're seduced by it," Erta snapped bluntly. "You know nothing."

"Erta! I . . ."

"Your mother brought you here because something stalked you. It was stealing away your very life, just as it stole away your cousin's."

"No," Pina protested yet again. She shook her head so violently the pins came loose from her hair and it tumbled down her back. "It's not the same thing. It's not!"

Erta grabbed Pina's shoulders and gave her a shake. "Control yourself," she ordered. "Get a hold of yourself and think; think about what has happened. Your mother brought you here to keep you safe. She came to me because she knows I can feel the presence of magic. And you are no longer safe here, Pina. I fear the thing, whatever it is, has followed you. Something isn't right in the forest. It's . . ."

"No!" Pina screamed her final protest. Pulling from Erta's grasp, she threw open the door and fled from the hut. She charged straight into the woods.

As Pina ran, a single thought played over and over in her mind. It wasn't true. There was nothing amiss, nothing. Only a dream. Only a dream . . .

The breath was knocked from Pina's lungs when she ran into the solid wall of human flesh. Arms encircled her, held her tightly. With a cry, she looked up into the face hovering just inches from her own . . . looked up into gold-flecked eyes.

The world spun away.

CHAPTER

24

He held her against him more tightly as her knees buckled, and smiled down at her.

Pina's heart lurched, then thudded wildly.

It wasn't just a dream after all. He was real. More than real. His physical presence was overwhelming. Trying to gather her scattered, shattered thoughts, Pina placed her hands flat on his chest and pushed away from him. He let her go, but continued to support her with his hands on her elbows.

"You . . . you cannot be," Pina stammered, despite the evidence. "You're a dream. Only a dream."

Slowly, carefully, he released her and took a step back. Pina noticed that he was, thankfully, dressed. Tight red leggings hugged his shapely legs, and he wore a white ruffled shirt, open at the neck. Something else was different from the dream of him as well.

He was not tanned, but pallid. His cheeks were not full, but sunken, and his lips were pinched, eyes dull. Pina's most basic natural instinct immediately took over. She extended a hand to him, her caretaking nature overriding all sense of caution.

"Are you . . . are you all right?"

"A dream?" he said, ignoring her question. His brow furrowed, finely arched brows drawn together. "You dreamed of me?"

Taken aback, Pina dropped her arm. "I, uh . . . Yes. Yes, I dreamed of you."

"Tell me this. Tell me of your dream."

The gold-flecked eyes were mesmerizing. Pina swam in their depths, losing sight of the surface of reality. She was compelled to answer him; there was no other choice, no other thought.

"I . . . I was here, in the forest," Pina began without further hesitation. "I saw a stag. It came right up to me. Then it changed. It . . . it became . . . *you*."

He sighed, the sound of his exhalation as soft and melodic as the whisper of a summer breeze. He nodded ever so slightly, gaze momentarily on something very far away. Seconds later, he refocused his attention on Pina with an obvious effort of will, and drew a deep breath.

"Do you believe in magic, Pina?"

She did not even pause to ask how he knew her name. It just seemed right that he would. Just as it seemed somehow right they should be having this conversation, despite that she knew, in another part of her mind, that it couldn't, shouldn't be happening.

"What . . . what kind of magic?"

"The magic of dreams."

"I'm not sure I . . . I know what you mean."

"I'm not sure either, Pina," he replied softly, evenly. His voice was as hypnotic as his gaze. "I am only certain of one thing."

Almost imperceptibly, his eyes widened. She was sinking deeper into the pool, farther and farther away from the surface. From breath. From life.

"I only know," he continued, in his quiet, spellbinding voice, "that I dreamed of you. As you saw me in your dream, so did I see you in mine. I dreamed of you, and I have not dreamed in so long that I have not even a memory of dreaming."

Pina was totally lost. She could no longer see the light at the surface of the pool. It did not seem extraordinary in the least to be speaking of dreams with the man who had come out of one. It did not strike her as dangerous to be alone with a stranger in the heart of the forest. A stranger who had, moreover, metamorphosed from a stag. All that mattered, all that was real, was his story, his plight.

"How . . . could you not dream?" Pina asked, concern for him filling her breast with a pleasant warmth. "Everyone dreams."

Once again he nodded, faintly. "Yes. You are right. Everyone dreams," he repeated. "And I must have. Once. Because I can remember being a young man. I had a family, a mother and father. I lived in a small village. I can remember being . . . normal."

Normal. The word repeated in Pina's head. Something beat at her brain, struggling to enter, like a small bird fluttering against a closed window, trying to gain entrance. Normal.

This was not normal.

A dagger of fear entered Pina's heart. She took a step away.

"Pina." His hand reached for her, his voice caressed. "Please, don't go. Please."

Pina trembled. But she did not take another step.

"You . . . you are not the . . . the same . . . now?"

"I do not even know what the 'same' might be," he answered eagerly, as if her continued presence relied on his most prompt response. "I recall so little of my life, as if I have lived it in a fog. The last thing I remember with any clarity . . ."

"Pina! Pina, where are you? Answer me."

Pina came up from her deep, dark well and broke the

surface, gasping for air. "Oh . . . Oh, my God." She took a step backward, stumbled. When he reached to help her, she recoiled. "No! Don't touch me!"

A look of inexpressible sadness crossed his handsome features and Pina's emotions wrenched. But this time they did not carry her away.

"Pina! Pina!"

Reality was a lifeline thrown by the old woman. Pina grabbed it and held on desperately.

She was alone in the forest with a dream incarnate.

Yes, she believed in magic. And in the terror of it.

He continued to hold out his hand to her, eyes beseeching.

Pina turned and fled toward Erta's voice.

CHAPTER

25

Tallhart stood motionless for long moments while the familiar, feral part of his mind took over. He felt the connection with her; it had not been lost. It had, in fact, been strengthened. He would be able to come to her. When night fell, and she relinquished control of her thoughts when she entered the place of dreams, he would be there. Waiting. His will created the void in that place; his will filled it with his presence. His will . . .

With a shake of his head, Tallhart tried to rid himself of the annoying buzz in his brain. It persisted, battering against the wild part of him, the part that constantly fought for survival; the part that *needed* to go to her. It was her very essence that would keep that part of him alive.

But now there was something else. The buzzing would not stop. He had to heed it, go to it, admit it into his consciousness. It had become more persistent lately, demanding his surrender. He bowed. And the memories flooded back.

"I have no name," he had said. He had found her; in the ancient way of his kind he had found her, and come to her. But she had not simply opened to him like the other blossoms he had plucked. Something elemental within her had resisted. He could not identify it; it was completely foreign to him. But he had had to acquiesce to it.

"I have no name."

"Of course you do. Tell me. Or you must leave."

Never, never had any of them spoken to him in such a manner. Never had anyone told him he must leave. It had opened something in him.

"I told you before . . . I don't know."

"Then I shall give you a name. At least until we find out who you are, and what has happened to you."

The crack had widened then; he had felt it most distinctly. The foreign thing, whatever it was, was flowing into him. And he had responded to it.

"You would give me something?"

"Yes, a name."

Such a small thing, seemingly.

"And what would you call me?"

"My father had a hunting lodge in the country. He often took me with him when he hunted stags. Your hair, the color of

your eyes, is so like the coloration of a deer. And you're so tall. I shall call you Tallhart."

The strange thing had threatened to overwhelm him in that instant. The unnatural feeling warred with the wild part of him, the essential part of him. But the battle only lasted a moment. The survival of his inner being was paramount, and took over.

He had given her the gift of sleep then, and had invaded it. He had taken sustenance from her soul, and left open the path to return.

Tallhart blinked and looked about him. Lost in reverie, he had forgotten where he was. He lifted his face to the patchy sunlight falling through the treetop canopy, and listened to the singing of birds and the chatter of squirrels, the rustle of small creatures in the undergrowth, and the susurration of leaves in a sudden breeze. He was in the forest. But how had he come to be here? The buzzing noise, sensation, inside his head pushed at him again, forcing him to remember.

He had come to her again, this time triumphant. There were no barriers to her soul. She wanted him, needed him, as he had designed. He had been able to take from her freely. Soon he would be able to take all she had to give, and he would be replenished. One more time, perhaps. Only one more time.

But it was not to be.

Unaware, Tallhart growled.

The way had been closed to him. A barrier had been erected, and the unidentifiable thing that had once entered him flowed strongly from it. He fought it, with all his power, all his might and will. He had even felt her straining to come to him.

But the power in the barrier had been stronger; he had lost. And when he had tried to come to her again, she was gone.

Again, still unaware, Tallhart let the anger form into a rumble at the back of his throat. A hare hiding in the shadows, frozen with fear at the instinctual recognition of a dangerous predator, sprang to life and fled. Tallhart noted its noisy passage, and was returned to the forest. How had he come here? The thing in his head nagged at him. One more time, he bowed to it.

He had been desperate to find her, and in acknowledging his desperation that crack in his being had opened a little wider. This was something he had never felt before. He had often lost his prey, lost the connection. Though weakened, of course, not fully sated, he had simply moved on to another. This time that had not been possible. Why?

He did not know. He knew only he must find her.

Using the feral essence, he cast about for her. Nothing.

Letting the new thing come to the fore, the small, new part of him, he had searched.

"I shall call you Tallhart."

The name had come from an assemblage of her memories. It had been a gift. She had opened a part of herself to give him that gift. It was enough of an opening to squeeze through. He had scented her on the path to her memories, and followed her to this place in the forest where he had cloaked himself in the fabric of her remembrances.

Tallhart smiled. It was not an expression of seduction, however, but of gladness. Though his lips felt stiff and uneasy with the emotion behind the movement, he let the smile widen. He threw back his head and gazed up at a patch of blue just visible behind the leafy curtains.

"I . . .I was here, in the forest. I saw a stag. It came right up to me. Then it changed. It . . . it became . . .you."

He had done it, even though he had not known he could. The 'how' of it was a mystery. It might be he had powers he did not realize. Or maybe it was as he had told her?

" . . . I dreamed of you. As you saw me in your dream, so did I see you in mine. I dreamed of you, and I have not dreamed in so long that I have not even a memory of dreaming."

There *had* been a dream, he remembered it now. It was how he had found her memory path. And it was the key; somehow; it was the key to unlock the knowledge of what was happening to him. *"The magic of dreams."*

He did not know what it was, and the wild part of him scrabbled rudely inside his head, clawing, begging for his attention. He would go to it soon; he had to. It would hold sway over him as it always did.

He just wanted to enjoy one more moment of freedom.

Tallhart breathed deeply, inhaling scents he had not even known he had once experienced and forgotten. He inhaled, memories pricking at him.

"Everyone dreams," she had said to him.

And he had answered, *"Yes. . . . And I must have. Once. Because I can remember being a young man. I had a family, a mother and father. I lived in a small village. I can remember being . . . normal."*

Elation filled him abruptly. He recalled something other than the wildness, the need, the thing inside that drove him! He remembered *self.*

And then, just as suddenly, the dark, wild essence came again, screaming, and bore him away.

CHAPTER

26

Heedless now of direction, Pina fled from the stranger in the wood. She could still hear Erta's voice, but it mattered not that she find her. She wanted merely to get away.

The edge of the treeline was just ahead. Pina stumbled from forest into the sunlight of the lawns and gardens surrounding the lodge. Pausing to catch her breath, she looked down and saw that the lovely off-white gown was stained and wrinkled. Worse, what was she going to say to her mother? How was she going to explain her appearance?

"Pina!"

She jumped and looked over her shoulder to see Erta had found her.

"Why did you run from me?" the old woman demanded.

Pina opened her mouth, but no words would come.

"Why?" Erta repeated sharply. "Especially when I had just finished warning you of the evil that has followed you!"

"And I tell you he is *not* evil!" Pina clapped a hand over her mouth, but it was too late. What was she saying, anyway? Hadn't she just run from him in terror? Pina watched Erta's eyes narrow.

"It's more than just a dream . . . isn't it?" she said slowly. "You've seen him, haven't you, Pina?"

How could she know? How could she possibly know? Ever truthful, admission was on the tip of her tongue. Then she recalled the beseeching look in his eyes as he held out his hand to her. Almost before she knew it, she was shaking her head.

There was a long moment of silence before Erta uttered her next words.

"You're protecting him," she said astutely. "Why?"

Pina's knees turned to water. She could barely stand. Licking her lips, she averted her gaze. Erta grabbed her wrist.

"Ow!" Pina tried to pull away, but the old woman's grip was vice-like. "You're hurting me!"

Erta made a rude noise. "You don't know what pain is," she spat. "Stupid girl!"

Her old nurse's words, her tone, reached deep into Pina's breast and clutched at her heart. She quit trying to resist the old woman, and a measure of the fear she had felt when seeing the stranger in the forest returned to her.

"That's better." Erta loosened her grip but did not let go. "Now, we'll go back to the lodge and . . ."

"No! No, please, Erta. Please, don't tell Mother. She's finally getting over Father, living her life again. Please, this will only upset her. I'll tell you everything, I promise, if you just leave my mother out of this."

There was another period of silence while Erta considered. She nodded abruptly and, still holding Pina's wrist, turned back into the woods toward the faint trail to her forest clearing.

Despite the heat of the day, Erta closed and barred the door, then the single window. Pina protested to no avail. Already warm from the brisk pace the old woman had set on the way back to her hut, Pina picked up a thick scrap of cloth used to wrap around the handle of the soup pot when it hung over the fire and wiped her dripping brow.

"Now, sit," Erta ordered. "Sit and tell me everything. As you promised."

"Everything." Pina repeated the word silently. What *was* "everything"? She had run into the stranger she had dreamed of. He was real, not an illusion. That's all there was.

Or was it?

"Well?" Erta prompted.

"Well, I . . . you're right," Pina conceded in a rush. "I saw him again. He's real — real, Erta! — not just a dream. He's real, and I spoke to him."

"Spoke to him?" The old woman's sparse, gray brows arched, deepening the canyons etched in her brow.

Pina nodded energetically, golden waves of hair falling about her shoulders. "Yes. He . . . he told me he had dreamed of me. He asked if I believed in the magic of dreams . . ."

Erta listened, rapt, while Pina related the details of the strange conversation. When she finished, Erta asked only a single question. "He said he remembers being 'normal'?"

Pina nodded once again. "He was going to tell me more, but I . . . I heard you calling, and ran away."

Pina watched Erta closely. Had she detected the white lie? Apparently not, for her thoughts seemed far away.

"Magic," the old woman muttered at length. "The magic of dreams . . ."

"Erta?"

The sound of her name drew her thoughts back to the present. She blinked and turned a questioning gaze on Pina.

"What are you thinking, Erta? What do you know?"

Erta rose stiffly from the stool she had placed near Pina's chair. She crossed to the window and opened it. A breeze immediately swirled into the room, freshening it.

Pushing sweaty strands of hair from her face, Pina rose as well to face the light and air pouring into the hut. The significance of Erta's action was not lost on her.

"I was right, wasn't I, Erta?" she asked softly. "There's no harm in him, is there? He's not evil. The magic isn't evil."

Erta's head snapped in her direction. "I said nothing of the kind."

"But you opened the window. Surely you wouldn't open it if you perceived a threat!"

Erta returned her attention to the square of sunlight streaming into the room. "There is no threat," she admitted, distantly. "Not now, at this moment. No."

Something leapt in Pina's breast. "You know something, Erta . . . you know!"

"I know little, very little," Erta murmured. "Dangerously little."

"But, you said . . ."

"I know what I said," the old woman replied brusquely. She turned from the window and took Pina's hand. "Come, child. There is something we must do."

"What . . . what are you talking about?" Pina stammered as she let Erta pull her out the door and into the sunlit clearing. "What do we have to do?"

"Many things before this night," she replied mysteriously. "Many things . . ."

Pina was astonished when Erta readily agreed Signora Galbi need not be advised of recent events. Or of the old woman's plans. Erta even helped her to straighten and brush off her clothes and repin her hair.

The three women chatted amiably for a time in the pleasant room where Francesca took care of her correspondence, although Pina had trouble following the conversation, even when the subject turned to the morning's incident with the elder Fontini. She was amazed Erta could be so calm and apparently unaffected by what seemed to be transpiring.

Magic. She had long known of the earth's natural magic, the land's essential forces. But this was something different. Pina cast a sideways glance at her mother and Erta, sitting side by side directly in a beam of sunlight falling through the leaded windows. She would be eternally grateful to Erta for affording her that balance in her life, along with her mother's religious and spiritual teachings. Even though she knew it had pained her mother to have Erta as her nurse, her father had been undeniably astute in his choice. Pina sighed.

She missed him acutely. Especially now.

Pina fidgeted her hands in her lap, drawing a look from Erta. The old woman smiled benignly at Francesca.

"It has been good to speak with you, Signora," she said, rising. "And it is good to see you embracing life again."

Pina watched her mother return Erta's smile, genuinely. "Thank you for the visit. And for the time spent with my . . . with Pina."

Erta acknowledged Francesca's generosity with slight inclination of her head. She and Pina left the cheerful room.

"What did you tell Mother?" Pina questioned as they walked the dimly lit corridors.

"What do you mean? You were there. You have ears."

Pina flushed. "I . . . my mind was on other things. How can *you* be so calm?"

"Because I have to be," she replied evenly, and entered Ramona's busy kitchen. After exchanging greetings with the woman, she asked for a few common ingredients, garlic chief among them, ostensibly for her soup pot. Pina hurried after her when she once more headed into the lodge's interior corridors.

"Where are we going now?"

"Your chamber. To look at your jewelry," the old woman replied enigmatically.

Pina opened her mouth, then shut it again. She would find out soon enough.

And she did.

Erta closed the door behind them and began at once to

rummage through the ivory-inlaid box on Pina's dressing table that contained her jewelry.

"Ah ha," she exclaimed, and triumphantly held up a small cross, inset with diamonds, on a thin gold chain.

Pina frowned. "What . . . what is that for? And the garlic, and herbs? What are you up to?"

"I am 'up to' your continued good health." Piling her treasures on the dressing table, Erta crossed to the shutters, now open, and examined them. "They might keep out a stiff wind and some rain, but not the creature that stalks you."

Pina's stomach clenched. "But I thought . . . I thought you said he wasn't a threat."

"Pray your memory gets no worse as you age," Erta said tartly, and returned to the objects on the dressing table. "I said he was not a threat now, at this moment. Tonight, however, is a different story."

"But, Erta, you don't even know if the man I saw in the wood is the thing that made me ill and . . ." She stopped abruptly, biting her lower lip, thinking of Valeria.

"No, you're right. I do not. But I intend to find out, and to do my best to protect you in the meantime."

"With soup ingredients?"

The old woman chuckled under her breath. The objects spread out before her on the table, she sat on richly cushioned stool.

"When your mother first brought you here," Erta began, "I examined you. Remember?" When Pina nodded, blushing, she continued. "I had thought to see the mark of the blood drinker, who comes by night to take sustenance from his victims. I saw nothing, it is true. Yet, your symptoms were so very like those I have heard described. So much so that I am not certain I did not miss something. Tonight, therefore, we will have with us the talisman used for centuries against this night creature." She touched the string of garlic and roughly tied, dried herbs, almost reverently, and smiled. "Soup ingredients."

"And the cross?"

Erta picked it up and let it dangle from her fingers. "Bend down here and let me put this on you."

Pina complied and Erta fastened the chain around her neck. Pina fingered it, brows arched into question marks.

"The cross is to maintain balance; something to protect you from my world, something from your mother's. The cross is an ancient symbol of good, just as the garlic and herbs are an ancient ward against evil."

Feeling suddenly weak with the realization that Erta really did expect something to come after her, Pina sank down onto the edge of her bed.

"And . . . and now what?"

"Now . . . we wait."

CHAPTER

27

It was the longest wait of her life.

Soon after Erta had put away her "tools for the night," Andrea came in to see if her mistress needed anything. Dipping a quick curtsy, she was suddenly overcome with a wide smile. Although the morning's visit from Antonio's father now seemed very far away, in light of other events, Pina was instantly returned to the reason for Andrea's expression of joy.

"Oh, Miss, I'm so happy for you."

Pina opened her arms and Andrea came into her embrace. "I'm happy, too," she murmured, and realized at last what a heavy burden had been lifted from her shoulders.

"He's gone, Miss Pina. He's gone from your life. You won't have to marry that . . . that monster."

Pina stepped away from her maid. "He's gone from *our*

lives, Andrea. He won't trouble either of us again."

Tears gathered at the corners of Andrea's dark eyes and she blinked them away. "*La Signora* was very brave."

"So were you."

There was no more to be said, and Andrea left to make the pot of tea her mistress had requested. Pina turned to Erta.

"A 'monster'," the old woman mused aloud. "Your little maid calls your ex-fiancé a 'monster'."

"And he is," Pina replied vehemently.

"In what way?" Erta asked thoughtfully.

Warming to the subject, Pina related the tale of her engagement to Antonio, the way he spied on her and tried to control her life; his rudeness to her mother and his treatment of Andrea.

"He's evil," Pina finished. "Truly evil, Erta. I can't believe my father was so fooled by both Antonio and his father."

"Because evil comes in many guises," Erta said quietly, looking Pina in the eye. "We are often fooled. Especially when the evil is cloaked in wealth, the trappings of nobility . . . or sheer, physical beauty."

Pina felt herself flush, remembering how she had gushed to Erta about how handsome the stranger in the wood was. She opened her mouth to protest, but the old woman raised a restraining hand.

"Say no more," she warned. "Andrea comes with the

tea. Just think on the irony of it, child. Just think."

Pina did think. Throughout the long afternoon she had little else to do.

After drinking several cups of tea, which Erta seemed to heartily enjoy, smacking her lips and smiling her toothless smile, she had left Pina with the excuse that she had preparations of her own to make for the night. When Pina had questioned her, she had replied, enigmatically, "I told your mother when you first arrived that your last bastion of defense against whatever this is would be the strength of your own mind and spirit. Mine, perhaps, as well. I must go now. I will return before dark."

And so she had gone, leaving Pina to ponder much. A light lunch with her mother was only a brief distraction, along with conversation about the correctness of the decision to part ways with the Fontinis. Pina could see her mother was almost light-hearted, and she was glad. But it pressed Erta's words even deeper into her thoughts.

". . . evil comes in many guises," Pina repeated to herself as she sat in her sunny garden and worked on a piece of embroidery. The stranger in the wood was beautiful, there was no denying it. Was he evil as well?

Every time the thought entered her head, Pina jumped

on the denial.

No, he was not evil. There was magic at work, yes, but not dark magic. Antonio was the evil one, not her handsome stranger.

And the more she thought of him, the more Pina's heart went out to him. He looked so sickly, and he seemed so lost. Why had she even run from him? Why had she been frightened? Obviously he needed her, needed her help. He had come to her, and she had fled. She felt horrible.

Furthermore, Erta had to be wrong. He was not the evil being who had, as they told her, come to her in Venice to sap her vitality as he had stolen away Valeria's life. He couldn't be. He was just a poor, lost soul . . .

Wrapped in her thoughts, Pina did not notice the inevitable ending of the day, the setting of the sun. Her first warning was the chill she felt when the long shadows of the ornamental fruit trees fell across her shoulder. Shivering, she gathered up her sewing and entered her chamber.

"Close the doors behind you," Erta ordered. "Lock them."

Completely unaware of the old woman's presence, Pina was taken aback. With a gasp, hand to her throat, she took a step backward.

"Do as I say," Erta snapped.

The relatively pleasant mood she had conjured, her sympathy for, and defense of the stranger, evaporated beneath the heat of the old woman's tone and expression. She whirled and pulled the doors closed, locking them. She watched as Erta shuttered the windows.

"Erta, what's . . .?"

"Nothing's wrong," Erta replied, anticipating her. "I simply prepare, as I told you we must."

It occurred to Pina, with a sense of increasing unease, that Erta had divined her mood — and was countering it. She tried to summon her earlier emotion but the old woman, and the coming night, held it at bay.

"What . . . what about dinner?" Pina managed to stammer at last. "Mother is expecting me to eat with her."

"No, she is not. I've developed an ache in these old bones. After years of nursing her child, *La Signora* has agreed to return the favor. You will sit with me this night and help apply a poultice. You will also brew a tea for me from herbs I have gathered."

"Erta, are you really . . .?"

"Of course not. Oh, I have aches. But I'm able to tend to them without help."

"Then why . . .?" Pina pressed her lips together.

Erta wanted her away from the lodge. What was she planning? The feeling of unease spread from the pit of her stomach throughout the rest of her body. How could Erta possibly think she'd be safer in the hut than in the lodge?

She had no more time to wonder. Grabbing her wrist,

Erta pulled her from her room.

The last of the day was no more than a pale glow on the horizon, quickly extinguished when Pina and the old woman entered the shadow of the wood. Dread hugged Pina's narrow shoulders. What if Erta was right? What if Antonio had not been the only evil in her life?

Small sounds in the undergrowth, harmless by day, became sinister in the darkness. The hunting cry of an owl, familiar in the safety of her bedchamber, was menacing in the gloom of the forest. Paths she knew well by day disappeared into the abyss of night.

Yet Erta's steps were unwavering. Deeper and deeper she moved into the forest, one hand gripping Pina's wrist, the other holding the canvas sack containing the herbs and garlic. With a deep, cleansing breath of relief, Pina saw the light from Erta's window pierce the darkness all around.

Once inside, Erta closed and barred both door and window, as she had done in Pina's chamber. Then she banked the fire and put a pot of water on to boil.

"Well?" Pina crossed her arms across her breast. "Are you going to tell me what you're up to?"

"Are you hungry?" Erta countered evasively.

The emotion building in Pina's breast overflowed.

"No, I'm not hungry! How can I have an appetite with everything that's going on? How can I feel anything but *fear* when you drag me through the forest in the dark of night, and tell me there's some kind of . . . of . . . blood drinker or something stalking me?"

The old woman's brows arched slightly. "Fear, child? Are you telling me now that you're afraid?"

"Of *course* I'm afraid. Aren't you *trying* to frighten me? And I'm . . . I'm angry. Why did you bring me here? *Why? What are you doing?*"

A slow smile spread across the old woman's wizened features.

"Good," she pronounced. "Now, you are ready."

CHAPTER

28

Pina did not think she would ever be able to fall asleep, despite Erta's preparations and ministrations. Although she had denied hunger, the old woman had warmed a soup that Pina found, reluctantly, to be irresistible. And then there was the tea.

Pina had watched Erta make it from what had seemed to be a collection of ordinary herbs. But now her eyelids seemed heavier than they should be as she watched the old woman putter about her small home, placing more herbs, and the strings of garlic, about window sill and door frame.

She should have known Erta was up to more than she admitted. But why give her a concoction to make her sleep? Wasn't it sleep that she feared? And dreams?

It was soon impossible to hold her head up from Erta's cot any longer. She relaxed back on the crude but comfortable pillow. Her eyelids fluttered closed.

Erta watched sleep carry her former charge away, aware when her breathing became deep and regular. The old woman turned her focus to her own breathing, a technique she had learned long, long ago.

Doubts, however, intruded on her concentration. Was she doing the right thing? Would she really be able to keep Pina safe? She issued a mental grunt.

Neither walls nor guards had kept her safe before, or any of the other girls. It was not strength of body that would prevail now, but of mind. Pina was as secure, physically, here in the hut, as she would be anywhere. Or, perhaps not.

With sinking heart, Erta remembered Francesca's tale of the war she had waged over the unseen predator — and had won. Would she be as strong? Would she be able to ward against the evil as Francesca had done?

No matter. It was too late now. She had made her decision and would live by it. Or die. Erta turned her gaze toward the shuttered window.

He — it — was out there. She had absolutely no doubt. The thing that had come for Pina in Venice had found her again. There was no other explanation for the stag, Pina's dream of transformation, and the man she had come upon in the wood. In her trusting, innocent heart Pina certainly wished it differently, but wishing could not make it so. The malice had come for her.

Resignation settled into Erta's body like an old friend. There was nothing she could do but her best, using the tools and knowledge of a long life. She took a few steadying breaths. Listened to the night sounds.

Her eyesight might be failing, but her ears were still keen. She heard the distant call of a nightbird, the flapping of wings, a high-pitched squeak. Gradually, the noises faded away. Now there was only the crackling of the fire, a pop and a hiss. The sound of a stick settling. Then these sounds, too, faded away. Erta heard only her breathing and the rhythmic beat of her heart. Vision narrowed, blurred, turned inward.

She had found her place.

Now, there was only the waiting.

It was black, everything was black. And she was falling. Falling . . .

Pina waved her arms and kicked her legs, limbs thrusting, clawing, seeking purchase. There was none.

She was doomed.

The breath was sucked from her very lungs as she plummeted. She was in the place of dreams, and it was empty, and she was going to die.

And then she saw a hand — pale, long-fingered — reaching for her. Reaching out to help her, to stay her fall, rescue her. With all her will, Pina surged toward it, groping. She clutched the hand, and it pulled her. The fall was ended. She realized her eyes were closed.

She opened them.

"Tallhart . . ."

"Yes." He fingered the oven V at his neck, but hesitated. Tallhart. That was the name she had given him. Her gift. "Yes. I am . . . Tallhart."

Her gaze devoured him. How hungry she had been for the sight of him! Now he was here, and as he had reached for her, to save her, so she extended her hand to him. He needed her. For his very survival he needed her, and she must help him . . .

"No!"

The shriek seemed to pierce Pina's brain. She clapped her hands to her ears. She watched Tallhart's eyes widen.

And then she was falling again.

Silent, mental scream still echoing inside her head, Erta felt Pina's essence hurtling past her, flying away. With all her might, all her incredible force of will, she extended her being toward Pina. But something blocked her, something as intent on Pina as she was. She had not frightened it away.

Erta was tiring. She began to be aware of her breathing. Soon she would slip away from the place she needed to be and would be unable to help Pina, to save her. Desperately, she narrowed her focus, tightening her concentration.

Out of the darkness beamed a tiny light. Pina.

Erta cast her awareness about her, shielding her. Something growled. The hairs on the back of her arms raised.

"Leave her!" the old woman's mental voice commanded.

A roar of anger nearly shattered her focus. Regathering energy, she wildly shot a bolt into the void.

The presence abruptly withdrew.

Erta was aware of her breathing again. She was slipping away from the "place." But Pina was with her.

The old woman shook her head and glanced about the room. She saw Pina's eyelids flutter. She released a long, slow sigh and rose slowly, shaky, from her chair.

"Pina, child. Are you all right?"

Pina swiped a hand across her eyes, pushed an errant lock of hair from her cheek. Tested her lips with her tongue. She nodded vaguely, and struggled to sit up. Throwing her legs over the side of the bed, she pushed to her feet. And smiled.

At something behind Erta.

CHAPTER

29

Despite the hour, the sounds of revelry continued unabated from the streets below. Drunken laughter, a snatch of song sung off key, a feminine squeal. Antonio grunted in the general direction of the merry-makers and turned abruptly from the window. The expression on his face was thunderous.

"You sniveling old fool!"

"Antonio . . . how dare you?"

"How dare *you*?"

Claudio Fontini drew himself up to his full and imposing height. "I suggest," he said with quiet menace, "that you pull yourself together and remember who's the father and who's the son."

"Or what? What, *Father*? What more can you do to me that you haven't done already?"

A tic worked in Claudio's jaw. "Shut . . . up. You're a fool, Antonio. No wonder Francesca and her whelp want nothing to do with you."

An unattractive flush spread over Antonio's pale features. Without another word he turned from his father, picked up the wine decanter and poured a brimming goblet. He raised it to his lips.

"Don't you think you've had enough?"

Only Antonio's eyes moved. He glanced sideways at his father, then tilted back his head and drained the glass. Immediately, he poured another.

Claudio threw up his hands and dropped heavily into an ornately carved chair. He shook his head and impatiently ran his hands through his hair.

"I should have seen it coming," he said, as if to himself.

"Seen *what* coming?"

Claudio leaned back and eyed his son. "Francesca's letter. The breaking of the betrothal."

Antonio made a rude noise. "Stupid bitch. She had no reas. . ."

"Enough!" Slamming his hands on the arms of his chair, Claudio jumped back on his feet. "I've had enough, Antonio. Let's stop playing games, shall we?"

Antonio became still. He lowered the goblet slowly to the silver tray, eyes narrowing.

"Why, whatever do you mean, Father?" he asked softly.

"Don't feign ignorance. It doesn't become you."

The corners of Antonio's lips tilted upward, but the smile didn't reach his eyes. "Then I'm afraid I shall have to appear . . . unbecoming. Go on, Father. Do say what's on your mind."

Claudio took a deep breath, trying to will away his anger. Better than anyone, he knew how useless it was to verbally spar with his son. But it was late and he was very tired. Tired, most of all, of cleaning up Antonio's messes.

"It's common knowledge, Antonio," he began at length, evenly, "that you have a penchant for . . . controlling women."

"Most women love it." The smile never faltered.

"And most of them would argue that with you."

"Who have you been talking to, Father?"

Claudio matched his son's expression. "You mean, who's been talking to *me*, don't you? Come on, Antonio. Did you think your little . . . secret . . . would stay safe forever?" With a kind of bleak satisfaction, he watched the flush return to color his son's face and neck.

"If you hadn't been incompetent," Antonio said tightly, "handling the situation, it never would have gotten around. Just as you were incompetent handling Francesca, and now . . ."

The slap took him completely by surprise. Antonio's head jerked back and he held a hand to his flaming, stinging cheek.

"You *idiot*," Claudio hissed. "You think to blame *me* for what you did? How typical, Antonio. How typical of you to just bull your way through life, taking what you want, discarding what you don't, and leaving me to clean up the rubbish heap."

"At least you're right about one thing." Antonio's hand dropped from his face and curled into a fist at his side. "She was garbage."

"She was a woman. And now she's dead."

"She was a *servant*!"

Disgusted, Claudio watched his son turn from a threatening, angry man into a petulant child. He threw up his hands and turned away.

"Don't you walk away from me!" Antonio shrieked. "Come back here!"

Claudio continued toward the door, footsteps heavy.

"Father!"

Claudio exited the room, leaving the door ajar.

Whirling, Antonio threw his goblet against the wall. It shattered against a mural depicting a group of happy picnickers in a pastoral setting. The dregs of the red wine ran down the skirts of a prettily dressed blond woman, staining them like blood. Antonio started to laugh.

So, Francesca thought the betrothal was broken? She didn't even begin to know what "broken" really meant.

In another wing of the villa, a frightened servant slammed her window shut and hugged herself, shivering. Then she clapped her hands over her ears.

But she could still hear the sound of laughter . . .

CHAPTER

30

Erta felt the hair on the back of her neck prickle. She turned around slowly.

The man was well-formed, handsome. Not a fearsome beast. But then, she had not expected that to be so. She did, however, note his pallor and the gauntness of his cheeks. His neck was corded and his chest, though broad, appeared sunken.

He was in need. Terrible need. And she was the only thing standing between him and what he desired.

"How did you get here?" Her voice sounded small and insignificant in the flickering light and shadow of the hut, facing the monster.

"I . . . don't know."

"Erta," came Pina's voice behind her, excited and fearful all at once. "This is the man I saw in the . . ."

"Hush, child," Erta said quickly, never taking her eyes from the man. "I know who it is. Be quiet. And stay where you are."

"But . . ."

"Pina."

She lapsed into silence as Erta continued to stare, unblinking, at the stranger.

"You know," she said. "Tell me."

"I . . ." His gaze flicked from the old woman to Pina. "I . . . I came . . . with you."

"Don't talk to her. Don't look at her," Erta commanded in an even tone. "Look at me and answer."

His gaze shifted back to Erta and she saw something in his eyes that gave her strength and a spark of hope. "How did you come here?" she repeated.

"I . . . I was searching for her . . . for Pina." He said her name as if tasting it. "And I found her in . . . in the darkness."

Erta heard Pina suck in a breath. She ignored it and nodded for him to go on.

"I . . . I held on," he continued. "But then something . . . happened. I'm not sure . . ."

"*I* happened," Erta said firmly.

It was Tallhart's turn to nod. "Yes. I remember. Then there was only darkness again. And then I was . . . here."

Erta was silent for a long moment. She did not know how it had happened. But there was much about magic she didn't understand. It was enough simply to believe in it. She straightened her back, squared her shoulders, and plunged on.

"You are here, and you've come for Pina. But you will not have her."

Only sadness was reflected in the depths of his gold-flecked eyes. "I do not want to hurt her," he said simply.

The thing Erta had seen in the creature that gave her hope shone from him once again. Yet, he was a seducer, she reminded herself. She must stay strong, guarded against his wiles.

"Do you know what you are?" Erta demanded sharply.

Again, only sorrow showed in his expression. "I . . . have need. I destroy to . . . to survive."

This time Erta could not ignore the sounds behind her. She turned to see Pina rising from the cot, tears streaking her face.

"No, child." She held out a restraining arm. Pina stopped and gazed at her piteously. "Don't touch him. Know him for what he is."

"But what is he?" Pina cried. "I don't understand what's happening . . . I don't understand any of this!"

Erta finally tore her gaze from the creature to look Pina in the eye. "This . . . being . . . took your cousin's life." Although Pina started to shake her head, the old woman continued relentlessly. "He is the reason you became so ill in Venice, the reason your mother brought you here, to the country. To get you away from him. To save your life."

"No." The whispered denial was barely audible. "It can't be. I . . . I don't remember any of that. This is the man I met in the forest . . . he's not evil. He's not!"

"Denying it will not change it," Erta said gently. "Look at him. Listen to what he says."

"It's not true." Pina didn't know why the fact was so important to her, but it was. Although she couldn't explain it, her heart had gone out to the stranger. She could not possibly feel that way toward a creature of evil, a murderer. She had to think of something so Erta would understand. She had to think . . .

A bolt of pain shot through Pina's temple, seeming to enter her brain. Wincing, she pressed her hands to her head. Before she squeezed her eyes shut, she saw a tremor of pain mirrored on the stranger's face.

Erta also saw it. A new spasm of fear shivered through her body.

They were connected. Somehow, the bond had been forged. Had this happened with all his victims? Was Pina irretrievably doomed? Or was it a mutation of the magic, something her interference had caused?

Nausea churned in the pit of the old woman's stomach. By coming between their essences when the creature sought Pina's life force, to suckle from it, had she caused them to

form a new kind of bond? Something completely different than the one between victim and predator? Or was it
something else, something she did not yet comprehend?

A groan from Pina brought Erta from her unpleasant reveries, and new worry replaced the old. She gently
gripped Pina's shoulders.

"What is it, child? What's wrong?"

Pina looked up slowly, blinking. Her expression was
one of wonderment. "I . . . I think I . . . I remember."

"Remember what?" Concern growing, Erta noticed
that the creature now had his eyes tightly shut as well, as if
concentrating with all his might.

Pina looked up, lips parted, eyes shining. "We were on
our way back from church, Mother and I." She shifted her
attention from Erta to the man standing in the center of
the hut. "I saw you," she said excitedly, "in the alley . . ."

"Yes." He nodded. "I, too, remember."

"You seemed so lost," Pina went on. "I . . . I wanted
to help you."

"You gave me a name. Do you remember that? Others
wanted only what I gave to them before I . . ." Tallhart faltered, brown creasing. He averted his gaze, then brought
it back to Pina. "But you were different. You reached out
to me. You gave me a name because I have — had — none.
None I could recall. You named me . . ."

"Tallhart," she finished for him. "Yes!"

A broad smile lit his handsome face, then faded. "Do you . . . do you remember . . . where we were when you gave me the name? Do you remember me coming to you?'

Pina's high, smooth forehead wrinkled in imitation of Tallhart's. She pressed her fingers to her temples, but the memory would not come. It seemed to drift around her in a fog, just out of reach. "I can only recall . . . naming you . . ."

Tallhart seemed to relax. He took an audible breath and let the smile return. "Yes. You named me. You gave me a gift. No one ever . . . cared. Ever gave me anything. You . . . you . . . helped me."

"Why should I not?"

"Because I . . ." Tallhart looked at the old woman, then back at Pina. His expression dissolved into grief. "Because she's right," he continued, so softly Pina had to strain to hear. "I kill. I must kill to live. I would have killed you."

Pina took an involuntary step forward and was instantly restrained by Erta.

"But you didn't," she protested. "And you're not trying to hurt me now, are you? You were alone with me in the woods and you didn't try to hurt me then, either. Did you?"

Erta was growing uneasy at the excitement in Pina's voice. But it was also infectious. She looked at Tallhart through new eyes. And saw growing amazement in his face as well.

"Tell me," the old woman said, "how you found Pina

when she left Venice."

Reluctantly, he tore his attention, and longing gaze, from Pina. Something seemed to soften in his gaunt but handsome features. "Because, I think, she gave me something no one else had ever given me before. Something real. Something more than desire. Pina . . . you cared," he said to her. "And I needed to have that back again, needed *you*. Needed you so much, I think, that I started to dream. I dreamed of this forest. I dreamed of the name you gave me. I recalled it — Tallhart. It was a name pulled from your memories, Pina, and I . . . I followed the path of those memories to this place, this forest. Yet, I had no form, and again, using your memories of the name you'd gifted me, I was able to take the body of a stag. I saw myself as you had described me when you named me, and became what you beheld.

"Then, all of a sudden, there you were, in my dream. Caring for me again. Although I was as I had envisioned myself, a stag. You were caring for me. And then you touched me. And now here I am . . . as you saw me in the forest. As you see me now."

"So," Erta said on an exhalation of breath. "It's as I suspected, as I feared. There was magic at work. The stag was not natural."

"There's nothing 'natural' about any of this," Pina inserted.

The comment brought Erta up sharply, returning her to reality, however stilted. "You are absolutely correct," she said. "We are faced with terrible danger, and yet we stand talking as if this is the most normal thing in the world."

"But I'm . . . I'm not," Tallhart blurted. "I'm not dangerous. I would never do anything to harm Pina.

"Yet, you even admitted . . ."

"Yes, yes, I am a monster. I must kill to live. But not Pina, not now."

Erta's eyes narrowed suspiciously. "What do you mean, 'not now'?"

All too humanly, Tallhart threw up his hands. "I don't know. I don't know what to tell you. What little memory I still possess is foggy. My former life, before I was . . . was . . ."

" 'Made'?" Erta offered.

"Yes, yes, that's it. Before I was 'made', I remember little. But I recall the sleep-like existence in which I now live. I know my . . . my nature. And my crimes. I know I use the avenue of dreams to commit them. I know I only need to touch, physically, my victim and I have in my mind a map to that avenue. It's always the same then. I come to them in dreams. And . . ." He shook his head impatiently. "But this is different, so different. I've never been able to come out*side* of dreams. But now . . . do you understand anything I'm trying to say? Anything at all?"

Erta never would have believed it, but comprehension was slowly dawning. Comprehension and . . . sympathy. Although she denied entirely his assertion that Pina was safe from his seductions. No, there was a great deal more she had to learn. Her greatest concession, this eve, was her willingness to learn it.

"I think I am beginning to understand," she conceded finally. "A little. I have believed in and studied magics all my life. *Natural* magic. This is foreign to me. But understand it I must. To protect Pina."

Tallhart's expression was so pitifully grateful Erta found it hard to refrain from consoling him. Instead, she waved him away.

"You must go. Despite your protestations to the contrary, I do not trust your nature. And I have much to think on. Much."

"Erta!" Pina exclaimed. "You can't just send him out into the night!"

"Never forget, child, that he is a creature of the night. No matter what else you might believe, or wish." She turned back to Tallhart. "Go. And since it seems you can bear the light of day, return to us on the morrow."

"Erta . . . !"

"Go, I said. Now."

CHAPTER

31

Night had come again to plague him. The wine was not making him sleepy, or even dulling his senses. Antonio heard every sound of drunken revelry and merriment outside his closed and shuttered window, taunting him. The air in the room was sultry and stifling and the upper portion of his *camicia* was wet with sweat. With a curse, he slammed his goblet down on the delicate, inlaid table by his elbow, and uncoiled from his chair.

Trying to seal out the world, and the joys denied him, was a waste of time. Antonio flung back the shutters and opened both windows. The gold brocade drapes immediately stirred with the rising night wind. Though balmy, it cooled the heat still rising from him. It did not, however, cool his temper. Pushing strands of listless, sweat-damp hair behind his ears, Antonio whirled from the window.

The sight of his unmade bed only served as fuel for the fire raging within. Brooding, nursing his growing rage, he had locked himself in his bedchamber, not even allowing the presence of servants. He had dined on the ever-present fruit in the hammered silver bowl on the long table between the windows, and had drunk the red wine kept in the matching silver ewer.

But the vessel was now empty. And his temper was over-full.

What the bitch Francesca had done and his father had allowed was unforgivable. Pina was to have been his bride. It was all arranged. Someone was going to have to pay.

Francesca would be the first. Then Pina. Antonio smiled. There was also the pretty little dark-haired maid who had spurned him. She, too, would learn what it meant to refuse Antonio Fontini. It would be good, oh, yes. It would be very good.

He could not depart in the middle of the night, however. The servants would talk. His father would know. And his father would know where he was going. He would try to stop him.

No, better to wait another day or two. Or three. Until his departure would not raise any questions he didn't want to answer. He only need say he was going about his business. Then he would ride out to the country and pay the Galbis a visit. Another smile curved the corners of

Antonio's thin, pale lips.

No one would get hurt. Not permanently, or in a way that was obviously visible. The women just needed to be taught a lesson. Nobody — *nobody* — turned their back on Antonio Fontini and got away with it. That other silly little servant . . .

Antonio's head snapped toward the door, as if he feared his accusatory father might enter at any moment. He forced himself to relax.

The common little bitch had deserved what she got. The only thing that made him think twice about indulging in such a satisfying pastime again was the difficulty even the august senior Fontini had experienced having the affair covered up. He might not be so successful next time. And Antonio enjoyed the life he led. Jail would not be at all pleasant. No. Although it was tempting, he would have to restrain himself.

Absently, Antonio picked up the goblet and raised it to his lips, annoyed when he remembered it was empty.

Damn. He would have to call a servant. Or get more wine himself, perhaps step out into the courtyard to more fully avail himself of the night breeze.

Replacing his goblet on the table, Antonio left his chamber and started down the curving marble staircase.

Angelina pulled down her skirts and shoved her most recent client away, both palms flat against his chest, when he tried to steal a parting kiss. Surprised, he stumbled backward and growled something unintelligible at her. She waved a dismissive hand.

"Go on. You got your money's worth. You want another kiss, you gotta pay for it."

"I paid too much already," the man grunted in response.

Angelina uttered a short, mirthless laugh. "Your cock didn't seem to think it was too much."

The man spat and turned on his heel. Angelina laughed again and watched her former client stagger out of the narrow alley. She wiped away his drunken kisses with the back of her hand. When she could no longer see the retreating figure, she headed for the mouth of the alley herself. The night was young yet. Young enough for two, maybe three more customers. She sauntered out into the street.

It wasn't as crowded as it had been earlier. Pickings were lean. She strolled on down the avenue and eyed the potential clients critically. Not only were the pickings lean, they didn't appear as affluent as she generally liked. Angelina tossed her head and frowned.

She was young and good looking, with wide hips and a generous bust. Her black hair was thick and curly, tumbling to her waist, and her dark eyes were long-lashed. Her skin, almost untouched by the sun, was as pale as milk, and when she pinched her cheeks, roses bloomed at once. She still had her health and kept herself relatively clean. She was better than the other whores, as she reminded herself often, and could do better than the others. She was picky about her clientele, charged a higher fare, and most often got it.

But the night's dregs didn't look as if they'd be able to meet her price. Making the most fateful decision of her life, she changed direction and walked back the way she had come. She would cross the grand and broad Plaza San Marco, absent of its pigeons under the dark of night, and head to a more affluent neighborhood. The sons of wealthy families often roistered late into the night, and by this hour were drunk enough to take their pleasure on the streets rather than the high-toned brothels they were wont to visit.

Heels clicking on the pavement, Angelina picked up her pace.

There was usually a flagon of wine in the senior Fontini's office. Knowing his father was long since abed, Antonio entered the room and refilled his goblet. Restless, he crossed to the window, but it had been locked for the night, drapes drawn. Too short-tempered to bother with the procedure of opening everything, and still warm, Antonio left the room and strode to the front door. As soon as he opened it to the night, he felt it beckon to him.

Antonio drained the goblet and, without looking, extended his arm to set it on a foyer table. It caught the edge and clattered noisily to the marble floor. He ignored it. The beast in him stirred. It needed to be fed.

Staying close to the building facades, or villa walls, gliding through the shadows, Angelina saw him well before he spotted her. He was exactly what she had been looking for: well-dressed in embroidered robes, the glint of rings on his fingers when he passed a lighted window, or streetlamp. As he neared, she saw he wasn't the most handsome of men, with longish hair, Spartan features, and slightly protuberant eyes. But it didn't matter. That wasn't the part of him she was interested in. Boldly, licking her lips, Angelina stepped from the shadows.

" 'Evening, my fine young gentleman," she purred. Canting the curve of one generous hip in his direction, she patted it with one hand while she fingered the cleavage visible above her low-cut blouse with the other. "Looking for company?"

Antonio halted and stood stock still. He could hardly believe his luck. The prey had come to the predator. He nodded briefly, a smile crawling onto his lips.

"Good evening yourself, pretty lady. And, yes, company such as yours would be delightful."

Angelina quickly glanced about for the nearest alleyway, what most of her customers preferred. Spotting a dark, narrow entrance, she jerked her chin in its direction.

"Pay for a nice room over there, my handsome *signore*?"

It was getting better and better. "As soon as I've seen the . . . décor."

"As you like." Quirking an eyebrow, a smile caressing her mouth, Angelina flicked a length of hair back over her shoulder and sashayed toward the alley. Antonio followed without hesitation.

His anger had finally been channeled in the proper direction. The heat of it still beat in rhythm with his heart, but now the core of it was in his loins. His cock stirred to life as he followed the whore into the shadows.

She heard his footsteps following close behind. Good. Angelina turned slowly, already extending her hand for the coin. She gasped when he grabbed her hand.

"Hey," she protested. "You said . . ."

". . . I'd pay as soon as I saw the goods." With his free hand, Antonio gripped the front of the whore's blouse and tore it downward. Her heavy white breasts gleamed dully in the dim light of the alley. When she squealed, his erection rose full blown. It pulsed, achingly, when he slapped her with the back of his hand.

For the first time in her career, Angelina felt fear. Although she smelled the sour odor of wine on his breath, this was not an ordinary abusive drunk. She tried to pull her arm from his grasp, and realized her mistake almost at once.

Soon he would have to take her, before wasting himself on the fabric of his garment. But he could exact a bit more exquisite pleasure first. When the whore struggled, trying to pull free, he backhanded her again, then grabbed her throat. He watched the scream die on her tongue.

It was almost more than he could bear. It was time.

Angelina's wrist was suddenly free. She put her hands on her attacker's chest and tried to push, but she was rapidly weakening. The fingers around her throat were choking the life from her. She was only fuzzily aware of her skirts being shoved upward, and being entered. From somewhere far away, she heard the words: "I . . . *I* am the man who will make you beg for more . . ."

It was over swiftly. Antonio slammed into the whore once, twice, three times, and reached his orgasm. Teeth bared in a grimace, he rode the wave, pulsing until he was dry.

The moment she had prayed for had arrived. In the

aftermath of his pleasure, the grip on her throat loosened. With all her remaining strength. Angelina shoved her attacker and twisted her head to the side. She was free! Stumbling, she started to run.

The rage returned. Filled him. Overflowed.

Antonio overtook the whore before she made it to the mouth of the alley. He tangled a hand in her long, flowing hair and tugged her backward into his arms. She flailed wildly, but could not reach him. All she could do was scream.

He silenced her quickly, slamming her face into the wall. He heard a crunch as her nose was destroyed. The joy was returning, his cock stiffening yet again. Power thrilled through him.

"Yes, it's me . . . I'm the one," he growled as he pounded her head into the wall over and over. "I'm the one . . . to make you . . . beg . . ."

She was dead weight in his hands. He let her slump to the debris-strewn ground. Antonio laughed, and without even bothering to life his *camicia*, finished himself off in a few short strokes. Still laughing, he strolled from the alley.

"Antonio? 'Eh, *mi amici*! A slurred, but familiar voice called from barely a few steps away.

Antonio froze. The molten lava in his veins instantly turned to ice.

"What are you doing, neighbor? Same as me? Coming

home late . . . and drunk?" The flaxen-haired young man's features seemed blurred by drink. He squinted at Antonio. "And with a lady?"

"Don't be absurd, Emilio," Antonio said curtly, and moved away from the alley.

"But I heard something. A scream of pleasure?" Emilio giggled, then hiccoughed. He staggered toward the entrance to the alley. "Something left over for me, perhaps?"

"Emilio . . ."

"Oh, my God . . . oh, my *God* . . .!

Antonio ran.

CHAPTER

32

It was a long time before Pina slept again, wrapped in one of Erta's old, shapeless night dresses. She had been a fountain of questions, overflowing. But Erta would answer nothing. There were mysteries upon mysteries here. She would wait for the sunrise and a new day.

As the moon neared the end of its journey, the night sounds faded away. Erta sat by the open window and listened through the scant hours before dawn when the forest finally, briefly, slept. Then the rustlings of the early risers began. Just as the scene outside her window took on definition, the first bird song trilled through the mild morning air. Erta rose to tend her fire.

The quiet at the end of night no longer upon her, her thoughts would no longer be still. She tried to keep them at bay, stay them until she could question the creature —

Tallhart, as Pina called him — further. But the questions were too insistent, hammering at her mercilessly until she relented and let them take her over. They came in a wave.

Erta had lived long and learned much. She had heard many legends, dark tales to scare little children; darker myths that went beyond. She had seen the truth of many. But this was outside her ken. Dreams.

"I come to them in dreams."

Erta shivered. She had seen the victims of the blood drinker, heard the stories of their terror and pain, had witnessed their deaths. She had, herself, seen the transformation of a man-wolf, and the carnage he had subsequently wrought. Those things were frightening, horrifying. You could run from them, however, lock your doors, protect against them. But someone who could steal into dreams?

The very thought weakened Erta's bowels. And the niggling of some unpleasant memory tickled the back of her mind. It was something she should be remembering, but could not. Was it because the truth, the remembrance, was too terrifying?

Because, uncomfortably, Erta knew it had something to do with dreaming. And what protection did someone have during the most vulnerable moments of their life? True, she had intercepted Tallhart last night. But she could not stand guard every night. And who could protect those who had no one to bide in the dark hours for them?

No. Erta shook her head. There was nothing more terrifying than this. And soon, too soon, she was going to have to meet him again. In the flesh.

A sound outside distracted her, and Erta crossed to her window. Had he come already? Dawn had barely pinked the far horizon, unseen, beyond the encircling wood. She could not even discern the separate boles of the nearest trees. What was out there? And what was she going to say if — when — it was him?

"Erta?"

She turned to see a sleepy Pina ease out of the cot, the folds of the night dress clutched around her slender form.

"Is he here, Erta?" she asked anxiously. "Has he come back?"

She shook her head. "I'll fix you breakfast. We have to talk."

Pina opened her mouth to speak, but promptly shut it again. Erta was right. They did have to talk. And she had a great deal to say.

First, however, she had to try and resurrect the gown she'd been wearing, and do something about her hair. Suddenly, her appearance seemed to matter very much.

In the end, there was nothing Pina could do to salvage

her clothes. She wished, desperately, she could run home to bathe and dress in one of her summery gowns. But she settled for another of Erta's shapeless shifts, belting it with a length of twine. If she went home, there would be questions. And she had absolutely no idea what to say to her mother.

Erta also had a brush Pina put to good use, and vigorously attacked her hair until it fell about her shoulders in shining waves. She turned from Erta's broken bit of mirror to find the old woman scowling at her.

"You prepare as if you go to meet a lover," Erta snapped.

Pina felt a furious blush rush to her cheeks and crossed her arms instinctively over her breast. "I . . . I do not!" she protested feebly. What was it that suddenly plagued the back of her mind? She turned from Erta.

"Come, child," the old woman said, softening. "Come and eat. We have quite an undertaking ahead of us."

Gaze riveted to the ground, Pina took a tentative step in Erta's direction, then halted. She looked up, through the window.

Erta spun as Pina dashed for the door, threw it wide, and raced into the dewy morning.

She shouldn't feel the way she did. By his own admission he was a monster, a murderer. Once more Pina tried to summon her outrage, but it would not come. Slowing, she approached him, almost shyly.

Resisting the urge to call out, Erta watched Pina and Tallhart. The words she had just snapped at Pina came back to her in a sickening rush. ". . . as if you go to meet a lover." Erta swallowed hard.

There was no mistaking it. The look they shared was not that of predator and prey, but of . . .

Erta shook her head. No. It was impossible. She mustn't think such thoughts. Clearing her throat loudly, she strode through the door and out into the clearing.

"Good . . . good morning," Tallhart offered tentatively.

Erta sucked in her breath. Closer to him, in the growing light, she could see how much more he had deteriorated during the night. That, coupled with the soft, almost apologetic greeting, tugged at her heart, and she immediately stiffened her spine. Ignoring his salutation, the old woman got right to the point.

"We have much to speak on. Let us begin at once."

To one side of the hut was a stump, a crude table and chair, and a small stack of firewood Vigo regularly cut for Erta. Erta took the chair while Pina perched on the stump. Tallhart crouched on his lean haunches, elbows on his knees, hands loosely clasped. With visible effort, he tore his gaze from Pina and looked up at the old woman.

"You did not come again to Pina in the night," Erta said tersely.

"I told you I would not."

Erta merely grunted. Tallhart lowered his head into his hands.

"Erta," Pina began carefully, but urgently. "Can't you see how unwell he is? How ill he looks? Please, don't . . ."

"You obviously have some control over what . . . you are," Erta interrupted.

Tallhart looked up. "Yes. I do. Although I did not know this before." He heaved a deep sigh. "Let me tell you how I passed the night . . ."

Tallhart began haltingly, his words coming with difficulty. Memory was hard for him still, holding onto his thoughts, bringing them back, being able to use them. Painstakingly, he related his labor of the soul throughout the night.

He was failing, his physical form was failing; he had needed to go to her and feed on her essence. The wildness had called to him, besieged him. But he had resisted it. He had denied it by holding on to reality.

"What reality?" Erta interjected sharply. "All about us is reality."

"For you, yes. For me, reality is hunting, staying alive. Until last night."

Erta's only reply was a raised brow. Pina sat forward, tense, bottom lip caught between her teeth.

Tallhart returned to his story, to the memories, the reality he had been able to capture.

"Since . . . since . . . *knowing* . . . Pina, I have been able to recall my village, being a boy . . . and my parents. I had sisters, and a brother . . ."

As he talked, Tallhart became more animated. His eyes brightened and seemed not quite so sunken in his pale, drawn face. Something warm and fluttery moved through Pina, and she leaned forward, fascinated by the very sound of his voice.

"My father was a carpenter," he continued. "He . . . he taught me." Tallhart paused and looked at his hands wonderingly. When he raised his gaze, his expression was alight with something akin to joy. "I made furniture . . . like my father. I made furniture," he marveled softly.

Pina's heart squeezed. He resembled a child opening a gift.

"And you're just now remembering this?" Erta asked, tone not as brusque as it had been.

Tallhart nodded almost imperceptibly, lips slightly parted. "Last night I remembered my family. I held on to them. But now I remember *me*."

As he went on, excitement spreading across his features, he spoke faster and faster.

"I was good at what I did; my father was proud of me. But I . . . I was vain." Tallhart's eyes clouded. He shook his head. "I liked the attention of women."

Something stirred in Pina. She watched Tallhart's

gaze narrow as he concentrated.

"I . . . there was one . . ."

"The one who made you," Erta supplied.

Tallhart nodded. "She came to me in the night. She . . . she came to me every night. She awakened the man in me. Finally, she introduced me to the act of physical love."

"Yet, she did not kill you," Erta said.

"This is the one thing I have struggled with the most, trying to remember. Why, why did I not die? Because I became her slave," he went on, "a slave of desire. I would willingly have died to have just one more night with her."

Pina thought she should be embarrassed, but she was not. Rather, she was aroused.

"But . . .? Erta prompted.

"One night she came to me and told me she must leave me. But she would grant me one wish before we parted, she said. And she asked if I was content with what we had, the passion we had known. Or, did I want more? Did I wish to spend the rest of my life seeking the physical love of beautiful women?" Tallhart paused and shook his head, as if trying to free a fragment of trapped memory.

"I . . . I was young, lusty. Foolish. I chose without thinking. I remember what I told her, the decision I made. She gave me a choice, and I took the path that . . . that sacrificed my soul."

Pina bit her lip. Tallhart didn't notice. He was entirely

lost in his memory.

"Did you not think anything strange about the way she came to you?" Erta asked. "At night?"

Tallhart jerked his head in her direction. "You must understand. Only now am I able to recall this happening. After I made my decision, I now know, my life became a waking nightmare. I meet a woman, then memory fades. I drift, grow weaker and weaker. Then I meet another, and grow strong again. But with no memory of our union. No memory of life itself. My existence was meaningless. Until I met you . . . Pina. At the time, Erta, when the one who made me came to me — and this is just conjecture — I think it must have simply seemed like a dream."

Pina was pulled abruptly from the almost trance-like state into which she had fallen. She glanced briefly at Erta, then back to Tallhart.

"But I . . . *I* don't even remember dreaming!" Pina blurted. "I just . . . became ill, my mother told me."

Pina had jumped to her feet. Tallhart rose and approached her, hands outstretched.

Erta opened her mouth to object, but shut it again. She watched, warily, the world she had known spinning out of control as Tallhart gripped Pina's hands.

"You don't remember?" he demanded.

"Nothing." It was barely a whisper.

Tallhart appeared to sag. But not with defeat. He

held her hands more tightly. "You don't . . . when I came to you . . . you don't . . .?"

She shook her head more forcefully. The scent of him, his closeness, rose to her — *man* scent — not a monster, the fabric of a dream.

"Pina!"

She pulled away, still holding his hands. She didn't spare a glance for Erta.

"Tallhart, we must help you . . . I know we can! You're a victim as much as . . . as *me*."

He shook his head, sorrow etched into every feature. "You can't help me . . . you can't. There's nothing you can do. I made my choice long ago. My soul is lost. It cannot be returned to me."

"There must be something we can do. Erta!"

The old woman remained silent, watchful. Then she said: "I have heard of this. It is legend as old as the land. I heard it first as a girl. I did not believe. I do not want to believe it now, but . . ." She made a noise in the back of her throat. "I did not believe the tale of creatures that could steal into your dreams. It was a story to frighten young maidens, I thought. Creatures that stole into your dreams, seduced you, sucked the vitality from you to keep them-selves alive. If alive is what you can call it.

"Yes. Yes, I should have known it all along," she con-cluded mournfully. "He is a dream thief. It is his nature to do what he does, to steal into dreams, steal away young lives full of promise. Steal away the lives, the dreams of youth. I should have known what you were . . . her symptoms . . . but I did not want to believe this evil . . ."

"He's *not* evil," Pina spat defensively. "He does . . . what he does . . . to survive!"

"And to survive," Erta put in, "you must leave."

The old woman's words sank in at once. Pina uttered a little cry and looked into Tallhart's eyes.

"Noooo." The word was a mere hiss of breath. "You can't leave. You'll . . ."

"Kill again," Erta put in. "He must kill, or . . .

" . . . or stay here," Tallhart whispered. "With you."

Pina's heart seemed to stutter and fail within her breast. Tallhart had moved so close to her their clasped hands were captured between their bodies. And in that moment she knew two terrible truths: If he stayed with her he would have to kill her to live; or he would deny himself, and die.

"No. You must go," Erta insisted. "You cannot stay. You cannot put Pina at such risk."

"She is not at risk, I swear to you. I would die rather than harm her. I *will* die."

It was Pina's turn to shake her head. It was all she could do. Tears clogged her throat, making it impossible to speak.

"It's best this way," Tallhart said gently, sadly.

"I can't watch you die!" Pina choked. "I won't!"

He felt like a newborn child. The world was fresh, barely discovered. As were his emotions.

Something built in Tallhart, something he could barely remember having felt before. Releasing Pina's hands, he put his arms about her and pulled her tightly against him. He heard the old woman's growl of disapproval, and cast her a glance over the top of Pina's head.

Erta settled back on her heels at once, lips compressed. She would not have believed it if she had not seen it. Perhaps she was wrong . . .?

But no. She saw it in his eyes, clearly, the message. She understood completely. And she understood how it had happened.

Pina was an angel of goodness. Just as there was more than one kind of magic in the world, there was more than one kind of miracle. The only problem now was how to guide Pina through what was to come. She approached the couple and touched their shoulders.

"Pina, come, child." Gently, Erta disengaged her from Tallhart's arms. "We will talk more later. But for now Tallhart must rest, and you must see to your mother."

Reality was a harsh intrusion. She didn't want to leave him, not ever. She had only just found him. And he needed her. He couldn't die! She wouldn't let him. There had to be a solution . . . there had to be!

"Erta, please, not yet. I don't want to go. I have to think, we have to talk . . ."

"Later, child."

"Yes." Tallhart stepped away and moved to the edge of the trees. Leafy shadows playing on his features obscured them, camouflaged the pain and resignation. The wind of his passage lifted the hair from his shoulders when he turned and disappeared into the wood.

"Tallhart!"

"Pina, no." Erta held her fast.

"I can't let him go to die. I can't!"

"He will return to see you again. I promise you."

The storm of weeping she had felt pushing to the surface of her scarcely controlled composure subsided all at once. Clarity brought the blessing of serenity. Pina knew what she had to do. She forced her body to relax and was rewarded when Erta dropped the hand from her arm.

"Are you all right, child?"

"Yes. Yes, I'll . . . I'll be fine." And she would be. "You're right. I should go back to Mother."

Erta didn't like it, the sudden capitulation. "I'll go with you."

"Thank you, Erta."

As they left the clearing and set out on the forest path, Erta had the feeling that all was not ending but, perhaps, only beginning.

CHAPTER

33

The heat of the day surrendered slowly to the cool of night. It wasn't until the shadows were so long they were losing their shape that Antonio felt he might be able to breathe comfortably again. And move.

He unfolded from his position, tucked against the base of a huge tree, and stretched his limbs. His stomach growled and his mouth was as dry as a desert. It had been two days since he'd had anything to eat besides fruit, even longer since he'd had something to drink other than wine. But he was about to take care of that.

Antonio made his way around the bole of the tree, positioning himself on the edge of the hill overlooking the modest farm. He had come upon it earlier in the day, following his flight from Venice. He grimaced, fists clenched.

Damn Emilio! And damn his own reaction to the fool. He had run . . . *run*. What had he been thinking? Emilio was drunk. He would have believed anything Antonio had told him. He could have wormed his way out of it.

But no. He had fled. And now there was no going back.

There was, however, something to move forward on. Antonio grinned wolfishly. It didn't matter any more what he did to the Galbi women. He could take them at his leisure, as he pleased. And then . . .

A furrow creased Antonio's brow. "Then" would depend on his father. But the old fool would help him one more time. He had to. Antonio nodded to himself. Yes, his father would help him. Their overland trade routes were numerous. His father could arrange to have him smuggled out of Italy, easily. The only problem would be deciding where to go. Antonio laughed. He'd think about that later. He had other things to do at the moment.

The shadows had disappeared. Dusk ruled, the most difficult time of the day to see. No one would notice him coming down the hill or, hopefully, see him crossing the open area to the farmhouse. Antonio started on his way. During the long hours of the afternoon, he had watched the farmer and his family, and he had made his plan.

The two horses he had seen earlier were in a lean-to shelter surrounded by a small corral. He eyed them speculatively. They were used to heavy work, he could see that, but were obviously well cared for. They pulled wagons, maybe a plow. Surely they'd be broken to ride as well. He decided on the bay. Its conformation looked like it might possess a bit more speed than the other. Next, he had to locate a saddle and bridle.

Antonio found them in a shed near the farm house. The harness and bridles hung from pegs on the wall while the saddle was mounted on a rack. Like the horses, the leather was clean and well-maintained. On the way out of the shed, he looked around for tools, any kind of implement that might serve as a weapon.

Leaning against the wall to one side of the door frame were several small tools, one of which was an axe. Perfect. He hefted it.

So far so good. The first part of his plan was working out just as he'd hoped. Now all he had to do was settle down and wait.

One hand pressed to his angry, empty stomach, Antonio made his way around the side of the house, pressed against the wall. He stopped when he could see the light coming through the single front window, and slid down to the still warm earth. He hoped the family were hard workers who retired early. He'd waited long enough.

But the stars were out, winking in a black sky, before the light was finally extinguished. Angry that the house's occupants had kept him waiting so long, Antonio pushed to his feet. He should go right in and teach them what it meant to defy Antonio Fontini.

It was foolishness, he knew. Everything now depended on sticking strictly to the course of action he'd devised. He'd have food, drink, transportation, maybe even clean clothes. Antonio looked down at his robe with distaste. Not only was it stained, but the front was stiff from his own bodily excretions. Yes, he'd have to try and get some clothing. The farmer, from what he'd been able to see, was about the same build, just a little shorter. Antonio leaned back against the wall and gazed up at the night sky.

When the sliver of a moon had risen to the top of its arc, he cautiously stepped up on the front porch and tried the door handle. It was unlocked. Stupid people. Opening the door slowly, fearing squeaky hinges, he peered into the darkened interior of the small front room. Two eyes suddenly glowed at him from out of the darkness, and he heard a low, breathy *woof.*

Antonio's heart froze in his breast. A dog. He hadn't seen a dog earlier, his mind was telling him even as he moved, swiftly now, toward the hearth where the animal lay. It struggled to get up, and he realized it was very old. It whined, with pain no doubt, a thin sound that turned into a growl. He watched the hackles on its back go up and knew that next it would bark. Antonio swung the axe.

A spatter of blood was added to the various stains on the front of his *camicia.* It didn't bother him in the least when he went to forage in the cooking area. At least the damn dog was quiet.

There was half a loaf of bread that Antonio immediately tore into. When he found the homemade sausage he abandoned the bread and gorged on the meat. He chased it all down with a pitcher of water, drinking right from the vessel. He belched noisily and looked up, alert to a sound from the back half of the house. Nothing.

Antonio looked down at himself again. He really should leave. Everything had gone according to plan. He could get away cleanly. Cleanly . . .

Antonio's eyes glittered in the darkness, accompanying his smile. What would Francesca think? And his bride? Dressed as he was, they would most certainly disdain him. He couldn't have that, oh no. He had to look his best. Suppressing a chuckle, he made his way toward the short corridor leading to the back of the house.

The first door on the left was ajar and he peeked around it. Two forms lay side by side on a low bed, apparently asleep. Antonio inched into the room and looked around.

Clothing hung on pegs, both a man's and a woman's. Leaning the axe against the end of the bed, he slipped the robe off over his head and left it lying while he snatched up the farmer's clothes. He had just pulled on the roughspun pants when the woman rolled over and blinked sleepily. Then her eyes widened.

Antonio grabbed the axe even as the woman shook her

husband awake. "Antonio!" she cried. "Antonio!"

How ironic, he thought as he swung the axe upward.

She only had time to scream and hold up a defensive arm. The blow sliced it off near her elbow. A bubble of laughter welled from Antonio's throat. When the husband came at him, roaring, he took him in the side of the throat. Then he finished off the woman.

"Mama?" came a tentative voice from down the corridor. "Papa?"

Antonio was glad he hadn't had time to pull on the shirt before the woman awoke. It was covered in blood. He exited the room.

Three small figures dressed in white, in graduating sizes, stood in the shadows. They held hands.

"Mama? Papa?" Antonio mimicked. He nodded toward the bedroom door. "In there." Pulling the muslin shirt over his head, he strode back to the front of the house.

It wouldn't take long to saddle the horse he'd selected. Then he'd be on his way.

To Pina.

CHAPTER

34

O ver the years, Francesca had learned to treasure the precious moments between waking and rising to begin her day. She savored the coming-awake process, the time when she was not yet fully aware, conscious of the stresses or grief, happiness or joy of the day to come. Simply floating, feeling the comforting luxury of her bed, her pillows, reveling in the special softness of the early morning light, listening to nature's music of the morning, smelling the perfume of whatever flowers had been placed in her room.

Lately these times had been even more special. Each day she awoke it was to joy, not grief. She was content to lie in bed a little longer and drift with pleasant thoughts, rather than jump up to start her day and distract her mind. Luxuriating in the simple feel of her skin, her body, Francesca ran her hands down over her ribs to her hips.

It was funny, she thought, how this part of a woman changed over time. When she had been young and supple, her hip bones had jutted proudly. With child bearing, during and after, they had disappeared for awhile, and even when they returned were not quite so sharp. Then she had lost her husband, her appetite, almost her mind. She had become thin to the point of emaciation. But no longer.

Francesca smiled to herself as she felt the flesh on her bones. She felt fine, healthy, happy, and she had much to be grateful for.

Pina had not only escaped her cousin's tragic fate, but had escaped marriage with Antonio. Francesca had absolutely no doubt, now, how grim that union would have been. Thank God the monsters had revealed themselves before it was too late. And thank God she had found the backbone to do something about it.

Francesca rolled over, preparing to rise, and pictured her daughter asleep in her room. Pina, with the bloom back in her cheeks, her hair lustrous, eyes bright and shining. She was quick to smile again, and Francesca fondly recalled how she had chattered away at dinner the previous evening. It appeared time with Erta had been well spent, and Francesca realized that the animosity she had once felt toward the old woman had completely dissipated. Eduardo really had known what he was doing when he had chosen Erta to care for their child. The only mistake, as far as she knew, he had ever made, was . . .

No, she wouldn't think of Antonio again. He, and his rude, overbearing father were out of their lives. Francesca pushed back the bed coverings and swung her legs of the edge of the bed. She would only think good thoughts for the rest of the day, maybe make some plans.

Francesca slid her feet into the slippers by the bed. Perhaps it was time to return to Venice and resume her public, as well as her private life. And a new, appropriate match would have to made for Pina. One that Pina, herself, approved.

She was pulling on her robe when she heard the sound. What was it? Someone pounding on the front door? Where were the servants?

The rhythmic hammering continued. Clutching the robe about her slim form, Francesca hurried out into the corridor.

When she reached the foyer, the noise had not abated. Stefano stood to one side of the door, Andrea the other. Stefano was pale; Andrea was wringing her hands.

"What is it?" Francesca demanded sharply. "Who's at the door? Why don't you open it?"

The pounding ceased for a moment, and Francesca's questions were answered.

"It's me, Antonio. You must let me in, signor. Please!"

"Antonio!" Francesca took an involuntary step backward.

"What should I do?" Stefano asked. "Should I open

the door? Andrea said . . ."

"Noooo," Andrea moaned.

Francesca shook her head. "No. Don't open it, Stefano."

"Signora. Let me in . . . I have to talk to you!"

Francesca found her voice. "There's nothing here for you, Antonio," she shouted. "Go away."

"I can't. Signora, please. Something terrible has happened. I must speak to you."

"No, Antonio. I will not open the door. Please, leave."

"But I have to tell you what has happened. It's urgent, signora, please . . . my father . . ."

That struck a chord in Francesca. His father. Much as she detested him, both of them, the parent in her responded. She started for the door.

"Signora, *no*! Andrea cried.

Francesca hesitated and looked from Andrea to Stefano. "Perhaps you should go get Vigo, Stefano. Andrea, go into the salon."

"Signora!"

"It will be all right, Andrea. Go on, do as I tell you." Francesca reached for the door.

Pina woke with an overwhelming sense of well-being. She

stretched and turned on her side.

Yesterday had been a day of wonders, miracles. If it hadn't happened to her, Pina Galbi, she simply wouldn't have believed it possible.

Tallhart was, indeed, a creature of magic. An evil being, Erta insisted, who had murdered Valeria, among others. A monster who survived by feeding on the essence of his victims. A taker of life, a thief of dreams.

Suddenly restless, although dawn was still imminent, Pina got out of bed and sat at her dressing table, smiling a secret smile at her reflection.

She and Tallhart had triumphed. The evil magic had been held at bay. A new, more powerful kind of magic was at work. Pina picked up her brush and worked at the tangles in her hair.

Despite the impossibility of it, the improbability, the sheer madness . . . she loved him. And he loved her. She knew it. What else could explain the incredible connection between them? Tallhart had said it himself: He had followed her by finding the path to her memories. Their minds had linked. And not just in dreams. Pina glanced out her window, no longer locked and barred against the night.

The colors of sunrise were just blossoming, and they seemed appropriate for her day. The lightening sky was cloudless, an intense shade of blue; perfect pastel pink limned the horizon, barely visible about the trees. It was the beginning of a new day, a new life and Pina picked a gown to celebrate it, pale blue with pink trim.

It was difficult, manipulating the tiny buttons at her back, and she thought about calling Andrea. But it was early yet, and Andrea worked long days. She'd manage herself. At that thought, something her father had once said came back to her:

"*Know your facts, keep your wits about you, and you can take charge of any situation in which you find yourself.*"

Well, she had her facts. She knew what Tallhart was. And she knew that he was *not* evil, no matter how Erta insisted. He had proved it by trying to deny his very nature in order to save her. He wouldn't leave her, either, even to save himself. Those were not the actions, the intentions of an evil being. She knew it, believed in it with every fiber of her being. Her wits were about her and she was, therefore, going to take charge of the situation. She recalled the exact moment when she had made the decision, speaking to Erta shortly before she had returned to her mother.

"Erta, if . . . if we do this night after night, if he resists coming to me over and over, don't you think it has to break the magic that made him?"

"I wish I could tell you, child. I wish I knew more, for both your sakes. But I *will* tell you this. I believe it too dangerous for you to put yourself at risk each night. Sooner or later Tallhart, or you, will weaken. You will not be able to help it. I can see what is between you."

Ah, Pina had thought, Erta acknowledged it as well. It was not her imagination, and it had given her strong surge of hope.

"Then you know that I'll do something, anything to help him. I cannot sit idly by and watch him grow weaker and weaker. Just as you see the inherent danger to me in his trying to resist coming to me every night, so do I see the danger to him. How long can he go on like this? There must be an end!"

"Perhaps," Erta had said softly, not for the first time, "that is exactly the end that needs to come."

"No. I will not let that happen. I *cannot*." Pina clenched her jaws. Her heart raced. "If I have to, I will give myself to him, Erta. I will give myself to him if only to save him, to keep him from . . . from fading away. I can't let him go. I won't be able to. I know it."

"Pina!"

The look of shock and horror on Erta's face had instantly caused Pina to regret her words. What had she been thinking? She hadn't needed to hear Erta's words — she knew how stupidly reckless she had been —but the old woman could not be told to hold her tongue.

"Have you lost your mind? You will be committing an act of suicide! Have you become so addled by this . . . this *creature* . . . that you would throw away your life? You would do this to yourself . . . to your *mother?*"

Pina had cringed under the onslaught. Erta was right; she had momentarily lost her mind.

But she had regained it.

Pina pulled a pink ribbon from a zebra wood box in which she kept all her ribbons and combs, and tied her hair back simply, then made a final glance at the mirror. Pleased, she noted she didn't need any makeup. Her skin was clear, there were no circles under her eyes, and lips and cheeks vied with the ribbon for color. She was in the peak of health.

She also loved Tallhart. There was a great deal of magic at work, there was no denying it, and this was a part of it. Pina had no doubt. She loved him, and she believed in the power of love and the purity of spirit. Nothing bad could come from something good, something as powerful as love. Yes, she knew what she had to do. It would save him. It would save them both.

Pina turned from the mirror.

And heard her mother scream.

CHAPTER

35

He had spent another night remembering, holding on to his reality, staying away from the girl/woman who had put a different kind of enchantment upon him. It had seemed a little easier; there had been more to hold on to. He was recalling not just the facts of his past, the people and places, but had been able to put himself into the scenes. However, he was weaker. There was no doubt he was failing more quickly now.

Tallhart sensed rather than saw the dawn. Curled atop the debris of the forest floor, his back to a mighty tree, he felt the coming of the sun although his eyes perceived no change in the darkness surrounding him.

A new day. Would it be his last?

Tallhart struggled to a sitting position. Dizzy, he leaned back against the tree trunk.

If it was, indeed, his time, he was ready to go. The

memories of self that had returned to him during the night were nothing to be proud of. Tallhart winced inwardly and closed his eyes.

He had had a decent and loving family. His parents had been hardworking and devoted to their children. He had gotten along well with his brother, and his sisters had adored and spoiled him. Through the long, lonely hours of the night, Tallhart had remembered how much he had loved his family in return. He remembered *love*.

So what had gone wrong in his life? When had he taken the turn that had led him on the road to destruction?

It had begun with his sisters and his mother, maybe, doting on him so thoroughly, telling him how handsome he was, how talented when he went to work in his father's trade. His older brother, he remembered, had not been as fair of face, and had no bent for the family artisanry, but had gone away to drive a wagon hauling goods from one town to the next. Tallhart had become the focus of his mother and sisters' attention then.

But he could not blame them. The fault was his own. He had come to crave the limelight, the adoration. It was a flaw in his own character and, as he grew older, he had learned to love, and crave, the attention of other women. The simple joys he had taken from life, his mastery of his father's craft, the love and warmth of family, became secondary to his sensual and sexual needs. Love had taken on a different meaning. Somewhere, somehow, he had lost the importance of it. Its loss had left him ripe to be plucked by the creature that had come for him.

Another wave of dizziness assaulted Tallhart, and he was forced to lie down again. Even when it had passed, he remained still, his eyes closed.

A new emotion touched Tallhart, although he became aware of it only slowly. He had never lost anyone, not anyone he had loved, had never experienced grief. But it was grief, he thought, he was experiencing now. He was mourning the loss of what could have been.

Tallhart groaned, unaware of the sound of his own voice, and pressed his hands to the sides of his head.

Pina. The very sound of her name brought back a flood of feelings he had forgotten he had known. They infused him, and left him filled with wonder. Was this love? Real love? Was this what if felt like to feel something for a woman other than simple lust? And if it was, how cruel was the irony?

Once again, Tallhart pushed himself up and leaned against the tree trunk. In a few moments, perhaps, he would be able to stand. He wanted to go to her one more time, before . . .

Tallhart would have shaken his head but for the dizziness he feared might return. Although, did it really matter? He was nearing the end, this was what it was like.

He had made his decision, now he must suffer the consequences. But the consequences were, perhaps, merciful. He would die. There would be no more victims. His half-life, waking nightmare would be over. Isn't that what he had wanted?

Or was it merely that he was unable to leave Pina, the one person in his nightmare who had ever reached out to him, ever cared? She was the very soul, the essence of goodness, all that was pure and right about the world. Even he, lost and evil creature that he was, had sensed, felt this within her. He was a monster, he had revealed himself to her, she knew her cousin was one of his victims. He was as tainted as she was pure. Yet still she wished to help him.

Tallhart sat up a little straighter.

Was it possible? Could her goodness be his salvation? Was there a chance for him?

Bracing against the tree, Tallhart rose. He would not know unless he saw her again, at least one more time. There might either be redemption, a slim hope at best, or a farewell for the only love he had known in his adult life.

For he knew it at last for what it was, the emotion burning within him. He straightened and took a step forward, mind reaching out to Pina, searching for her that he might come to her. He probed, reached, and . . .

. . . her terror hit him like the force of a blow. Tallhart

reeled.

She was in danger, in terrible danger, and frightened for her life.

Staggering, he broke into run.

Pina entered the foyer to see a scene so shocking it took her breath away and weakened her knees. Stefano lay on the floor, bleeding profusely from a horrid, gaping wound in his shoulder. He appeared to be unconscious, Tita at his side desperately trying to staunch the bleeding. Ramona stood at the threshold to the salon, face ashen, eyes bulging. She held out a restraining arm, preventing her husband from passing her. Shaking, mouth agape, Pina inched forward.

"Stefano . . ." she whispered. But there was worse horror.

Tearing her gaze from the tableau on the floor in front of her, Pina looked past Ramona and Vigo. The world came to a halt.

It was too surreal. The pale green velvet drapes had been pulled open and the room was bathed in buttery sunlight streaming through the wall of windows, casting warmth on the soft pastels that were her mother's favorites. Delicate chairs, seats and backs covered with embroidered silk in hues of green and blue, edged in gold. Intricately carved and inlaid tables supporting vases of summer blooms and fanciful *objets d'art*. Paintings depicting pastoral hunting scenes, or serene and elegant still lifes.

And her mother, in her morning robe, standing in stark terror beside Andrea. Tears streamed down the maid's cheeks, and even from where she was standing Pina could see she was shaking. Shaking and staring, wide eyed, at the man with the axe, holding it menacingly, its blade dripping crimson.

Antonio.

In a far away part of her mind, Pina wondered if what she was feeling or, more exactly *not* feeling, was what it was like to be in shock. She simply stood there, numb, trying to take it all in. And then her mother's gaze flicked in her direction. Francesca drew in her breath, looked quickly back at Antonio, but it was too late.

Though it felt like a lifetime, it had only been a few moments since Pina had entered the foyer. Moments that would play and replay for the rest of her life.

Antonio saw her. A slow smile crept over his mouth, lifting his sagging, sallow features.

"Ah," he breathed. "At last. My bride has arrived at last."

Dreamlike, Pina watched Ramona and Vigo shrink away from the threshold, as if standing between Antonio and the apparent object of his desire threatened their very lives. Even Tita had stilled, halting her ministrations. Pina heard Stefano moaning softly.

"Come in, my dear," Antonio said. "Please, join us. We've been waiting for you."

"No." Francesca shook her head frantically. Antonio stepped forward and slapped her with his free hand and she fell back, steadying herself against a chair.

Pina pressed her hands to her mouth.

"Come in, I said," Antonio repeated. The smile was gone. His eyes were hard and cold and dead.

Pina found herself moving forward, step by agonizing step. Her gaze locked with her mother's, who continued to almost imperceptibly shake her head. Forcing herself to look away, she concentrated on the man to whom she had once been betrothed.

The smile, which did not reach his eyes, was returning. He stepped away from her mother, as if to greet Pina. Just over the threshold, she stopped.

"That's better," Antonio said. "Let me get a good look at you." He glanced up and down at her figure. "Very nice, very nice, indeed. All you need now is a cloak. We wouldn't want to get any travel dust on that lovely gown. I am *so* glad you dressed appropriately this morning. It will save us time."

"Where . . . where are we going? Was that her voice?

Had she just heard herself speak?"

"Well, I'm not quite sure yet. The point, at the moment, is simply to get away. After I teach your mother . . . and that useless little whore . . ." he said, indicating Andrea, "the lesson they deserve. I *am* glad you arrived in time to observe."

Andrea's knees abruptly gave out and she sank to the floor. Antonio frowned.

"Stand up," he ordered. "Stand *up*, I said!"

Pina watched her mother help Andrea back to her feet. The two women clutched each other.

"That's better." Antonio returned his attention to Pina. "Now, where was I? Oh, yes. You were going to come with me. When I've finished with these two, of course."

"Don't touch them. Please," Pina heard herself say. "I'll come with you. Willingly."

"Naturally. Because I do believe you've seen the error of your ways, haven't you? It was wrong, very wrong of you to spurn me."

As he spoke, Antonio approached Pina in an almost leisurely fashion. It was all she could do to hold her ground, to keep from turning and running for her life. Antonio stopped mere inches in front of her, the axe still held in a threatening position. Fascinated, Pina watched a single drop of blood drip from the edge of the blade.

Abruptly, Antonio grabbed her chin and forced her gaze back to his. "Look at me," he hissed. "Look at me, and never turn away again."

Terror began to penetrate Pina's shock. Antonio was insane, she realized. And capable of anything. He leaned closer to her, and it was all she could do not to shrink away from his rancid breath. He licked his lips, and his hand traveled from her face to her neck. He smiled again.

"You're beautiful," he whispered. "So beautiful. You're mine, and you want me. I know you do. And you will have me . . . soon." Antonio's fingers trailed from her neck to the exposed flesh above her bodice.

Pina managed to repress a shudder. But when his hand cupped her breast, nausea nearly doubled her over.

"Maybe we shouldn't wait," Antonio breathed. "Maybe you should come with me now. Have a taste of what's in store for you. Because I *am* the one who will make you beg for more . . ."

"Oh, my God!"

It was Andrea. Antonio spun, face contorted with anger. Francesca gasped and Ramona uttered a small, startled cry.

"Oh, my God," she repeated. "I remember now . . . I remember. Oh, God. It was you. You murdered Catarina, my friend. She said . . . she told me . . . right before she died . . .those words. A friend of her employer's son, he was after her . . . he . . . Don't go with him, Miss Pina . . . don't . . ." Andrea suddenly broke down, sobbing.

Despite Andrea's broken recitation, Pina understood exactly what had happened. She also understood they were all in mortal peril. Dread flowing through her veins chilled her heart and the very marrow of her bones. Horrified, she watched Antonio stride away from her, axe lifted.

Andrea screamed and turned to Francesca, who hugged her tightly to her breast.

"No, Antonio! Stop . . . don't!" Pina flung herself after him and caught him around the waist. And then something very strange happened.

A balm seemed to flow through her, replacing the dread. She felt calm, almost serene.

Tallhart was coming. And she knew what she had to do.

The abruptness of her attack had slowed Antonio. Pina loosened her arms from his waist and let her grip become an embrace. She ran her hands seductively up his back.

"Antonio," she purred. "What are you doing? Why are you wasting time? I thought you wanted to be with me."

"Pina," Francesca choked. "Pina, no . . . "

She ignored her mother. Her prayers were answered when Antonio did, too. He turned to face her, and she willed a smile to her lips.

"I know what you're doing," Antonio replied smoothly. "I'm not stupid. I am, in fact, quite clever. So clever that I know what would be worse than physical harm, or even death, to your mother."

With a suddenness that amazed her, Antonio gripped her wrist with his free hand and twisted her arm behind her back. She sucked in her breath on a strangled cry.

Maneuvering Pina, helpless in his grasp, he turned them both to Francesca and Andrea.

"If anyone makes a move, if I hear a sound, if anyone tries to interfere . . ." Antonio stopped for a moment, and grinned, ". . . I'll kill her."

Without another word, he whirled and dragged Pina from the room.

Tallhart continued to run, stumbling in his weakness. He had reached the edge of the wood and saw the lodge across the expanse of lawn and gardens. She was in there, he knew, and she was in danger. Terrible danger. But how could he help her when he didn't even think he could make it the final distance to the house?

Falling to his knees, Tallhart uselessly cursed the frailty that afflicted him. Something horrible was going to happen to Pina and he was powerless to prevent it. Unless . . .

The idea gave Tallhart a surge of hope, of energy. He pushed to his feet and tried to concentrate, to recall and follow the memory path he had used once before.

The world around him seemed to become very still. The chatter of squirrels and the chirping of birds faded away. No longer did his nostrils detect the perfumes of summer, or the fertile loamy scent of the forest. His flesh no longer felt the heavy, velvety touch of summer's warmth. All his being was focused on *becoming* . . .

Pina quickly realized that fear, resistance, were exactly what Antonio wanted. What he needed. When he demanded she lead him to her chamber, she complied without hesitation. It seemed to take some of the starch out of his sails, and the painful leverage he had maintained on her arm eased somewhat.

Still, he propelled her down the corridor in front him until she indicated the door to her room. Antonio shoved her up against it while he fumbled with the latch, then pushed her through the door.

Pina stumbled and grabbed the corner of her cheerfully painted armoire. It seemed to mock her. Antonio slammed her door and she heard him turn the key in the lock.

Hurry, Tallhart, she prayed. *Please, hurry.*

Antonio strode across the floor and grabbed her arm again. When she offered no resistance, he growled and threw her on the bed. She lay still, on her stomach, scarcely daring to breathe. Once more he gripped her with rough hands and turned her onto her back.

The anger was fading, and with it his desire. Looking down at Pina's passive, almost serene expression, Antonio was baffled. Why didn't she fear him, shrink away, fight?

Well, if she wasn't afraid now, he could change that.

Pina watched Antonio lean the axe against the side of the bed and loom over her supine form. His teeth were bared in a grimace, a farce of a grin. So focused was she on his tortured mien, she didn't see the blow coming.

Her head snapped painfully to one side when his fist connected with her jaw, and she choked back a cry. Gathering her calm about her again like a mantle, she turned her face back to Antonio. He hit her again.

This time Pina couldn't stifle her groan of agony. Her jaw felt as if it had shattered; her entire face was aflame. Tears stung in her eyes. Through them she saw Antonio's expression light with triumph. Dropping her gaze, she also saw the growing bulge tenting his trousers. Her heart increased its beat.

Tallhart . . .

He finally had her where he wanted her. Antonio pulled off his shirt and cast it aside, then groped for the buttons at the front of his pants.

Instinct, self-preservation, took over at last. Pina rolled over, drew up her legs, and pushed to the opposite side of the bed. Jumping off, she ran for the doors to her garden.

Antonio was right behind her, too close. Near panic, Pina threw herself at the double doors and groped for the latches. Uttering small, animal-like sounds she wasn't even aware of, Pina somehow fumbled the doors open and staggered through them into the sunlight. She felt Antonio catch the back of her dress. Sobbing now in an extremity of terror, she saw something else as well.

A stag was loping across the lawn, headed in their direction. Though he was lean, appearing almost starved, he carried his head, and his magnificent rack, held high. Even as Pina watched, he increased his stride. Her heart swelled.

"What . . .?"

It was the last word Antonio would ever utter. With a mighty leap, the stag bounded over the ornamental tubs delineating the perimeter of Pina's garden. Almost at once the beast reared up and struck at Antonio with its front legs. When the man was down, the hart lowered his head and attacked with his formidable, and deadly, antlers.

Pina had to turn away as the animal mangled Antonio beyond recognition. The last sound she heard him make was a gurgling groan. She sank to her knees, hands pressed to her face, and began to pray for his immortal soul.

CHAPTER

36

Despite her mother's assurances, Pina feared for her health. Francesca lay back against her sheets, her complexion whiter than the bleached fabric. Her lips were so pale they were undefined. Pina lifted the wine once more to her mother's lips.

Francesca turned away. "No, please. No more. I've had enough."

"Do you feel sleepy yet? You need to rest, Mother, to get over the shock."

Tita bustled into the room and Pina noticed, gratefully, she had changed into clean clothes.

Francesca lifted a fraction from the embrace of her pillows, lines of concern creasing his brow. "How is he?"

Tita wiped nonexistent dirt from her hands onto her spotless apron, briefly outlining the bulge of her belly. She smiled grimly.

"He'll make it. I set his collarbone — thank goodness it was a clean break — and stitched him up."

Francesca relaxed back into her pillows. "Thank Heaven."

Pina thought she saw a little color return to her mother's face.

"I just . . ." Tita glanced quickly at Pina, than back at her mistress. "I just need to know what to do about, well, you know . . ."

"The body?" Pina asked crisply. When Tita reluctantly nodded, she said, "Can you . . . clean it up?"

"I already have. And wrapped it . . . him . . . in a sheet."

"God bless you," Francesca murmured.

Pina put down the wine and took her mother's hand. "Would you like me to write a letter and have Vigo take it to Signor Fontini?"

Francesca shook her head weakly. "No, I'll do it. It's my duty to inform him that . . . that . . ."

". . . his son was killed by a rogue stag," Pina finished for her.

Francesca exhaled a long breath. "No matter how despicable a man he was, still . . . what a horrible way to die."

"It was very quick, Mother."

Francesca squeezed her daughter's hand. "I'm so sorry, so very sorry you had to . . . to suffer his . . . his attack. And so sorry you had to witness his death, my dearest daughter. But a miracle, a miracle from God surely, that the beast happened along when he did."

"Yes, Mother," Pina agreed softly. "A miracle." She watched her mother's eyes flutter closed, then barely open again. "Try to sleep now, Mother. I'll have Tita draw the drapes. Go to sleep, and I'll go and tell Erta what's happened."

"Yes. Yes, that's a good idea, dear. Just a little nap, and then I . . . I'll write to Claudio . . ."

Pina waited a few minutes more until her mother's breathing was deep and regular. As Tita closed the curtains, Pina gently disengaged her hand from Francesca's and tip-toed from the room.

Pina was nearly sobbing with fear and frustration when she pulled her mother's chamber door closed behind her. She tried to drive the horrific scene from her mind, but, as she ran down the corridor, it replayed relentlessly in her memory.

As she had told her mother, Antonio's death had, indeed, been swift. The stag had caught him entirely unaware. And although the remains were grisly, Pina knew his suffering did not last long. But it was not Antonio's anguish she was concerned about.

The lodge seemed empty of servants. Tita, of course, would remain busy tending both her mother and Stefano. Ramona and Vigo had taken an hysterical Andrea to her quarters to ply her with tea laced with belladonna. Pina flew down the hallways without seeing a soul.

Everything seemed so normal as she reached the front of the lodge. Drapes were drawn wide, windows open to the summer warmth and sunshine. One part of her mind becoming very quiet as she raced past the room where the terror had begun, she noticed a petal drop from a collection of blooms and fall gently to the table top. Then she was at the door.

The air was sultry and still. Pina's face beaded with moisture and she felt the upper half of her gown dampen, but she barely slowed. Picking up her skirts, she ran with a renewed burst of speed toward the perimeter of the woods. The images in her mind continued to assault her.

It was not the picture of Antonio's end, however, that tormented her, but the stag's debilitation. How the noble beast had managed to do what he had done would forever astound her.

As the animal had come closer, Pina had been able to see how frighteningly thin it was; its coat was dull and lusterless. Even its eyes seemed glazed. She knew Tallhart was in very desperate straits. She prayed she would find him quickly.

Without regard to her clothing or person, Pina crashed into the forest undergrowth. "Tallhart!" she cried. "Where are you?"

There was no response and she ran on, heedlessly. With

every step, her hammering heart sent greater fear spurting through her veins. Was he all right? Did he live? Or was the defense of her his final, desperate act?

"Tallhart!"

The only sounds she heard in reply to her call were the noise of her passage. Twigs snapped underfoot and branches lashed her body. A flurry of birds rose, startled, from the treetops and from somewhere in the near distance a crow offered its raucous cry. Pina halted abruptly.

If she kept on like this, she would never find him. Running in a blind panic would help neither of them. Focusing all her concentration, trying valiantly to still her wildly beating heart, Pina tried to access the quiet place in her mind.

It didn't take long. Strangely, it had become easier and easier to do of late. She found her place. And listened.

Pina heard him almost at once. His voice was weak, barely audible. But she heard. Hesitantly, she started off in a new direction.

The stag was down when she first caught sight of him. His front legs were folded neatly beneath him, but his back was twisted and his rear legs sprawled to one side.

"Oh, my God," Pina murmured, and sank to the fragrant, needle-carpeted ground by the animal's side.

The great beast rolled its eyes in her direction, then gave a long, deep sigh and rolled over completely on its side, front legs now extended and head bent awkwardly to accommodate its huge rack of antlers. Its tongue protruded and its breathing seemed labored and shallow.

"No, oh no," Pina whispered. She ran her hands over the stag's back, fingers trembling. "Please, don't die. Don't die. Tallhart . . ."

Did the animal blink? Did she see a sign of life in his large, dark eye?

"Tallhart!"

The stag attempted to lift his head, tongue still lolling.

"Don't try to move. Just concentrate . . . think. Come back to me. Please, come back to me!"

The very air suddenly seemed to shimmer. Pina gasped and sat back on her knees. What was happening? Was he trying to assume his human form? She clasped her hands tightly, squeezed her eyes shut and tried to find him in her mind, to aid him, give him focus and bring him to her.

Pina heard sounds of struggling and opened her eyes again to see the stag trying to get to its feet. Alarmed, she watched it plant its front feet and heave forward, pulling its rear legs up under it, pushing mightily to stand erect. Even as it found its balance, the air around it shimmered again and the animal began to lose its form. Before her eyes, it appeared to rear up and as it stood upright, it metamorphosed exactly as it had done before, forelegs becoming arms, back limbs the legs of a man. Tallhart emerged. And immediately fell to his knees. Pina put her arms around him.

"No . . ." His voice was barely a whisper. "You mustn't. I . . ."

Pina held him more tightly, willing her strength to flow into him, his heart to beat as strongly as hers. He was so frail, so enervated, he could not resist her, but was quiescent in her embrace.

Pina's fear for Tallhart began to ebb. And as it receded, she felt it replaced by something else.

"Pina, no . . ."

So. Tallhart felt it, too. Pina's pulse picked up its pace once more, the boldness of her plan sending fire through her veins. She turned her head slightly, the mere fraction of an inch. Her warm breath caressed the flesh below his earlobe. Tallhart shivered in her arms.

"You need me," Pina breathed. "Let me help you, Tallhart. Please." She felt him shake his head against her. "Yes," she countered. "Yes. I want to help you. I *can* help you."

"Pina, no, it'll put you in danger. I can't . . . can't do that . . ."

Once more he tried to push her away. Once again she resisted his feeble attempts. She let her lips touch the smooth column of his neck.

This time Tallhart shuddered almost violently. Pina could virtually feel the surge of energy flow through him.

"Yes," she whispered. "Yes . . ."

Despite the heat passing between them, Pina felt the first flicker of fear stir to life in the pit of her belly.

What was she doing? She was a virgin, a young woman raised in the most sheltered of circumstances. Why, she had never even kissed a man before!

Then she remembered Tallhart as he had once been, as he had appeared at the side of her bed, straight out of her dreams. She remembered the way he had looked, so handsome and virile, curling hair touching the top of broad shoulders. Narrow waist and well-made, muscular hands. In her memory she watched him, long-fingered hands reaching down to caress . . .

Pina moaned, and the sound of her voice, vulnerable and needy, was like a lance through him. She felt him stiffen, then relax into her arms. His hands moved over her back. His breathing became deeper, more normal, as he responded to her.

"No," Tallhart repeated, hands moving from her back to her upper arms. "You don't know how dangerous this is, Pina. You don't understand."

"Oh, but I do . . . I do."

Abruptly, Pina pulled away, her hands placed like Tallhart's on his arms. The biceps seemed to swell beneath her touch. She gazed up into his eyes, pained anew by how sunken they were, and dull..

"Listen to me, please. I . . . I know you need my . . . my essence . . . to survive. And I would give it to you, gladly."

"Pina!"

"No, listen."

"No, *you* listen." Stronger already, Tallhart felt the recently familiar emotion pushing itself out of his breast and up into his throat. It threatened to strangle him and made it impossible for him to speak. He cleared his throat.

"You've given me enough already, Pina. More than anyone else," Tallhart managed to choke. "You'd be risking your life with what you're thinking."

"You saved it," she replied simply. "It belongs to you."

He could only shake his head, slowly. "No," he repeated at length. "I cannot, will not, let you do it."

"But look, look at you, you're stronger already! And I . . ."

"You have already started to lose the bloom in your cheeks," Tallhart said grimly, and touched her face with the back of his hand. "You do not see it, but I do. And soon you will feel it."

"But we're in the light of day . . . this is different! You didn't come to me at night, didn't steal into my dreams to take something from me. The sun is shining on us, Tallhart. And I am giving myself willingly!"

"I . . ."

"Tell me this has happened before, I dare you! Tell me

you came to someone in the light of day, openly. Tell me, Tallhart," Pina demanded.

His lips parted, but he did not speak.

"And tell me anyone . . . *anyone* . . . has come to you like I have."

"Pina, you know . . ."

"Yes," she interrupted. "I do know. I know you will die unless I . . . *we* . . . do this."

"And you know, in your heart," he replied softly, "that it would be the best thing for all if I . . ."

"Absolutely not." Pina removed her hands from Tallhart's arms and jammed them on her hips. "How is simply giving up the *best thing*? How can you want to die when you're just learning that you *lived*? Don't you want to live again?"

"Of . . . of course I want to live," Tallhart stammered. "But not like this. And certainly not by taking . . ."

He stopped, too acutely, uncomfortably aware of what he had been about to say. And too deeply, horribly aware that he did, very much, want to believe that what Pina said was possible.

But he couldn't allow himself the luxury. Once more, Tallhart shook his head. "The danger to you is too great," he said firmly. "We cannot even consider this."

"Did you ever think you could transform into a stag?" Pina continued mercilessly. "Did you think you'd find yourself trying to protect someone's life, rather than take it?"

Tallhart opened his mouth, then closed it again. A spark, small but warming, had flickered to life in his breast. But no, she was too precious. He couldn't allow himself to believe, to hope. And then it struck him . . . how long had it been since he'd even remembered what it was to believe, to hope? To feel the emotions? Any emotions?

All of a sudden it was too much. Tallhart was overwhelmed. A wave of dizziness assaulted him and he staggered. Pina caught him in her arms once again.

"Are you all right?

He nodded, swallowing. "I can't . . . I just can't . . . I mean . . ." Tallhart clasped his hands behind his head and grimaced. He felt as if something huge within him was pushing, trying to get out. Abruptly, he clutched his belly, bent double, and fell to his knees.

"Tallhart! What's the matter?"

Head hung low, he panted, struggling for breath. Gulping great mouthfuls of air, he was finally able to look up. A lock of damp hair straggled across his forehead.

"I . . . I don't know . . . I . . ."

Impossible hope flooded Pina's entire body. She grabbed his shoulders. "You're changing," she asserted. "Something's changing." Improbable joy tingled from her toes to her fingertips. Gently, she took his chin in her hand and forced him to look at her. "Tell me you believe in magic," Pina demanded breathlessly. "Not the magic that made you, but *my* magic . . . the magic that will free you."

"No . . ." It was scarcely a hoarse groan. "Pina, please, no . . . you can't."

"Come to me tonight," she insisted, her features enchanted by the smile of pure happiness on her face. "Come to me, and you'll see. We'll fight it, Tallhart, the evil. We'll win, you'll see. We'll win . . . love will win . . ."

Both were captured suddenly . . . captured and held motionless by the very word.

Love.

Pina inhaled sharply and pressed her hands to her lips, eyes wide.

Tallhart experienced a moment of elation . . . followed by powerful sickness, nausea. He fought it, climbing unsteadily to his feet. The wildness within him, the beast, clawed at him madly.

She was his. Without effort, the victim was his. The battle was over. He had been invited.

He would come.

`Tears springing to her eyes, Pina watched Tallhart vanish into the trees.

CHAPTER

37

Erta straightened, one hand to the small of her back, and turned from Stefano's bed to the hovering Tita. "You did well. I couldn't have done better myself."

Tita offered the old woman a tight smile and bobbed her head nervously.

"Keep the shoulder immobilized," she continued. "Change the bandages every day and keep the wound clean." Erta moved toward the door and Tita followed. "How is *la signora*? Did she eat any dinner?"

"A little bread, a piece of bread."

"Good. I'll see to Pina now and look in on Signora Galbi once more a little later."

"Shall I make up a room for you? Will you stay the night?"

Erta stopped in the corridor, as if considering. The dim, wavery light of a wall sconce played over her deeply lined features. At length she nodded.

"Yes. It will be better if I stay tonight. Thank you, Tita."

The portly maid hurried off in the direction she had just come, and Erta went on to Pina's bedchamber. She knocked once, lightly, and entered the room.

Pina did not look up from the dressing table where she sat, chin propped in one hand, staring out the open doors to her garden.

"Pina, child," Erta said in a kindly tone. "Will you talk to me now?"

"I spoke to you already," Pina said in a curiously flat tone.

"You told me what happened, yes."

"Then what more is there to say?"

Erta heaved an audible sigh. "Much, I think. What are you planning, child?'

Pina swiveled slowly on her dressing table stool and looked up at the old woman. " 'Planning'?"

Erta emitted a mirthless chuckle. "Come, child. I never thought you believed me stupid."

A veil seemed to fall over Pina's expression. Nevertheless, she offered a faint smile. "I know you're not stupid, Erta. But I told you everything."

"You found Tallhart, in animal form, in the forest. He transformed again. He was . . ."

"So ill and weak!" Pina exclaimed, suddenly coming

alive. She jumped up from the stool. "I have to help him
. . . I *have* to do something."

"I ask again," Erta said calmly, "what are you planning?"

Pina turned away abruptly and walked to her open
doors. It was almost impossible for her to tell a lie. She
certainly couldn't do it looking Erta directly in the eye.

"Nothing," she replied at length. "How can I plan
anything? I don't know what to do."

"I've said before," the old woman went on gently, "that
this might be the best . . ."

"No!" Pina rounded on Erta. "Don't say it. Tallhart
said the same thing, but I won't believe it. Besides, what
will happen to him if he just . . . fades away? Where will
he go? What happens to his *soul*? What if he faces only
darkness? Obliteration?"

"Perhaps," Erta replied, so quietly Pina had to strain
to hear, "it will be a blessing for him. Perhaps it is the
peace he seeks. It might be that eternal dark is preferable
to an eternal waking nightmare."

Pina's lips parted but she did not speak. She couldn't.
The horror of what Erta had described filled her with unut-
terable dismay. In place of her voice, two fat, scalding tears
slid down her cheeks.

Erta visibly sagged, as if the life had just run out of
her. Her stoop was accentuated; she shook her head slowly,
sadly. Her appearance shocked Pina so profoundly she mo-

mentarily forgot her concern over Tallhart. Pushing to her feet, she started in Erta's direction.

But the old woman waved her away, head still shaking. "I'm sorry, child . . . so sorry." With gnarled and spotted hands, she dashed away her own sudden tears. "Your father was such a great man, so wise. Both your mother and I believed . . ." Erta pulled a scrap of linen from the shapeless bodice of her garment and scrubbed it over her face. She took a deep, shaky breath.

"We believed in his . . . his wisdom. I know your mother trusted his judgment in his choice of . . . of a husband. Yet . . ." Once again she shook her head. "Such evil. Such unspeakable evil."

"Erta . . ."

"But who is really evil?" She went on as if she hadn't heard. "Which one? The one who kills to live? Or the one who lives to kill? The world has turned upside down, Pina. I don't know any more. I don't know . . ."

Not only was the world turned on end, its very foundations seemed to be crumbling. To see Erta, her rock, as she was, shook Pina to her very core. Trembling, she sank back down on her stool.

Pina's movement caught the old woman's eye and she appeared to pull herself together somewhat. She straightened, blew her nose and returned the square of linen to her bodice. Her eyes narrowed.

"You are the key to this, child," she murmured at last. "You are the balance, I think. We, all of us, must trust in your goodness, your purity and innocence. The entire world must, ultimately, trust in this balance of good and evil."

Pina sat, transfixed, as the old woman continued to pin her with her intense, narrowed gaze.

"I will remain here tonight, should your mother . . . or you . . . need me," Erta said finally, voice sounding strained with exhaustion. "Good night, child." The old woman started for the door, then turned.

"Sleep well."

Pina remained motionless for a very long time after Erta had left. She felt as if the continent on which she had been living had shrunk to a tiny island and she was alone, trying to find its center. She lost her awareness of time and simply sat, lost in her thoughts, floundering and fearful.

Her father was gone; only his words and wisdom remained, and even that was questionable now. Her mother's strength was nearly spent; it was now time for the child to protect the parent. And Erta . . . Pina's stomach clenched. Even Erta was wallowing beyond her depth. Pina was alone. All alone.

And she had told Tallhart to come to her.

Reality crashed over her in a numbingly cold wave. Nausea churned in her belly and her skin dampened with clammy sweat. Slowly, she turned toward her garden doors.

The world was fading, losing its definition. Softly, gently, the summer evening moved into night, shedding its gauzy veil of heat and the lethargy of the sun-drenched day. Things would move more quickly now, the creatures of darkness, the hunters, predators. The prey would scurry, hide, run for their lives. Night was coming swiftly now.

Somehow, Pina found the power to rise. She started to close the doors, but halted.

If he came to her in the flesh, would she not allow him to enter? She knew she would. No emotion, nothing she was feeling now, was greater than what had grown, unbidden, in her heart for the thief of dreams.

And if he came to her in those dreams . . .?

Pina turned away from the doors and began to light the candles in her room, her wards against the darkness, as the night deepened.

CHAPTER

38

I n the end, she did not know how he had come to her. She was teetering on the very narrow, fine line between waking and sleeping, in a place where the mind assessed but did not judge. Emotion held no sway. On the one hand, she knew that if she surrendered to sleep the avenue to her dreams would be opened. But if she awakened . . . what?

Pina did not know, and had no curiosity. She simply . . . *was*. Waiting.

And then she heard her name, someone calling softly. "Pina . . ."

She opened her eyes.

The sight of him appalled and Pina's heart squeezed painfully. His body was almost unrecognizably lean. It almost appeared he was sucking in his cheeks, so sunken were they, and his eyes gleamed dully. He was more skeleton than flesh. Yes his power was not diminished.

Pina immediately felt a melting in her core; she was helpless to prevent it. When he raised his long, elegant fingers to the base of his throat, she licked her lips. When his fingers trailed down his chest, heat suffused her body and her legs trembled. It was as if she had become a marionette and Tallhart pulled the strings. Pina felt herself rising from the bed.

At the same moment, she heard the warning bells clanging in her brain. The sound seemed to reverberate throughout her body, tingling through her limbs, bringing her to sharp awareness of her reality.

Tallhart had come to her. She longed for him. But he did not come as her tender lover. He came as her killer, and she must do all in her power to resist not only him, but the force of her own desire.

"Tallhart . . . no."

"You want me." His hand continued to drift downward, almost lazily.

"I want you to . . . to love me."

Something flickered in his gaze. Confusion?

"I want you, yes, but not like this."

An index finger hooked in the waist band of his tight, black leggings. Pina resisted the urge to follow his hand and kept her gaze riveted to his.

"I . . . I want you to love me," she repeated.

"Come to me, Pina."

Something elemental and demanding moved through Pina, countermanding his order. She shook her head slowly.

"Come to me."

"No," she whispered. "Come to *me*."

That look again. Something changed in his expression. His entire essence seemed to . . . *falter*.

"Come to me, Tallhart. Come to me and . . . kiss me."

"Kiss . . . kiss you . . ."

Pina lifted her arms. Opened them.

He was buried in rubble. Something had collapsed and covered him. The beast. It had exploded from within and covered him. There was no light, no air. Only the terrible, suffocating weight of his need.

Through his eyes, Tallhart saw her. She was beautiful. Desirable. She would fill him, provide him what he needed and then the crushing burden would be lifted for a time. But she had to come to him.

The wildness flowed through him strongly. The heat of it gathered in his loins, insistent. He watched her lick her lips as he moved his hand downward, and let a small smile of triumph alight on his lips.

The sense of imminent victory, of fulfillment, did not last. Something was wrong.

Tallhart watched her lips move. She was speaking. At first the words shattered against the ruin of his humanity that surrounded and encased him and fell away in broken shards. But they came again, insistent, and this time he heard them.

"I . . . I want you to love me."

At first the words were meaningless, but they began to take shape in his mind. They took on form and substance. They *meant* something.

Love.

The yearning in him, the desire, started to shift. The heat in his loins diffused and drifted through his form, filling him. Touching his heart.

Through the crush of rubble, Tallhart saw light. His lungs filled with air. Purpose flooded his very veins. Drawing together the last of his failing strength, he gave a mighty shrug . . . and was free.

He literally fell into her embrace.

Pina staggered, both with Tallhart's weight and the abrupt awareness of what had just happened. Her world came sharply back into focus and Pina clutched him tightly in her embrace.

"Tallhart. My love."

He was weak, so weak, but not unable to hold her. His arms moved; his hands caressed her back.

"Oh, Tallhart. Thank God. Thank God." Pina closed her eyes but the tears managed to squeeze between them. Her cheeks were damp and salty when his lips found them.

Cupping her face in his palms, Tallhart kissed her until her tears had dried. She laughed lightly, a sound of pure joy that pulled something within him taut as a bowstring. Desire surged again, strongly. He found her mouth.

One of the hardest things Pina had ever had to do was place her hands against Tallhart's chest and push him away. Her laughter subsided, but a small smile remained. She gazed up into his gold-flecked eyes, brighter now.

"Walk with me," she murmured. When she offered her hand, he took it.

The garden doors were open, as Pina had left them the night before. As dawn tickled the sky with fairy-feathers of pink and salmon, she led Tallhart outside, through the garden and beyond. Dew dampened the hem of her nightdress and felt slick and cool beneath her bare feet.

A distant part of her mind registered what she was doing and wondered at it. Another part held up the memory of what had transpired here just yesterday, but she did not heed it. The rightness of what she was about to do was freeing. Nothing constrained her. She gave herself permission to revel in the joy of the moment only.

Hand in hand Pina and Tallhart walked across the expanse of lawn to the edge of the woods. With the coming o the light it was coming to life. Small sounds from the underbrush and from the treetops above filtered down to them Shoulders touching, they entered their woodland paradise.

They continued until they found the clearing where Pina and Erta had come upon Tallhart as a stag. Releasing his hand, Pina turned to him and looked up into his eyes She took his face in her hands . . .

. . .only to see his expression darken, furrows creasing his brow.

"Tallhart . . . what . . .?"

He grasped her wrists and pulled her hands from his face. "You don't . . . you don't understand what you're doing," he rasped. "Remember what Erta . . ."

"Erta may know legend," Pina interrupted. "She may know the stories of dark magic. She may even know more about you than you do. But she does not know more about you than I."

Tallhart's eyebrows formed twin, worried question marks.

"I know the truth about your body," Pina whispered. "About your soul." Once more she took his face in her hands, raised on her tip-toes, closed her eyes and lifted her lips to his.

His response was not hesitant, confused, or reluctant.

but instantaneous. With a ragged, indrawn breath, he pressed his mouth on hers. His arms went about her slender form and he drew her to him fiercely.

Pina had to fight to maintain her grip on reality, to right her swimming senses. Passion threatened to overwhelm her as she felt him grow hard. And she could not lose herself, she couldn't. Or Tallhart would be lost with her and they would both be doomed.

But Tallhart's hips ground into hers and she felt herself drowning. Desperately, she pushed away from him and gasped for air.

"Stop. Tallhart, stop. You must listen to me."

He groaned and threw his head back, eyes closed. Then he looked at her and his vision cleared along with his mind. Pina saw it and allowed herself an inward sigh of relief.

"You must listen to me," Pina repeated. "You must . . . you have to stay . . . stay *in yourself.* You have to remain aware. Do you understand?"

Tallhart hesitated, then nodded heavily. "But . . ."

"No, listen." Briefly, she touched a finger to his lips. As certainty and clarity washed over her, the blood in her veins almost seemed to sing with the beating of her heart. "There's more than one kind of magic, Tallhart. There's the magic of love. And I believe it is the stronger." Pina took Tallhart's hand and pulled him back to her.

"What . . . what are you saying, Pina?"

"You know what I'm telling you. Look at the sky." She gestured, and obediently he gazed upward. "The sun shines, Tallhart. You are not coming to me in the dead of night, in my dreams. This is not a dream, it's real. And it's love. It is the magic that, in the light of the sun, will free you."

There did not need to be more words between them. The moment had long been preordained. Only the magic had changed.

High above in the treetops a jay scolded. A startled squirrel darted away from them on an overhanging branch, and sent a small shower of leaves down upon them. Sunlight poured upon them and the trees encircled them, sentinels, patient, watchful guardians. Pina laughed, her spirit so light she feared it might fly away.

"This is right, you know. This is absolutely right."

"I cannot know," Tallhart replied softly. "I know only that my desire for you, my feeling for you, is beyond anything I have ever known. And I fear for you."

"Don't fear for me. Love me."

He was very tall. Pina placed her hands on his chest and raised her face to his once more.

"Pina, I don't . . . I don't know that I'll be able to stop myself again."

"You will, Tallhart. You will. You will love me, not in

dream, but in reality. You will break the curse. It will end."

He shook his head, terror for her building to a painful mass in his chest. "What if . . . what if you're wrong?"

"I am not wrong. Love me."

Pina did not pause to wonder how she knew what to do. It was instinctive. It was necessary.

She moved one hand from his chest and slipped it into his shirt. She teased one nipple erect, then the other. Tallhart moaned as her hands slid downward.

He was ready for her, hard and hot beneath her probing fingers. "Love me," Pina breathed.

Tallhart reacted so swiftly, so violently, it took her breath away. His arms fastened around her waist and he drew her tight against him once more. He covered her mouth in an explosion of passion, crushing her lips while he thrust into her abdomen.

Pina's reaction was easily as intense. Though she had no conscious memory of it, the memory exited nonetheless: She had waited for him, wanted him, for too long. She had coveted his body, longed to touch it, feel it beneath her hands. Had yearned for his lips on hers.

But in dreams. This was reality. And it was to be his salvation. If she could hold on . . . if *he* could.

It was running away with them, the passion. Tallhart growled in the back of his throat, more animal than human. Fear uncoiled in Pina's belly and snaked through her limbs.

She struggled suddenly in Tallhart's arms. Turning her head away, she avoided his mouth and beat upon his chest.

"No . . . stop. *Stop*," Pina cried. "Tallhart, listen to me," she panted. "If you take me like this, you'll kill me! Don't you understand?"

Gradually, his hold on her loosened. Pina was able to breathe again. She looked up at him.

Already the change was obvious. His lips were full and red, his flesh toned and bronze. And she felt weakened.

"Kiss me gently," she whispered, her words a plea. "Kiss me as if you love me . . . as I love you." Pina closed her eyes. She felt her entire life swaying on the edge of a cliff.

It might have been a butterfly brushing against her mouth, so light was his touch. She felt the warmth of his breath pass over her cheek and he kissed one eyelid, then the other. With the tip of one finger, Tallhart tilted her head back and Pina felt his tongue dart at the hollow of her throat. She groaned and her knees grew weak.

It was her turn to be the aggressor. Pina found Tallhart's lips. Her hands unlaced his shirt, her fingers caressed the smooth, firm flesh of his chest. She traced the outline of his musculature and felt the softness of the downy line of hair that ran downward to the place on which her entire being was focused. With a tug, she lifted his shirt and he helped her by pulling it over his head.

Desire was a live thing that inhabited her body. It writhed within her, blurred her vision, and sapped the strength from her limbs. She kissed Tallhart's face, his neck, his chest. Then she felt him fumble with the tiny buttons at the front of her night dress.

She willed herself to be still until he had them undone. The dress dropped from her shoulders and became a silken puddle at her feet.

A low rumble came from somewhere deep in Tallhart's chest. His fingertips caressed her nipples, then he cupped her breasts, testing their weight, glorying in her beauty. The purity of what she offered. It stunned him momentarily, and he stood motionless.

Pina regarded him through half-closed eyes, seeing his longing for her was evident. The weight and power of his manhood strained against his breeches. Pina reached for the waistband.

And then they were together as nature had intended man and woman, lovers, to be. Flesh glided over flesh like silk. Hungry mouths kissed and nipped. Pina felt Tallhart's hands seemingly everywhere at once on her body as he lowered her to the grassy carpet, bodies straining in unison to merge.

Stretched out at last, Tallhart cradled her against his body, and she felt the ground warm beneath her back. Its sweet pungency filled her nostrils. And then it was the musky, heady scent of him as he lowered himself down onto her.

There was only one part of her body now. All sensation focused in a single area, all heat emanated from a single spot. Instinctively, Pina arched her back to meet him. One arm pillowed her head while with the other he separated her knees, and she reached down to feel him, hard and pulsing in her hand. A sound came from her throat she did not realize was her own voice and she guided him to the part of her that burned. Only he could quench the fire.

Pina felt the tip of his engorged member brush against her nether lips, wet with her passion. She cried out as he delved, then thrust into her so powerfully he nearly lifted her from the ground.

She was ready, so ready the pain was minor. Moist, slick, hot, they moved together. He filled her, body, soul, and heart. The world went away. There was only the man, his scent, his motion, the feel of his breast sliding against hers. The sound of his voice now, mingling, entwining with hers as they cried out together . . .

Exhausted, Tallhart collapsed on Pina's body, then rolled to the side. She remained within his embrace and touched his features with wonder.

He was fully restored. For one long, fearful moment,

Pina was afraid he had taken his strength from hers. But her body remained unchanged, and the only weakness she felt was the languor of satiation.

Pina's heart soared. She pushed herself up on one elbow and rolled into Tallhart's sprawled form.

"Open your eyes," she breathed. "Look at yourself. And look at me."

Tallhart obeyed, looking down at himself. He sat up and examined his hands, turning them first one way, then the other. He let his gaze devour Pina, from her dainty toes to the glorious mane of golden hair that fanned out around her.

"I . . . we're both . . . whole . . ."

"Yes." Tears of joy sprang to Pina's eyes. She sat up and wound her arms around him, laying her cheek on his shoulder. "You're free, Tallhart. Free . . . and I love you . . ."

CHAPTER

39

It was near dark when Pina finally awoke. The grass beneath her had lost its warmth and she felt the cool of the earth from which it grew. It was late, so late. Her mother . . .

But nothing mattered. Only Tallhart. And what the magic between them had achieved. Pina stretched her hand to the side, fingers groping only emptiness.

She sat bolt upright and realized he had covered her with her night dress. She threw it from her lap and jumped to her feet.

"Tallhart!"

There was no answer. Fear thrilled through her. *"Tallhart!"*

Terror numbed her fingers and she fumbled with her gown. Precious moments were lost as she struggled with the buttons. Leaving half of them undone, she started to run.

Branches slapped against her face, drawing blood. Pina barely noticed. She ran until she thought her lungs might burst, and saw at last the dim outline of Erta's cottage. "Erta!" she screamed, silent praying the old woman had returned to her cottage. "Erta, where is he?"

Erta met her at the door. She was strangely calm in the face of Pina's incipient hysteria.

"What do you mean, 'where is he'? Were you not with him?" she asked sternly. "Were you not with him all this time I worried and had to calm your mother with lies?"

"Yes . . . yes, but . . . but he's gone!" Pina pushed past the old woman and cast wildly about the interior of the tiny hut, as if she might find him there in spite of Erta's words. "Why didn't he come here? Why isn't he here?"

"Hush, hush now, child." Erta closed the door behind her. "Calm yourself. Talk to me. Tell me what happened between you."

"You *know* what happened," Pina sobbed. "And it worked, Erta, it worked. Look at me, I'm fine, and Tallhart is restored . . . it worked!"

Erta nodded slowly, a great well of sadness in her eyes. "Yes, I suppose I know," she admitted. "It was inevitable. I know you would do anything to try and save him. It is your nature, your essence." Erta made an effort to smooth Pina's disheveled hair, but she pulled away.

"He loves me, I know he does," Pina continued desperately. "He held me, and I . . . I fell asleep. When I awoke he was gone. Erta, where is he? Please, tell me where he's gone!"

"I don't know, child." The old woman clasped Pina's arms and felt her trembling. "I don't know what to tell you."

"What am I going to do?" Pina twisted away. "How am I going to find him?"

Erta had no answers, but she had a solution.

"What are you doing?" Pina demanded frantically.

"Making you tea," she replied calmly.

"I don't need tea. I need Tallhart!"

"Hush, child, and sit." Erta pushed Pina gently on the shoulder, and the exhausted girl sank into the chair by the hearth. The old woman turned her back, poured a measure of tea leaves into the pot . . . and something else, something she took care to conceal from her former charge. "Here you are. Drink it. It will make you feel better, I promise."

Reluctantly, Pina took the cup and raised it to her lips. At least it was something to do. She sipped at the tea. It was something to do while she tried to think where Tallhart might have gone, how she might find him.

Erta grabbed the cup just before it slipped from Pina's fingers. Using all of her frail strength, she put one of Pina's arms across her shoulders and half pulled, half carried her to the narrow cot. She straightened Pina's limbs and covered her with a thin blanket.

She wasn't sure, but she thought she might know what had become of Tallhart. And if she was right, he would come to Pina in one last dream. With a heavy sigh, the old woman pulled her chair to the side of the cot and sat down to wait.

It was like, yet unlike the times before, which Pina was suddenly able to recall with startling clarity. She woke and saw him standing by the cot where she must have fallen asleep. She saw Erta, dozing, head bent to one side. Pina rose from the narrow bed.

"Tallhart." His name was a prayer on her lips. Her heart surged with joy and relief, and she moved toward him.

"No, wait." He held up a hand to stop her.

But Pina would not be stopped. Her fear had been too great. She thought she had lost him. She crossed the remaining distance between them and put her hands on his chest. They went through him as if he had been made of smoke.

"What . . . ?"

"You're dreaming, Pina," Tallhart said gently.

"No." She shook her head in denial. "You're real. You're here. I'm awake."

"Look behind you," he replied so softly she was scarcely able to hear.

Pina glanced over her shoulder and caught her breath sharply. Her still form lay beneath the thin blanket. A hot floor of fear poured through her veins.

"No," she said again, denying it with all her heart. "No, you're real. The dreams are over. Reality is my love for you, yours for me. Tell me it's true!"

"It is true," he agreed quietly. "It is true that the dreams are over, true that I love you. That is what I have come to tell you. And to tell you always to remember, Pina, that love never dies."

"What . . . what do you mean?" Terror rose in her throat, threatening to choke her.

"Our love is real. It has freed my soul, my love, to go to God . . . where it belongs."

"Nooooo . . ." Tears poured from Pina's eyes and stained the front of her night dress.

"When I was made," Tallhart continued softly, "the dream thief took only my soul. My corporeal body was left behind. Only the magic animated it, only the dark magic gave it its semblance of life."

Pina slowly shook her head. "No," she repeated dully. "No, you're not dead. You're not."

Tallhart's only response was a sad smile.

"But I love you," Pina whispered hoarsely. "I love you."

"As I love you. With all my soul, Pina. And because of that love, I am able to give you one final gift."

Tallhart raised a hand to Pina's forehead. Though it seemed he touched her with his fingertip, she felt nothing. And then knew nothing.

"I love you." The whisper of his voice lingered a long moment after his image had vanished.

Brilliant bird song filled the morning. It flowed through the open window along with the sunlight. Pina awoke and stretched languidly. She yawned.

"Well, it's about time," Erta remarked. "I've made you breakfast. Get up, lazy girl."

"Erta, what happened? Did I fall asleep here last night?"

The old woman's sparse brows arched almost imperceptibly. "You don't remember?"

Pina sat upright and stretched again. "I remember only coming to visit you. I'm so happy to spend time with you again, Erta," she said earnestly. "I'm so glad Mother brought me to the country to recover from that silly illness. And to come to her senses about Antonio."

She rose from the bed, then hugged herself and shivered as if experiencing a chill. "It's horrible, though, isn't it? The way he was killed by that . . . that rogue animal."

"Yes," Erta murmured. "Pina, do you . . . do you recall

anything about your . . . your illness?"

"No, how could I? Mother said I was really quite sick."

"But you're fine now." It was a statement, not a ques
tion.

"Oh, yes. Perfect. I feel . . . I feel *wonderful*, Erta
despite all that's happened. I feel . . . ready to start my life
all over again!" She started to turn away, then whirled
back to the old woman.

"Oh, and Erta, I had the most amazing, fantastic
dream last night . . ."

BLAZE OF LIGHTNING, ROAR OF THUNDER

Helen A. Rosburg

Louisa Rodriguez was out on the desert gathering fuel when the scalp hunters came, massacred her family and all the people of her village, shot her in the head and left her for dead. Regaining consciousness, she buried the people she had loved, and when she was done she stripped off her bloody clothes and walked naked into the mountains. Where she was reborn.

When horse wrangler Ring Crossman came across the half-wild woman in the western wilderness, she would not tell him her name. So he gave her one. Blaze, for the lightning like streak of white in her long, black hair where a bullet had creased her skull. He gave her his heart, too, although he knew there was no room in her life for anything but revenge.

Vengeance consumed Bane as well. His life was devoted to finding the man who raped his Apache mother and fathered him. Then The Bringer of Thunder, as he was called by his people, crossed trails with the only human being whose thirst for a man's blood was as great as his own. And when they discovered they stalked the same prey, the destructive power of the storm they unleashed consumed all around them, including themselves.

ISBN#1932815643
Silver / Historical Fiction
$9.99US
December 2006
www.helenrosburg.com

By Honor Bound

Helen Rosburg

Bound by fate. Bound by love. Bound by honor . . .

Honneure Mansart, orphaned child of a lowly servant, neve
dreamed that she would one day find herself at the glittering palac
of Versailles as a servant to the young and lovely Marie Antoinett
future Queen of France. Nor could she have imagined the love o
her life would turn out to be her beloved foster brother Phillipe, wh
also served the young princess. Their lives were golden.

But the young princess, Antoinette, has a mortal enemy i
Madame du Barry, the aging king's mistress. And Honneure ha
a rival for Phillipe, a servant in du Barry's entourage. Together th
women scheme to destroy both Antoinette and Honneure. The
Louis the XV dies, and his grandson inherits the throne. Mari
Antoinette becomes the Queen of France.

Honneure and Phillipe, their lives inextricably entwined wit
those of the king and queen, find a second chance together. Yet a
France's political climate overheats, sadness and tragedy stalk bot
couples once again...tragedy, and a terrible secret that might lea
Honneure to the guillotine in the footsteps of her queen.

ISBN# 097436391X
$6.99
www.helenrosburg.com

A PERFECT TEN!

"In my opinion, BY HONOR BOUND is a must-read for any romanc
fiction fan, and assuredly deserves the distinction of a Perfect 10. It's ju
that good!" —*Romance Reviews Today*

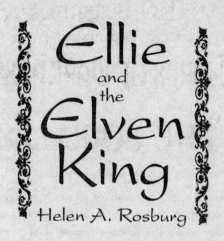

Ellie
and
the
Elven
King

Helen A. Rosburg

Ellie's Mysterious sister died and left her everything: money, a fabulous horse farm, and a husband. But not just any husband . . . Ellie and the Elven King.

An adventure into fantasy, romance, and the magical hearts of horses.

ISBN#0974363901
Platinum
$24.95
Available Now
www.helenrosburg.com

L.G. BURBANK

PRESENTS

LORDS OF DARKNESS

VOL I:

THE SOULLESS

AN UNLIKELY HERO...

Mordred Soulis is the chosen one, the man ancient legends
claim will save the world from great evil. There's only one
problem. Before Mordred can become the hero of mankind,
he must first learn to embrace the vampyre within.

A FORGOTTEN RACE...

With the help of a mysterious order, a king of immortals and
a shape-shifting companion, Mordred is set on a dangerous
course that will either save the human race or destroy it.

A TIMELESS STRUGGLE...

Journeying across the sands of the Byzantine Empire; in the time
of the Second Crusade, to the great Pyramids of Egypt and then
on to the Highlands of Scotland, Mordred will face the Dark One.
This evil entity is both Mordred's creator and the Soul Stealer
he has become. As champion of mortals, Mordred must accept
his vampyre-self... something he has vowed never to do.

ISBN#1932815570
$11.99
Available Now
www.lgburbank.com

HOLLY TAYLOR

Night Birds' Reign

The legend is as old as time . . .

The High King is dead. The land is in peril. A child has
been born to save his people. But a traitor lurks with evil in his
mind and murder in his heart, dogging the footsteps of those
who protect the babe who would be king.

But magic is at work, high magic.

Gwydion the Dreamer awakes, screaming, from a
prophetic dream of tragedy and loss, a dream peopled by kings
of the past. Though he thinks he is not ready, the Shining
Ones lay a task upon him: protect young Arthur; and locate
Caladfwlch, the lost sword of the last, murdered High King
of Kymru.

Dodging assassins to find the woman who holds the key
to unlock a horrible secret, and fighting the longings of his
own shattered heart, Gwydion sets out upon his odyssey. And
finds that fate cannot be fulfilled without sacrificing the life of
someone he loves . . .

ISBN#1932815538
Silver / Fantasy
$14.99
October 2005
www.dreamers-cycle.com

For more information

about other great titles from

Medallion Press, visit

www.medallionpress.com